Copyright

Copyright © 2021 by Alisha Sunderland

All rights reserved.

No part of this publication may be reproduced, distributed, or transmitted in any form or by any means, including photocopying, recording, or other electronic or mechanical methods, without the prior written permission of the publisher, except as permitted by U.S. copyright law. For permission requests, contact Alisha Sunderland at AuthorAlishaSunderland@gmail.com.

The story, all names, characters, and incidents portrayed in this production are fictitious. No identification with actual persons (living or deceased), places, buildings, and products is intended or should be inferred.

Book Cover by JV Arts

Editing by Literary Maiden Editing

American Werewolf In Space

Alisha Sunderland

Dedication

To Michelle
   For always being my biggest fan

Contents

Content Warning	IX
1. Chapter 1	1
2. Chapter 2	12
3. Chapter 3	23
4. Chapter 4	32
5. Chapter 5	45
6. Chapter 6	54
7. Chapter 7	63
8. Chapter 8	74
9. Chapter 9	85
10. Chapter 10	100
11. Chapter 11	117
12. Chapter 12	135
13. Chapter 13	154
14. Chapter 14	160
15. Chapter 15	171

16.		184
17.	Chapter 17	198
18.	Chapter 18	206
19.	Chapter 19	216
20.	Chapter 20	225
21.	Chapter 21	233
22.	Chapter 22	244
23.	Chapter 23	251
24.	Chapter 24	259
25.		268
26.	About Author	281
27.	Afterword	282

Content Warning

Readers be advised: this book contains graphic violence, gore, predation of humanoid sentient aliens, torture, death, child injury and death, civilian casualties, body dismemberment, preparations for war, mentions of PTSD, mentions of the possibility of sexual assault, mentions to past drug use and sex work, graphic sex, illness, genetic modification, kidnapping, and tentacle sex.

One

Go out looking for *trouble and trouble will find you.*

It was one of my mom's favorite things to tell me when I left her house. Blah. Blah. Blah.

Trouble found *me*. It wasn't my fault I beat the shit out of trouble and ended up in jail. Puny men. They whine so much when you break their legs.

So *weak*.

It was only two broken bones. Someone had called the cops, and then there was more fighting and more complaining about 'resisting arrest.' *It's not resisting if you win.* Then ten male cops wrestled me into the back of the car and I didn't kill them all. Mostly to avoid my mother's wrath, but it still counts. I went quietly, like a good citizen. They should thank me.

The last thing I remembered was being stuck in a jail cell with Patty the Prostitute.

Again.

Patty and I went way back. I'd busted up some dude smacking her around, and she'd told the cops his neck was snapped like that when she got there.

Good people, Patty.

I went to sleep on the cold metal bench in Eddy County lockup waiting for my mom to bail me out, like usual. Only I woke up in the dark and with a hangover I didn't drink for. I was also naked. I didn't remember getting naked or drunk enough to pass out. This cell was not the familiar dinky cell I was used to. It was more like a cage.

A strange whirring sound filled the space around me, pounding into my skull in time with my heartbeat. The smell of rot was thick in the air. I rolled to my side, sat up, and puked all over the floor, adding to the already rancid smell.

My head spun and I groaned. I laid back down and rested for a few minutes with my cheek against the cool metal of the grate floor. When my head stopped spinning, I risked lifting it to squint into the darkness. In the corner, was the shadowed outline of a body. They smelled alive, maybe they knew what was going on. Hopefully, it wasn't The Worst Nightmare. A government lab that somehow got to me while I was in jail. That would be bad. Really, *really* bad.

I crawled around my splattered vomit and nudged the body with a shaky hand. It was Patty. She didn't move after I gave her a hard shake. My heart jerked once. I checked her pulse and found it steady. The breath I'd been holding burst out of me with a soft whoosh of relief. She was just knocked out, probably drugged, like me. Alcohol would never get me this sick. I'd have to drink a whole town, and still not be this bad.

Alright. Assessment time.

All my fingers and toes? Check.

Drugged and taken to a secondary location? Check.

About to be murdered and featured on 60 minutes? Probably check.

Except they took *me*. Me! Who, by physiology, *can't* be drugged. Or at least, not by anything I know of.

Oh, God. It *was* The Worst Nightmare! I was in some government lab and they were going to vivisect me! Use my blood and parts to make super soldiers.

My breath panted out of me. There was a roaring in my ears, and cold sweat drenched my body. The logical part of me that wasn't freaking out—deep, deep down—was worried I was about to hyperventilate and pass out.

"Shhh."

I jumped, peering into the dark. The voice had come from in front of my cell. Only shadowed shapes stood out against the black. The drugs were making my eyes slow to adjust, but I was less shaky, so they were wearing off. That was good, except I was going to be starving in about five minutes. Bet they wouldn't feed me in this stupid government lab. Yeah? Well, jokes on them! I would munch on a person *so fast*! The Donner Party had nothing on my will to survive.

"Be quiet." Another hoarse voice whispered in the dark. Good thing too. I'd been spiraling down the rabbit hole there for a second.

"Who's there? Hello?" I whispered back. The scratch, scratch sound of movement came from in front of me.

"Don't make any loud noises."

It was a woman's voice, trembling and thick with tears. There was fear in her voice, making the tone shrill even at a whisper. I was starting to smell the fear now, too. The sickly sweet scent hung in the surrounding air, faint, but growing more noticeable by the second. Pretty powerful drugs they'd pumped me full of, to be dulling all my senses this much.

"Why? Do you know where we are?"

Her obscure shape was getting lighter, more detailed. I blinked a few times, rubbed my eyes, and there she was. She was in the middle of her own cage across from mine, sitting cross-legged on the floor with her thin arms wrapped around her breasts. She was dirty and her cheeks were sunken like she hadn't been eating. Her skin was deep brown, and she had close-cropped dark hair. Her eyes were black reflective pools in the dark when she turned her head to look in my general direction.

"We've been taken." She drew in a deep, ragged breath. "I think I've been here for around a month, but I'm not sure. I was the first on the ship. Don't make any loud noises. They will shock us if you do, then they won't feed us for a few days."

Taken?

Ship?

Oh, don't tell me.

"This isn't a government lab?" I asked, dread pooling in my stomach.

Please be a government lab.

I didn't mind vivisection.

Honest.

"You—we—were taken by aliens."

My heart plummeted like a brick, the shock stiffening my spine into a hard line. She dropped that insane information bomb almost casually, but tears had gathered in her eyes. She'd been here a whole month already.

Poor thing.

She'd probably had to do this song and dance over and over again with each new abductee. Because there *were* others. Twenty girls in the gloom of what must be a cargo hold. That strange hum? The engines of a spaceship. A fucking *alien* spaceship.

That government lab was looking better and better right about now.

"You woke up a lot sooner than the others have." She sniffed, running a hand through her short hair. "Usually takes a few days. The girl in there with you will be out for a long while. She'll wake up though. They all do." She wrapped her arms around her legs and rested her head on her knees.

"I'm Callisto, but you can call me Callie. They took me from my hotel bed at Nellis Air Force Base in Las Vegas. Where are you from?" she asked, still whispering. There was only a narrow walkway between us. I could reach out and hold her hand. It sorely tempted me. Her dark brown eyes appeared bottomless, filled with fear and sadness that were sparking all kinds of protective instincts inside me.

Keeping her talking was the next best thing. She might not want the touch of a stranger, no matter how comforting they were trying to be.

"I'm Jack. I was nabbed from a jail cell in New Mexico, along with my friend Patty here," I said, pointing at Patty's prone body on the floor; remembering right after I did that she couldn't see me so I let my hand drop. I waited a few seconds, but she said nothing more.

"Are you in the Air Force, Callie?" I asked, just to get her talking again. The whirring sound of the alien ship combined with the muffled whimpering from the other cells was making the panic bubble up again.

She hesitated for a beat before answering me. "Yeah. I'm a pilot." She licked her lips and wiped at a tear tracking down her cheek. "My roommate from Nellis was taken with me. Her name was Callie, too. We'd laughed about it when we first met." Her voice wobbled, and she sucked in a breath. "They took her from our cell about a week ago. We heard screaming. I don't think she's coming back," Callie said, her voice cracking again.

Jesus. This was *fucked*.

"What did they look like?"

I wanted to know, to be prepared so I wouldn't freeze in shock if they came into my cell. It could happen to even the most badass person on the planet. New, shocking things could make your mind blank for a few precious seconds, and it could be the difference between living and dying. I was a mean bitch with big teeth, but aliens were a whole new ballgame.

Callie buried her face in her knees and said nothing. Her shoulders shaking with silent sobs.

I closed my eyes, tilting my head back. I was an ass. "I'm sorry about your friend," I whispered to her. I should have led with that.

"They aren't little gray men, if that's what you're expecting," another girl whispered from the cell to my left. I opened my eyes to look at her. She was lying on her back with her hands folded across her belly, just staring at the ceiling.

"They look like us in a nominal way. Bipedal. Two arms with normal five fingered hands. They stand slim and tall. It's their faces that are truly strange, with a circular mouth like a cookie-cutter shark and shark eyes, very black, no pupils. No ears, and no hair," she droned on, almost like she was recording it.

I narrowed my eyes at her.

"Are you a scientist?" I asked.

I didn't like scientists.

She huffed a quiet, sad laugh and sat up. Her hair was short and wild around her face. She might be a blonde, but I couldn't tell for sure with all the filth covering her.

"Medical examiner. Sorry, it's easier if I pretend I'm at work. I'm Sam. Dr. Samantha Johnson," she said, waving a hand in the air in a halfhearted wave. "I'm from Atlanta. They took me right from my desk. I woke up here about three days ago," she explained, her voice breaking, and I heard her swallow hard.

"I'd say it's nice to meet you, Sam, but it would be a fucking lie."

She snorted softly and laid back down.

I stood and had to hunch to avoid cracking my head against the weird bumpy metal that made up the top of my cozy little cell. I paused to see if I was going to be sick again. Nope. Good as new. My stomach cramped a little. Burning calories from ridding myself of the drugs. It was going to get uncomfortable soon, and I was betting they wouldn't be handing out any snickers bars to return me back to normal after I got all hangry.

I checked Patty again, touching her forehead with my fingertips. She was still out cold.

Lucky bitch.

Okay, what now? Looking up I saw what was a metal alien version of popcorn ceiling and that the walls, just a few inches from the bars of the cages, were matte black. Rough grate metal floors. And, of course, our lovely little five star accommodations. Ten cages. Five on each side of the aisle, with two or three girls in each cage except for Callie's. She was all alone. I reached out and tentatively touched a fingertip to the bars. It didn't shock the shit out of me. That was good.

I grabbed a bar with each hand and pulled them apart, stopping when they moved easily so I didn't leave a noticeable difference. Alright, so human strength bars. Things were looking up! It had to mean these aliens were about human strength too, right? If they were crazy strong, they'd have super metal or something. Sounded logical. We'd go with that. Now, so long as they didn't have laser weapons that would burn me to ash before I could try to fight them, this might be doable.

"Did they have weapons?"

Callie was the one who answered me. "Yeah, guns of some type and a cattle prod-like thing." She stood to face my cage, giving me my first real good look at her. She was maybe five six, and built like a runner, slim but muscular. Her face was drawn, but I'd bet when she was healthier she was still severe looking. Her RBF was probably top tier. As of right now, that bitch face was directed at me, her full lips pulled tight in a scowl when she gestured at me with her chin.

"Why? Are you thinking of doing something? I tried that. They took the other Callie and hurt her as punishment. While they were frying me with their cattle prod, she tried to get them off me and they took her," she said. Her voice was rough and cold, her knuckles white where they gripped the bars.

I raised my hands in surrender even though she couldn't see them.

"Okay, okay. I understand," I said. And I did. She probably blamed herself for getting her friend taken, and she would blame me if I got anyone else hurt.

I wanted them to work with me, but I'd worry about that later. I wasn't about to be cut up, or sold, or both. Maybe they wanted our organs? Did they know what I was? All the other girls were human.

"Did they take any blood? Scan us? Anything like that?" I asked.

Callie shook her head. "I don't know. We were all unconscious when we were brought on the ship. Nothing hurt when I woke up besides my head and stomach. I don't think they did."

Yeah, I'd feel it if they had probed me. Hopefully.

Okay. So not super smart scientist type aliens then. Just smugglers. Most likely sex traffickers.

Huge mistake bringing me on board this ship.

Also, *aliens*! I could have an internal freak out while planning a daring and violently bloody escape, right? Yes, right.

Okay, Plan. Planning was good. I could plan.

I took a deep, calming breath and sat crossed legged on the grate floor. So uncomfortable. The skin on my ass was being smashed through the little holes. I was going to look like I'd had an ass grabbing competition with an octopus and lost.

Focus, Jack!

I pushed aside the hysteria bubbling in the back of my mind.

Callie said she was a pilot. Maybe she could fly this thing? She said I woke up fast, and Sam said she was brought on roughly three days ago. Wait, no. She said she *woke up* three days ago. So say, three days unconscious, three days awake, that might mean maybe a week in between abductions? How anyone was keeping track of the days was beyond me. There was no light inside the ship to mark the passage of time. Maybe they were counting?

Callie said it had only been a few hours for me. Maybe we were still somewhere on Earth? Or at least close to it.

Guards would have guns and cattle prods, and drugs. Couldn't forget about the drugs. Hopefully, they don't use darts or something that could tag me from a distance. I was strong, and I was fast, but if the other girls didn't help, it would just be me against many. I didn't want to bust out of here just to be knocked out and the others punished for my escape.

I could take ten human men on and win, no problem. But aliens of unknown strength and numbers? Better make it fast.

"Callie?" I whispered, about to ask her about darts, when the door opened to my left at the start of the aisle between the cells, flooding the hold with bright white light. It looked like a solid wall. So, seamless doors?

If I went by movie logic, probably biometric scanners or some shit. I was going to need one of their bodies.

Through the bright doorway came an honest to god, bonafide, fucking shark-faced alien. He was wearing a black ninja costume, minus the mask, that emphasized how slender and wrong they looked. Saliva flooded my mouth, tasting sour with my fear. Goosebumps spread across my skin, all the hair on my body standing on end. It was a horror show. My heart pounded painfully in my chest. I froze, perfectly still, like a cornered animal confronted by a hunter, and watched the aliens with hard eyes.

Jesus, Mary, and Joseph.

It was like Sam said, they were tall and crazy skinny, with flesh-colored skin, a round mouth filled with teeth, and flat shark eyes. They had bald, creepy heads.

Kill it with fire.

I stifled a hysterical giggle before it could escape.

The alien walked down the aisle, hitting the cage bars with his cattle prod and making a gurgling sound when the girls screamed.

He was laughing at them.

My muscles swelled up and roiled. I gritted my teeth to stop it.

Be cool.

Watch.

Wait.

The alien paused at each cage and looked at the girls in them for a moment before moving on to the next until he came to Sam's. He stared for several minutes, making clicking noises.

My stomach clenched.

Oh god.

Please don't take her out of the cell.

Another alien came in carrying a girl over his shoulder. He moved past Sam's cell, mine, before stopping at Callie's. She scrambled to the corner when he turned to face her cell. He whistled and four bars slid down from the ceiling and into the floor. The girl's body hit the metal floor with a thud when he tossed her in. He then whistled again, and the bars went back up. He walked back down the aisle and out of the hold without looking at any of us.

Full house again. So much for my week between abductions theory.

It was time to leave.

The alien that was staring at Sam hadn't left.

He was holding his crotch and gurgling. Sam pressed against the back of the cage, as far back from the creepy gurgling pervert as she could get. She was trembling and sweat rolled down her temple, trickling down her neck while she watched the alien.

Okay. If he took one step into that cage, it was claws and blood. Screw the not-really-a-plan plan.

He didn't. He grunted, then turned and walked out the door. It closed and left the hold back in darkness. Sam let out a gasping sob of relief and curled up in a fetal position.

I curled my hands into fists and concentrated harder.

Plan A: Bust the girls out, especially Callie. Kill all life that isn't human or me. Preferably with fire, but fangs worked too. Fly the spaceship back to Earth. Get off the ship and pretend this all never happened.

Good plan. It was a great plan!

Plan B: On the off chance that we have left beautiful Terra Firma, I bust out solo. Go full beast mode. Tear everything that isn't human or me apart. Get Callie to learn to fly a super advanced alien spaceship. Go to Earth. Get off the ship and pretend this never happened.

Plan A sounded better.

I scooted over to the bars across from Callie and was about to whisper to her my brilliant plan when blue strobing lights and a whomp whomp alarm started going off. My heart skipped a beat, my muscles going rigid with tension. That couldn't be good. I got a solid grip on the bars and looked at Callie. She was looking at me with wide eyes. I reached out my hand through the bars and she grabbed it in hers. I leaned down to pull Patty's unconscious body to me with my free hand and clutched her to my side. When I looked back up to Callie's pale face, the ship lurched violently forward and everything went black.

Two

I FELT LIKE SHIT. Again.

This time, though, it was the fault of the wormhole. How did I know? Shark alien number two had come back, threw us all a pill and shocked the shit out of us until we took it. It had been the rudest awakening of the century for poor Patty. She'd come awake swinging, cursing out the shark asshole. She'd tried to yank the cattle prod out of the aliens hands and she'd been shocked again for good measure, but he'd been a little nervous about it. Patty did not react how people expected her to in any given situation. It's what made us such good friends.

All the girls started screaming and crying once the pills had been swallowed. I'd had to curl up in the fetal position to avoid screaming right along with them. Once the blinding, agonizing pain of having our insides rearranged subsided to manageable levels, he'd told us we'd jumped through a wormhole; he'd given us nano robot things to adjust our biology and install translators into our brains.

My body had *not* responded well to the alien superbug. I'd vomited up a bunch of little robot sludge and then slept for days.

When I woke up, my stomach cramped badly enough that I'd thought I might die. Hunger gnawed at me. Patty had saved my ration bars like the absolute doll she was. Or was it ration paste? Ration oatmeal? Gross stuff that started as a soft bar and then turned to oatmeal when you bit into it.

It tasted like dog food smelled. Whatever. It was food, and I ate all there was and drank the water in a bucket the sharks gave us that she'd also saved for me. I refused to think about the fact that this was also the bucket we shit in. They'd come to get it every two days and bring it back full of water. Very accommodating, these aliens.

I sighed, leaning against the bars next to Patty, stretched my legs out and closed my eyes. I just needed to rest some more, then I'd bust out. For sure. In five minutes.

Patty snickered and I opened one eye to glare at her. The running lights on the aisle floor were on now so she would see the full power of the stink eye I was directing her way.

"Your legs are huge. I don't think I've ever been this close to you before. You really are a giant." Patty pointed at her leg beside mine.

She was right, but *rude*. She was a petite woman, standing at maybe five feet tall and about a hundred pounds. Made me wonder why I had been taken at all. All the other girls were normal sizes or petite. I stood six foot six inches with two hundred and thirty pounds of muscle. My *biceps* were probably bigger than Patty's thighs.

Maybe some alien creep liked his women strong?

I'd tear his face off and eat it.

I grinned and flicked Patty's leg.

"Quiet, little person, or I might decide to eat you for the extra protein."

Patty snorted out a laugh and leaned against me with her head resting against my arm, her long brown hair tickling my skin. The brown hair was the only thing we had in common. Patty was a pretty woman, with a round face that made her seem sweeter and younger than she actually was, with pouting lips in the shape of a perfect cupid's bow. She had those big blue eyes that made you want to trust her. You'd never see the knife coming, too busy being charmed by her sweet, innocent face. She was also only a few years younger than me at twenty-five.

I had a hard face, with high, sharp cheekbones that could take a punch without bruising, and a slash of a mouth with a stubborn chin. My brown eyes were filled with malice on a good day—I charmed no one. They usually turned and ran in the opposite direction.

"I'm glad you're here with me, Jack. Not that I'm happy you got taken, but I feel better having a friend with me."

I grabbed her hand and gave it a squeeze.

"While I wish I could get off this funhouse ride and go home, I'm glad I can be here with you too, Pat. I got your back," I said. I'd looked out for her back home and I would especially look out for her here.

She squeezed my hand back and closed her eyes. I leaned my head back against the bars and did the same. I still felt like trash from the pill.

"Why do you think we're naked?"

Patty, asking the important questions.

"I mean, they abduct us in clothing and then take the extra time to undress us without doing anything else? Why?" she continued.

I shrugged. "I don't know. A wild guess?" I held up my free hand, made a fist and started ticking off with each raised finger. "Either we're being sold for our parts and it makes things faster if we're already naked. Or we are being sold on an auction block and they want to better view the merchandise." I opened my eyes and paused, taking a breath before giving her the most likely answer. "Or it could just be because it makes us feel small. It makes you feel vulnerable and afraid. If I was a skinny shark asshole, I'd want to make extra sure my captives didn't try anything. Don't want to damage the goods by disciplining them all the time. Killing one or two is fine if it keeps the others in line, but yeah, naked and afraid helps prevent that."

It was just too damn bad for them that my kind were naked often. I didn't pay nudity any mind. I was furious for the other women, though. We ladies had to stick together, regardless of the species.

Patty lifted her head from my arm and looked up at me. "Pretty smart for a drunk and disorderly giant, aren't you?"

I chuckled, and she shot me a grin before putting her head back against my arm. She still had my hand in a tight grip—for all her outer calm, her fear still lingered in the air around us. It mixed with mine, tangy and sour. I was big and strong and a monster, but aliens were a pretty big deal. We were somewhere—who knew where—in the universe, and my plan wasn't really a plan. It was wild hope and savagery. The fear had settled into the back of my mind like a tumor, just waiting to grow and take over. I didn't react well to fear. Usually something got torn to pieces.

"You know, this cargo hold is pretty small even for a human plane. You think this is just one room in a larger area? Like maybe there are more of us?" Sam said from her cage. Her voice was still shaky, but she'd uncurled herself and was sitting up again. With the light on I could see that her hair was indeed a light blonde, with wild curls coming to just under her jaw line. She was very young looking, like life had never touched her with a hard hand before. Though a sharp intelligence shone in her brown eyes, adding an air of mystery to her sweet face.

"Who knows? Let me break out of here and I'll find out for you," I said. I was half joking but testing the waters, too.

"You got an actual plan, Amazon?" Callie asked, scorn dripping from her voice.

With the lights on, there had been a few jokes about the giantess in the cage. I didn't mind. Let them laugh a little.

"I might. I'd need your help, though."

My back was to her, but her gaze burned into my skin.

"You thinking I can fly this thing?" It wasn't really a question, more like she'd read my mind and thought I was an idiot.

I shifted a little and looked over my shoulder at her.

"Are you willing to try?" I asked her, the challenge clear in my tone. *Come on, tough girl, show me some grit.*

We stared at each other for a full thirty seconds before she nodded stiffly. Alright. Game on.

We'd been talking pretty loud and I heard the rest of the girls shifting to pay attention to our conversation.

The new girl in Callie's cell has been crying on and off, but no alien had come to dole out electroshock therapy, so I'd figured the shark assholes didn't care anymore now that we'd left Earth. I hadn't gotten around to asking her name so I could tell her to shut up. None of us had bothered after the first few hours of no punishment. There had been more introductions while I was out and Patty had filled me in, but I'd been miserable and ignored her.

"How are you gonna get out of the cage? You gonna manifest destiny yourself outside?" Patty asked me, poking a finger from her free hand into my arm.

Now, do I just come out and say I was a huge monster with big teeth, hulk strength, and I was going to wrench the bars apart and slaughter the crew? Or do I let them wait and see? I mean, we were already on an alien ship. What's one more 'monsters are real' revelation?

Patty wouldn't blink. Hell, the truth would probably motivate her to get everyone on board with my spree killer plan.

I lifted our joined hands and stared at them, then looked at Patty's face.

She was thinner than she needed to be. Patty had lived a hard life. Harder now that she'd been taken. She deserved the truth, with no hem-hawing around to ease anyone into the fact that monsters were real. We just didn't have the time, and anyway, aliens were real so why not me too?

Still staring into Patty's sad blue eyes, I held my free hand up in front of her face and shifted it. There was no sound of bones cracking. No Hollywood skin flaking. Just smooth transformation, soundless and beautiful. In an instant shaggy brown fur erupted from my elbow to my hand, which ended with long fingers tipped with black three-inch claws.

"I'm one of the monsters, Pat," I whispered.

Patty stared at my claws with wide eyes. She dropped my hand that she'd been holding, reaching out to touch my changed arm. Her hand was steady as she ran her fingertips along my claws and through my fur, then looked at me and smiled. It was an evil smile, her eyes taking on a gleeful glint.

"You gonna kill them all, Jack?" she whispered back.

"Yes."

"You know, this explains a lot."

"The snapped neck thing?" One of my better moments. What an asshole. What kind of man beats on a woman, let alone a woman as small as Patty?

"No. The aggressive wild energy I've always felt around you. Used to scare me, you know, but you always had my back. Never judged me for what I was. I'm not scared anymore. Can't wait to see you, the real you." She entwined her fingers in my clawed hand and leaned her head back on my arm.

Well, damn. I might cry. Did we just become best friends?

Well now, she's gone and done it.

I was going to kill them extra hard for fucking with my bestie.

"Holy shit," Sam whispered. I looked at her and she was staring at my hand in Patty's, her face pale and mouth slack. She was shaking again.

"Werewolves are real. Aliens are real. This is fucked." She looked at me and winced. "I mean, not you. Get us out, Amazon wolf lady. Wreck shop. The weird ship has set sail and I'm not gonna freak out now. So cool. Yeah. What's the plan?"

"Rijitera is what my people call ourselves. Werewolf is so corny," I corrected with a smile.

Sam laughed nervously and shrugged. "I'll call you whatever you want if you get me out of this cage."

I looked out at the other girls and there was fear, sure, but also hope. Better the monster you know, I guess. This went way better than I'd figured it would go. And they say women are weak.

Bullshit.

Men would be screaming at me, calling me a monster and shit. Making committees and taking votes for burning me at the stake while they sat in their cages.

"So what's the plan, Amazon?" Callie asked, standing up and waving at me to get on with it. There she was. I'd known there was a badass hiding behind all that fear and grief.

I let go of Patty's hand to stand as well. The others followed suit.

I met everyone's eyes for a moment and then let a savage grin spread slowly across my face.

Alright then.

"Callie. I'm gonna need you to fly this thing like we talked about." She crossed her arms and nodded at me. I swept my gaze around. "Now ladies, I think the door scans them or something. So we need one to come in here."

"Are you going to take one hostage?" someone asked.

"No. I'm going to kill him and use his corpse to open the door."

A few laughed, and I grinned back at the faces watching me. "Callie is gonna take his gun and stay here and shoot anything that isn't me that comes through those doors after I leave. If they knock me out with drugs, keep fighting. In my shifted form, I should burn it off fast. Don't give up. I'll come get y'all when I'm done. Callie is gonna see if we can't fly this thing back home."

Callie nodded. "Better keep one alive, just in case I can't. Make him fly it."

Good point.

"Alright. One gets to live. I'm gonna get out of this cage. Don't freak out when I turn. Or do, actually. I need y'all to scream bloody murder when I say so." I grabbed the bars with both hands.

Please work.

I pulled hard and the metal groaned. They bent, but not enough. Alright. I let the change rise from under my skin and heard Patty take a sharp breath and step away from me.

I was six foot six when I was a human. As a fully shifted Rijitera I stood at seven and a half feet tall and at least a hundred pounds heavier.

Brown coarse fur rolled over me like a wave and muscle and bone slid into my new shape. It was smooth like butter and felt divine. I had always felt more like myself in this form. Humans got our descriptions mostly right, though some were better than others. Pointed, slightly curled ears, big wolf's muzzle filled with fangs, and clawed fingers and toes.

The only difference was that I was armored over my vulnerable belly, throat and spine with brown scales, kinda like a pangolin and they blended seamlessly with my fur. It was the only thing the myths got wrong. My eyes were the same in either form, brown and human looking, but they burned with an inner light which freaked people out.

It was a skill, really.

I hunched, avoiding the low ceiling and wrenched the bars with new strength. They snapped from their moorings. *Yeah, baby!* I tossed them aside. The deep clang of the bars hitting the metal floor echoed in the hold. I paused, listening. No sounds came from outside and I jerked two more out.

When I turned and looked down at Patty, she was grinning like a crazy person. I gave her a wolf smile, my teeth gleaming, and she laughed.

Not to be dramatic, but I would die for her.

Stepping out into the aisle, I looked around. The aisle was T shaped with the cages on either side. I needed somewhere to hide.

Mmm.

"Crush the lights and go back into the corner by the door," Callie said, pointing at the running lights in the aisle.

Ah. Smart.

"Cover your eyes," I said. My jaws didn't work well for speech, so it came out garbled.

Callie cringed. "Holy shit! You can talk like that?"

I snorted and started slashing at the lighting tubes along the aisle floor with my claws, walking as I went to get them all.

Sparks and bits of metal flew, and the hold plunged into darkness again.

I heard a few whimpers from the girls when the lights went out, but they stopped as soon as they started. Not very good for calling attention to ourselves. I backed into the corner between the wall of the hold and the front left cage and faced the door, crouching down, ready to spring. Silence that almost had an echo filled the room, and I rolled my eyes.

"Scream," I growled out.

The girls delivered, letting out days and weeks' worth of fear and anger with their combined voices.

I flicked my ears back against the sound and waited. Only a few minutes of screaming bloody murder had the door opening and two shark aliens stepped into the hold. The door closed behind them before they figured out the lights weren't working.

I jumped.

The girls were still screaming when I tore into the aliens with fang and claw.

The first alien hadn't seen me coming at all and I nearly decapitated him with a single swipe. Warm fishy smelling blood sprayed all over me.

The second alien warbled in alarm and raised his gun to shoot me. I jerked it out of his hands and tossed it behind me.

He turned to run, but I grabbed him by his skinny shoulders and lifted him up, cramming his creepy head into my jaws and biting down. His head crunched like a grape, flooding my mouth with brain, blood, and bone. It tasted just like fish.

I'd been hungry forever.

I tossed him to the floor and started eating the rest of him in a frenzy. Tearing his clothes and biting into his soft stomach.

I was glad the lights were off or it would have scarred these ladies for life. Well...scarred them more than being taken by aliens had already done.

Unfortunately, I didn't have time to eat the whole of him. His weird ass organs were going to have to do. His heart had *not* been where I thought it would be.

The screaming had stopped and the only sound in the hold was the squelching of me chewing.

"Um, Jack?" Callie called from her cage, her voice uncertain.

I swallowed and stood. Right. Less gorging and more escaping. The door was closed, so I turned, reaching for the nearly headless corpse of the first alien to jerk it up in front of the wall. The door slid open.

Success!

Grinning, I dropped the corpse and started wrenching cages open until I got to Callie's.

"Were you eating it?" she asked, sounding sick.

"Hungry," I said with a shrug. I would not make excuses for what I was.

"That's gross, Jack. You don't know where he's been," Patty said, laughing. She patted my arm as she squeezed past me, completely unbothered by the blood and gore all over me.

Die. For. Her.

The women were moving into the first few cages to be together. Some were holding each other and trying to avoid looking at the disemboweled half eaten corpse in front of the door that was being illuminated like some trophy for all to see by the ray of light shining in from outside.

Sam, Patty, and Callie followed me to the door where I reached down and slid my snack alien out of the way to pick up the gun, placing it in Callie's hand.

She gripped it like a professional and gave me a nod.

"I'll be back," I said with a toothy grin. I couldn't manage the accent with this mouth, but the open-mouthed way I had to talk gave it the same effect.

Sam and Patty snickered.

"Go get 'em," Sam said. She was a little green around the gills.

Maybe I shouldn't have eaten the alien.

Patty mouthed for me to be careful and gave me a thumbs up.

"Fuck them up!" One of the other girls called out and chuckles filled the room.

Aw, that warmed my heart. I picked the corpse up again and walked out the door.

Three

THE PASSAGE OUTSIDE OUR hold was huge, the ceiling much higher, so I could finally stand at my full height and my spine cracked in several places when I did. Why were there different ceiling heights? To make it more uncomfortable for tall, beautiful women? What a weird design flaw for an alien spaceship.

There were other doors lining the wall along the same side as ours, but the other wall was just pipes and metal. Smooth metal floors disappeared around a rounded bend.

I turned to the open door at my back and set the body down on the inside so the girls could get out if they needed to. Pale faces watched me as I took a step back, the door closing them into darkness, causing my gut to clench.

Please be safe.

I needed to hunt down the crew and then check the other hold areas for more women.

I took a deep breath through my nose, scenting. I smelled our former guards in the hallway, but there were other scent trails leading forward. They were fresh. Maybe only a few hours old. At least four new aliens.

Here fishy, fishy. *Mama's still very hungry.*

I padded on silent feet along the far wall and peeked around the corner. Nothing. Just an endless hallway.

There were a lot of doors here. Hopefully not a lot more women.

At the end of the long hall was a huge, reinforced metal door. So this entire area was cargo. I was betting this door led to the main part of the ship. Crap, I hadn't brought a body with me to open it.

I turned back to get one when I heard footsteps and chittering from the other side.

Shit.

I looked around for a place to hide and then up, a grin stretching my lips. I jumped and hooked my claws into the ceiling. It was a good twelve feet up and dark, perfect for some ambushing. I swung my body until my clawed feet stabbed into the metal. I could totally spider my way around. It would up the creepy factor. Just call me a Xenomorph and get the flamethrowers.

The door opened with a hiss of air and in walked another shark asshole.

He had a tablet looking thing in his hand. He wasn't armed, and he wasn't paying attention to his surroundings. These aliens really needed to work on their security.

The door closed, and I waited for a beat before dropping silently behind him.

I landed in a crouch and did my best slow rise and hiss. No one said I couldn't have fun while escaping. He turned slowly, gurgling when he spotted the dark form of a fanged monster rising to tower over him. I snapped out my hand, wrapped it around his throat, and lifted him. He clawed at my hand, whistling at me.

It was really too bad that the alien superbug didn't stick and give me that translator.

I brought him close to my muzzle, pulled my lips back from my teeth, and hissed again. Man, I wished someone was recording this for posterity. His struggles increase, and I wish I had an inner mouth for the skull fucking scene, but a snapped neck would have to do. Playtime was over. I squeezed until his neck crunched, and then turned to raise the body in front of me to open the door.

Nothing happened.

I slammed him into the door a few times and it still didn't open.

What the hell?

I grunted and tossed him aside. Hands on my hips, I studied the door with a scowl.

I tried pulling it open.

No give.

I growled at it.

It didn't open.

I clawed at it and broke a nail.

Still nothing.

I was pacing in front of the door when my foot hit the tablet, and it spun away.

Maybe that opened it?

I picked it up off the floor and turned it over to see that the screen had a bunch of buttons at the bottom. In the middle was a green triangle. No way did aliens use green to color their open buttons like us, right? I pressed it, and the damn door opened.

Aren't they supposed to be super advanced and shit?

Green buttons to open doors? I was kinda disappointed in them.

Wide stairs were just past the door, a lot of stairs and then another door that the tablet opened. Still no guards patrolling. They were really lax in their security. No artificial intelligence speaking out over the ship's intercoms, alerting them to intruders or anything.

What a letdown.

Through the door was another lighted walkway with huge round windows on one side.

Windows showing space.

Space.

I rushed past the windows. I really didn't need to see endless void and not a big, beautiful Earth. It made bile churn in my stomach. Rage sparked along with the nausea. I should be on Earth. My blood heated at the thought, my hackles rising.

The hall ended at another big door. There were a lot of sounds on the other side of it, whistles and croaks of alien conversation.

I bared my teeth and pressed the fucking green button.

The door slid open and a dozen or so armed aliens sat at an oval metal table whistling at each other in what I assume was conversation. The room looked like a guard station or break room. Did they really put all their armed guards in one place? Are none of them patrolling?

Amateurs.

One of the shark aliens looked up at the sound of the door opening and gave a shrill whistle at the sight of me.

I threw the tablet and hit him in the head hard enough for black blood to spray all over his buddy in front of him before he slumped forward over the table.

Everyone looked at their dead companion and then at me.

I barked at them.

They jumped up, reaching for guns, but I was already in the room, claws flashing and teeth biting into fishy flesh. Something punched into my back and burned. An alien behind me had finally gotten his gun up. I lunged at the alien shooting at me and swiped my claws across his face.

He screamed, shooting widely in an arch as he fell, hitting another alien in the leg. I crushed his skull under my foot and turned to the wounded one. He was scooting backwards, dragging his ruined leg and shooting. The bullets burned into my chest and stomach.

Bullets! Not lasers. I was so let down by these aliens. You have a damn spaceship, but your guns shoot bullets?

I snarled at the gun, ripped it from his hands, and shot him with it.

The rest of the aliens were firing their weapons at me and whistling from the other side of the room, all bunched up together and trying to get the other door open in a panic.

I tossed the big table aside and started slaughtering them, letting all my fear and rage out. Blood and wet flesh rained all around the room until it was just me, panting in the carnage.

It only took a minute. Fights never lasted very long. One minute you're in a room full of asshole aliens laughing and no doubt excited about the full cargo hold of money making humans, and the next you're trying to stuff your guts back inside while a monster loomed over you, watching you die slowly and then it was eating your dead body.

Gotta reach my calorie goals, especially with my body working to push the bullets out.

Plus, these alien shark guys were tasty. Like catfish.

When I had my fill of the choicy parts, I picked up my tossed, bloody tablet. Didn't have a scratch on it. The thing was heavy duty. They had bullets, but indestructible tablets?

I just didn't understand these aliens.

One stupid green button later and the second door they'd tried to escape out of opened up into the cockpit. Or was it the bridge? Control room? I shrugged to myself and peered inside.

It had a huge windshield looking out into space and there were very important-looking aliens inside, all wearing shiny uniforms and pressing buttons at consoles. Very Star Trek-like. Must be a good soundproof door because they didn't seem like they'd heard all the shooting and screaming from the guardroom.

I killed them all.

Ripped them apart and bathed the bridge in their blood. Space really pissed me off.

I moved on across the room into another hallway that led into a mess hall. I killed the crew sitting at their lunch and the cooks in the strange-looking kitchen. I found the crew quarters past the mess and killed the two aliens in their beds and then moved on to the poor soul doing inventory in a storage unit and killed him, too.

Past the crew quarters and the storage room was another gigantic door that led back into the big hallway of the cargo hold. The ship made a loop then, easy enough to remember. I backtracked through the bridge and found another biometrically locked, seamless door behind the Captain's console.

I picked up a body to open it, and stepped through into a hallway. The hallway ended in stairs that led to another biometric blast door the size of a bank vault. Inside was the engine room with vaguely catwalk type walkways suspended over pulsing engines that were submerged in a clear liquid. Three aliens were working on a huge computer monitor in the suspended square space over the engines.

I tossed two of them into the water below the catwalks. They screamed once, and then their bodies froze. So it was liquid nitrogen coolant stuff.

Cool.

It was then that I remembered I was supposed to leave one alive. I'd already killed all the aliens on the bridge.

Whoops.

The last alien in the engine room I picked up by its throat. It was its lucky day. It kicked and squirmed, whistling at me furiously so I shook it hard enough to threaten a snapped spine, and the shark stilled. I carried it back through the long halls, down the stairs to the cargo hold, and started opening doors to check for prisoners.

Three extra rooms held crates and nothing else. One was our room, and I moved past it without opening the door. The room to the right of ours was empty.

It was the last room I went to check that the alien Designated Survivor really struggled. He did not want to go into that room. I gave him a rough shake and pressed my teeth hard into the skin at his temple so he could feel my growl through his thick skull. He stopped struggling.

I held him up, and the door opened.

The room looked similar to ours, only no cages, and it had high ceilings. In the center was a glass tube lit up with orange lights.

Inside that tube was a monster.

It was trussed up like Hannibal Lecter, face mask and all. Only its straight jacket had metal bands suspended from the ceiling by chains inside the tube. It lifted its head when I approached the glass and stared at me. When our eyes met, a jolt of awareness sparked through me. Unease whispered at the back of my mind, but I pushed the feeling away.

Four eyes shining through the mask glowed a pale yellow. They were elongated almond-shaped with smaller secondary eyes directly behind the primary ones. It had horns with hard ridges that ran from the forehead, between the horns, and disappeared down its spine. I leaned in closer to the glass for a better look and realized the face *was* the mask. A horned face that looked like a half mask you'd see on Halloween. Black plates covered the entire upper half of its face, starting from below the cheekbones.

It looked like it made up the top part of its mouth, too, but the lower jaw was smooth, shiny black skin, the mouth just a seam between skin and plates. A mouth that was filled with nasty looking needle teeth that it showed me in a snarl, its face plate lifting up and away from its black gums almost like a shark's mouth with the gums pushing out a little from its face to give me a very in-depth view of the many, many teeth.

It lunged forward in the chains and lit up like a rave. I jerked back away from the glass with a yip, my heart in my throat, and shaking hard enough to make my teeth chatter.

Bioluminescent yellow lines and dots ran along its body, outlining rigid muscles. It allowed me to see the whole of what I was looking at; the thing was massive. Taller and broader than even my shifted form.

It had *tails*. Three of them. They thrashed around on the floor in a hostile warning. Its shiny black skin caught the glare of the orange lights of its cage, making it gleam in the hold's gloom. The hard muscles of its wide chest and thick neck flexed as it strained against the metal crisscrossed around it, arms and hands bound in manacles, its claws flexed, sickle-shaped and at least three inches long. They looked like they could do some serious damage.

Just what the hell were the shark assholes thinking, having this thing on board with their terrible security?

It was standing on legs similar to mine in my current form, but its feet only had three clawed toes. Freaky.

We were so fucked if this thing got out.

I crouched into a defensive position when the beast spoke.

Even through the thick glass of its tube prison, it was like a mountain was trying to talk to me. The vibrations of its voice rattled in my chest. It sounded straight up like Black Speech from Mordor and that was all the sign I needed to get the fuck out of this room.

It roared when I ran out into the hall and let the door shut behind me.

I held the trembling body of the engine room shark asshole up and shook him.

"The fuck is that?" I shouted into his face. I was sweating, the churning in my gut threatened to bring up all the good alien shark meat I'd eaten. Nightmares. I was going to have so many nightmares about that thing.

He whistled and garbled at me which was useless. I needed the girls to translate.

I moved to our cargo door and banged on it. "It's me. Don't. Shoot." I didn't need them killing my shark before I could ask him very prudent questions about the Terrible Terror in the other room.

I held him up to the door and when it opened, Patty rushed out, dipped around the dangling shark, and wrapped her arms around my waist. She didn't seem to mind the blood getting smeared all over her.

"Holy shit, Jack. We heard the gunshots and the screaming. The roaring shook the damn walls. Are you okay? Are they all dead?" she asked, stepping back away from me to eye the shark in my hand.

"Yes. This one's for questioning."

Callie stepped out behind Patty with a gun in hand, and I dropped the shark onto the floor. He crumpled into a heap at our feet.

I grunted before shifting back into my human form and pointed at the alien at my feet. "What's in the other room? Ask him what it is!" I was shouting at Callie, but this was the time for panic. That thing was terrifying.

The shark asshole started whistling at Callie and waving his hands.

She scowled at the shark and looked at me. "He said it's an Orixas. They're transporting him for some crime boss or king or something. The translation wasn't clear. He said they're paying them for the cargo. He's begging us not to let him out."

The alien croaked, and warbled some more, starting a hissing/hiccup cadence as he shook. He was crying. Great. He hadn't cried when he watched me killing his people, but he was going to cry just thinking about the Orixas getting out? That was not a good sign. Not a good sign at all!

"He said it's an At'ens. He said it like it was important. He put a lot of emphasis on the word," Callie said. The word she said also sounded like a Mordor word. I didn't like that *at all.*

"What is that? What does it mean?" I asked the alien.

The alien pointed at the Orixas's cargo door and whistled.

"He said it'll kill us. It'll kill us all," Callie whispered, her face blanching.

We all stared at the door.

We were so fucked!

"Let's stay away from its room. We have other things to worry about now. Come on, I'll show you the bridge and we can see if we can turn this thing around and go home," I said, picking the shark up from the floor and pushing him to walk in front of me.

The girls followed behind me.

Why did I feel things are about to go from bad to worse?

Four

CALLIE COULDN'T FLY THE ship. The ship being the only advanced alien tech the sharks owned apparently, so it was too advanced for Callie to make head or tails of it. The Designated Survivor was an engineer, and also didn't know how to fly the ship. Probably shouldn't have murdered all the fancy aliens on the bridge. My bad. My extra special bad.

We spent the rest of the next few hours moving bodies into the airlock in the cargo hold and, with a little instruction from the engineer shark, shooting them out into space.

We'd found some ninja costumes in the storage room by the mess hall, and got dressed after showering in the tube showers in the sleeping quarters. They used some sort of cold gel to wash with and not water. It was an all around unpleasant experience that got my skin clean but matted my poor hair further than it had been.

That hadn't been my only complaint. The black fabric of the alien clothes had a lot of stretch to it, but not enough to go over my frame. The pants I had managed to squeeze into, they were tight and I'd had to cut the bottom so they'd go over my calves, but no way was the top going to stretch over the muscled expanse of my shoulders and arms. Not to mention the boobs. I was built like a warrior, but I had boobs. The shirt just wasn't up to the task. I tore it into strips and fashioned a band to cover my breasts. One girl said she could try to make me something out of the crinkly sheets on the beds, but we hadn't been able to find anything resembling a needle so far. I didn't trust the sheet fabric to stay knotted together when she suggested we just tie it, so I was stuck with the bandeau for now.

Another girl took command of cleaning all the blood and bits and gathered a group together to help. I went along with the cleaning crew since it was my mess. We found cleaning supplies in the kitchen. An actual mop. Like a human looking mop. No fancy alien cleaning bots, just rags, disinfectant spray, and a fucking mop. I hated it here.

You lied to me, Ridley Scott.

We got the bridge mopped up and the one bedroom with the two aliens I'd murdered in their beds, but the security break room was taking forever, so I'd left the engineer cleaning that on his own with two girls armed with guns guarding him. The feral look in their eyes while they watched him would keep him in check better than the guns themselves.

We gathered everyone else in the mess hall, eating the weird food we'd found in the kitchen after I taste tested everything since it probably wouldn't kill me if it wasn't good for us. Everything went down and had stayed down with no side effects after an hour, so everyone was now enjoying some much needed dinner. We were a subdued bunch for having broken out and taken an alien ship. Learning we still couldn't go home had crushed a lot of hope.

Did the Big Bad in the tube cage need to eat? I mean, he was as much a prisoner as we were.

After everyone went to sleep, I'd venture into the hold to figure out if he needed to eat or not. Enemy of my enemy kinda thing.

We definitely didn't want him to be our enemy. These kinds of things always got out. I'd seen that movie and refused to be that stupid.

Callie pushed the metal plate away from her and sighed. "These meat square things aren't half bad. The weird pink root vegetables taste like ass, though. But I'm full for the first time in over a month so I guess I can't complain."

Patty was sitting next to her and popped a pink veggie slice into her mouth. "Tastes like a celery had a baby with a pumpkin. It's not that bad. I bet if we cooked it up with some spices, it would be delicious."

There had been no spices. Just square red meat cubes and the pink root we'd boiled in water on the electric stove that looked like a cross between a grill and a laptop. It had taken forever to figure out how to turn it on. At least their water faucets and toilets all work the same as ours, with actual water and not the gel crap.

"I'm just glad to have clothes on again. Never thought I'd be so thankful for pants," Sam said.

The four of us were sitting at the table, going over various plans. We'd kinda morphed into the command group and the others looked to us for answers.

We'd come up with a lot of nada.

The ship's flight deck, as Callie called it, was completely alien. The only truly alien thing we'd found aside from the ship itself. I was still salty about the green button and the lack of cleaning bots.

The engineer had said the ship was on an automated course to its original destination for cargo drop. Us and the Big Bad down in the hold. It had taken several translations to work out his alien time vs our Earth time. We thought roughly three weeks until some alien overlord boarded this ship and tried to take us again.

"Everyone should get some rest. There are enough bunks in the bedrooms. I'm going to take some food to our creepy alien guest downstairs."

Sam and Callie looked at each other, then at me.

"You sure that's a good idea? What if it breaks out when you try to feed it?" Sam asked.

"I will not let it—him—starve. We aren't the shark assholes. He's a prisoner too," I said, voice firm.

They looked troubled, but both just nodded and stood.

"We're all bunking together in the first room when you're done. I know you're a big, scary monster, but be careful," Callie said, and she went to herd the other women into rooms so they'd sleep.

I needed to go grab the engineer to open the doors and have him show me how to feed our scary guy.

"You said he talked? Want me to come with you to translate? Maybe he knows something about the ship," Patty offered.

I looked at her and nodded. "Yeah. That's a good idea. I thought about that earlier, too. An enemy of my enemy, ya know?"

"We need all the friends we can get."

I went and gathered some meat cubes into a metal container and followed Patty out of the mess hall.

We headed to the security room to relieve the girls of guard duty so they could eat and catch some sleep.

The shark had done a pretty solid job of cleaning up the place. Blood still spattered the ceiling and walls, but the floors were clean of blood and pieces of alien. The table and chairs were righted.

He whistled at us and bowed.

"He said he's ready to be of service and grateful for his life," Patty translated.

I didn't give a shit. I sneered at him and pushed him to walk in front of me.

When we got to the cargo hold door containing the Terror, the engineer balked again.

"If you don't move your ass, I'm going to eat you," I snarled.

He moved.

The door opened. The orange light of the glass tube really added an extra ominous feeling to an already fucked room.

Patty gasped when she caught sight of him. "Jesus. What is that thing?" she whispered, stepping into me.

Her hand found mine, and I gave it a squeeze before letting go.

"Let's see if he's hungry," I said.

I approached the glass tube, aware of his glowing eyes glaring a hole through me. My heart was really getting a workout through all this. I couldn't remember it ever racing so much in my life. There hadn't been anything but our own government to fear and they would have had to go through my mother. Mom wasn't here to be the biggest, scariest monster in the room anymore. This alien was. I clenched my teeth to keep them from chattering and took a deep breath.

"Do you eat? Are you hungry?" I asked when I was inches away from his prison.

His voice rumbled out, making me shudder. He was the Dark Lord, for sure. I just knew it.

I looked back at Patty.

"He said release him," she said. Her face had paled to ghost white, and her heart was pounding. The acrid scent of her fear swirled in the room, mixing with mine and the sharks.

"Are you going to try and kill us? We're prisoners too. I killed the crew when I broke out so I really don't feel like being waxed this close to freedom. We need help with the ship. Promise you won't hurt us, and I'll think about letting you out," I said, keeping my voice as calm as I could.

The shark warbled and whistled in protest.

"Be quiet!" I snapped at him.

The Orixas started speaking again, his lines lighting up. The ridges on his head pulsed in a light display with flashes and brief pauses.

"He said, he gives his word he will not harm us. He can fly the ship," Patty said. She looked at me and shrugged. "What do you think, Jack?"

I was thinking I'm going to let him out. We really didn't have a choice.

Jesus Christ, I was going to let him out.

Please, please don't kill us.

I'd fight him. I'd die for sure, but it might give Patty enough time to lock down the hold. If that was even an option.

"Can the hold door lock?" I asked the shark. He whistled in response and Patty nodded yes.

"I want you to lock this hold door open. And then you and the shark lock the blast doors to the main hold. If I don't come to bang on the door in ten minutes, get the girls and lock yourselves in the sleeping quarters," I said.

Patty had a gun. She could keep the shark under control.

"How do I open the cage?" I asked.

He warbled and rocked his head no.

"Either you tell me how to open this cage or I'm going to crack open your skull and eat your brain in front of you, then I'll figure it out on my own," I threatened, taking a step towards him and he scrambled to a control panel I hadn't seen on the floor. He waved me over and pointed at two buttons.

More buttons.

"He said push the larger one to open the tube, and the other unbinds him," Patty explained.

The shark stumbled to the door to jerk a panel off, revealing a lever that he pulled down, locking the door in place.

"Go. Seal those doors," I ordered.

Patty took a deep breath, gave me a crushing hug and then nudged the shark with her gun to make him walk, and they disappeared down the corridor.

I turned and waited. The alien regarded me with his yellow eyes, tails thumbing the cage floor.

The sound of metal sliding against metal came from the hall. Doors locking.

"Alright. Don't eat me."

The alien chuffed.

I blew out a breath before walking to the panel on the floor, and pushed the larger red button.

The tube opened with a hiss of air, and the orange light started flashing.

I looked at the alien.

He rattled his chains in impatience.

Please don't let this be a mistake.

I pushed the second button, and the restraints clicked and fell away.

The alien promptly crumpled to the ground in a heap of hissing, angry male, and thrashing tails. With tentacles. The metal bands must have had them locked down because there were four of them. They rested close to his tails on either side of his spine and gave the illusion that he had more tails than he did; the tentacles being more slender and shorter broke that illusion when you were this freaking close to him. The tentacles ended in three-pronged finger-like appendages at their tips that formed a stiff spear-like beak when they were closed together. His extra limbs were lined with dots that strobed in a fading pattern with the rest of the lines along his body.

How cool. Freaky, but cool.

"All the blood rushing back to numb limbs is painful, huh? Yeah, I've been there. Just rest for a second and flex your fingers and toes. The feeling will come back," I said, helpfully. He wouldn't eat someone who was helping, right? That would be rude.

He spoke in a low tone and did what I said. Flexing the claws on his hands, his hard finger-like tentacle tips, and then his feet.

I stepped closer to him, and that's when it hit me. Like a punch to the gut from a prizefighter.

His scent.

Christ.

He smelled *good*.

Really good.

I closed my eyes and basked in it.

When I opened my eyes again I was almost nose to nose with him and the sight of his face so close to mine froze me in shock. I must have crawled to him without realizing it.

He had vertical pupils in his glowing eyes.

What the fuck?

What the fuck.

I scrambled back away from him, breathing hard. I was sprawled on my ass against the door frame by the time I realized he hadn't moved.

"Oh shit! Sorry!" I said, hands palm out in front of me like that was going to stop him if he decided his personal space had been violated.

He chuffed and rose to his feet.

My mouth went dry seeing him standing outside the cage. He was huge. Truly huge. He was also very obviously male. I would think something as big and alien as him would have internal junk.

Nope.

His cock was external. It was also proportionate to his size. That said, it was also huge. Even flaccid, the thing was a hammer.

For Christ's sake! Stop looking at it.

I couldn't, though. It was beautiful.

His shape wasn't that much different from a man. Except for the ridges, and the bioluminescent bumps running around it in a spiral pattern, and the frills around the head. His balls were external too and perfectly shaped.

Saliva flooded my mouth. *Oh god, what was wrong with me?* I knew, though. I knew what this was. But you know what perfectly rational people do? *Deny. Deny. Deny.*

The deep bass of his voice jerked my attention away from his cock and up his body.

He had his arms crossed in front of his chest. He had really, really nice arms. Big biceps. Magnificent chest.

Stupid hormones.

Literally five minutes ago, I'd been terrified, and now I was panting over his chest. My mind was muddled, *off*, like I'd taken too many blows to the head.

"Um. Sorry? You're not going to kill me now, are you?" I asked, forcing my eyes to stay on his face. It was an actual struggle not to look back at his crotch.

He chuffed again and extended his clawed hand to me.

I stared at it for a moment, then slowly extended my hand to grip his fingers. There were six of them. His hands were hot, and it made a nervous giggle try to bubble up out of my throat. I had to press my lips into a hard line to keep it down.

He pulled me to my feet.

"Thanks," I said.

Again, I was staring at his chest.

His very close chest.

His skin was shiny, and smooth like oil, and he smelled so damn good. Before I could stop myself, I pressed my nose into his chest, breathing deeply. His skin was scorching hot, but so soft, stretching over his muscles like silk over stone. He smelled like musk and sex and war.

Before I could do something truly insane, like climb him like a tree, he gripped my shoulders and gently pulled me away from him. He said something in that Mordor voice, but I didn't understand. For the first time, I wished the superbugs had worked.

"I don't understand. I don't have any translating bugs inside my body," I said, frustrated. I felt like stomping my foot like a toddler.

He nodded his head and released me. He walked around me, through the door, and looked back at me. When I didn't move to follow him, he reached out with his tentacle and wrapped its three-pronged grabby things around my wrist. They weren't as hard as they looked and they must have joints or something because they could close all the way around my wrist like actual fingers. It weirded me out, but I managed not to rip it off me.

He tugged me after him and I followed like a good little doggy, off to the side so I didn't get taken out by his tails. My restraint should earn me a medal. A Nobel Peace Prize, really.

I took the time to study his back while we walked. The ridges from his head ran all the way down his spine to the base of his tails. They started small over his head and got larger the further down his spine they went and they glowed between the seams. His tails had the same glowing spiraled dots as his tentacles. He had a larger middle tail with two slightly smaller ones flanking on either side and they must be really flexible with the way he was rolling them around. He also had excellent control; he hadn't smacked me with them yet.

He made no noise when he walked. For a being that had to weigh a ton, that was pretty amazing. You'd never hear him coming. You'd just be dead.

Shuddering, I questioned my sanity for the millionth time, but he still smelled like sex on a stick! I wanted to rub up against his back like a cat in heat.

I looked at the tentacle and its finger things wrapped around my wrist.

He had really excellent control over these, too.

My dirty, *dirty*, completely cracked mind went straight to the gutter.

I needed my head examined.

When we came to the locked blast door, he let go of my wrist and stepped to the side. I rubbed my skin where he'd gripped me. It was hot from his touch and I was so totally not aroused by that.

Not. At. All.

Giving myself a little shake, I brought my fist up and banged on the metal door.

"It's me. We're good. Open up," I called. *We were not good. I wanted to fuck an alien. Send help.*

The locks disengaged, and the door slid open.

On the other side, Patty and the shark stood, with her pointing the gun at him. She turned when she spotted us and raised the gun halfway in the big bad's direction. I shook my head at her and she frowned, but lowered the weapon. There was no telling if the gun would even hurt him or not. Enemy of my enemy is my friend, and we don't shoot our friends. No matter how scary they were.

The shark squealed and tried to run for it when he spotted the Orixas beside me.

He didn't make it two steps before tentacles snatched him into the air. The Orixas started shaking the shark and roaring at him in his language.

Damn. Black Speech was sexy.

Oh. My. God. Snap out of it!

"He's asking for his weapons and armor. He's also threatening to rip the shark into teeny tiny pieces if he doesn't comply," Patty said, eyeing the big alien with a mixture of wariness and glee.

Patty was a bloodthirsty woman. My bestie was better than yours. She was staring at him, though. A hot, oddly territorial flash of anger flooded my mind. I didn't want Patty seeing his goods. I had to stifle a growl. Never mind that she was watching him shake the shark and not eyeballing his body.

I knew what this was, and it was impossible, and *freaking me the fuck out.*

The shark was whistle-gurgling frantically and the Orixas finally dropped him. He turned back into the cargo hold abruptly and I jogged after him as he glided straight to the room with all the crates. The doors didn't open for him, so he just punctured the metal with his claws and ripped the seamless door right out of the wall.

Damn.

His strength was incredible.

It was also still terrifying. It was good to know I hadn't completely lost my mind.

He entered the room to start ripping boxes open with his claws and rifling through them with his hand tentacles. His bioluminescence cast eerie shadows on the walls. He let out a weird chitter when he found what he was looking for, straightening to hold something up in his hand. It was a red metal torque.

When he clipped it around his neck, a red liquid that looked a lot like blood spread from the torque, spilling down his body to cover him from neck to toes, and molded to him. The liquid defied gravity, not a single drop fell from him, with only his tails and tentacles remaining free. The liquid shivered and then solidified into a matte red armor like nothing I'd ever seen. It was segmented with a porous fiber at his joints. It looked hard, but thin, and moved with him like a second skin.

Super advanced alien tech.

Finally!

His armor lit up exactly where his luminous lines and dots were on his body. The overall sight was intimidating as hell. He was already big and scary. Armored up?

War God.

"I always did like a man in uniform," I said, smiling at him while I ran my eyes all over his sexy new look.

He didn't acknowledge my comment, just continued to dig into the crate. His arm muscles flexed under the armor.

I had to press my thighs together against the arousal building in my core.

He was a goddamn alien!

My hormones obviously didn't care. My resistance to the whole alien sexy time was really wearing thin. I was a weak woman. My hormones were flooding me with the 'feel good juice' to lower my inhibitions. It was perfectly normal for my species, but that didn't mean I had to like it.

At least his dick was covered. I couldn't see even a hint of a bulge.

He turned to hold his clawed hand out to me. In his palm sat a round metal marble.

When I just stared at it, he grumbled and stepped close to me, picking it up with his tentacle. He pinched my chin gently with his fingers, tilting my head to the side and placed the marble into my ear. The marble was hot and the heat of it expanded to cover my ear in a flash of movement. I jerked my head out of his hand and reached for my ear. The metal had filled the inside of my ear completely, but I could still hear normally.

I blinked and looked at him in confusion.

"Do you understand?" he asked in his Mordor language.

The marble was a translator. How cool.

"Yeah, I understand you," I said, grinning up at him.

He nodded and started towards the door, where we left Patty and the shark. "Come," he ordered.

Gladly.

I snickered to myself. I was going to hell.

He glanced down at me, but said nothing.

Patty was still waiting for us with an exasperated look on her face. The shark was crying again.

"Can we figure out what to do with him?" Patty asked.

She didn't comment on or acknowledge the new armor at all. He deserved recognition for pure badassery, but without looking at him. That made me feel stabby. Patty just stared at us expectantly.

"There is a panel to the left of the cargo doors. Place him into one and pull the panel. He cannot open it from the inside," the Orixas answered.

Patty sighed in relief and pulled the shark up by his shirt and dragged him through the door.

I turned to the Orixas.

"I'm Jack," I said and extended my hand towards him to shake. "What's your name? I can't keep calling you the Big Bad or Terrible Terror," I said with a smile.

He glanced at my hand but didn't take it.

Instead, he bowed slightly at the waist and met my eyes.

"You may call me General At'ens."

Five

The General had been at the Captain's console for an hour, pressing buttons, muttering about outdated ships, and cursing the sharks with some very colorful language.

His scent was driving me insane.

I had never been so sexually frustrated and confused in my life.

I mean, he didn't even have ears! His nostrils were two pronged holes in his face that opened and closed with each breath. I should not want to bump uglies with him.

But I did. *I really, really did.*

I wanted to scream and demand he bend me over the console.

I did not.

I just stared at him like a stalker and growled under my breath while he continued to push buttons, oblivious.

He probably didn't even find me appealing. If he was strange to me, I imagine I looked strange to him. Probably more so, what with my tan skin's lack of light show capabilities. His ridges, from his head down to his spine, pulsed in rapid light patterns when he was agitated, like now.

It was mesmerizing.

"Problem, General?" I asked. My voice came out way huskier than I wanted.

He looked up from the console. "I have sent a message to my ship and changed our course to my ship's last known coordinates. However, we are further away than I expected, and this ship's transition drive is inadequate for the jump. We will have to travel two sectors before we can make the jump to my ship. It will take many days," he said, anger and frustration coloring his words. His lights strobed faster and his tails shifted on the floor behind him.

I shrugged and stood from the little chair I'd been sitting on while I creeped on him, and stretched my arms over my head. Time to make a retreat before I crawled into his lap.

"Nothing we can do about that. Might as well eat something and sleep. I'm exhausted. I'm gonna go find a bed," I said, and started walking across the flight deck towards the sleeping quarters. I kept my steps slow and deliberate, so it didn't look like I was tucking my tail and running.

I paused and looked back at him when I remembered none of the girls knew he was out. They'd freak if they woke up and he was looming here, putting on his threat display. They'd probably try to shoot him.

"Uh, General At'ens?" I said, thinking quickly. "Maybe you sleep in a room and wait until I can tell the others you're helping us before you come out? I'll bring you some food. It would avoid the panicked screaming."

His lights dimmed and stopped pulsing. I hoped I hadn't offended him. I opened my mouth to apologize, but he raised his hand and stopped me.

"I will lock the doors behind you. I do not require sleep for many days. I will wait." He paused, his lights glowing faintly again. "Thank you. For releasing me," he said, voice solemn.

I gave him a small smile. "Hey, no problem. Us alien abductees have to stick together."

I turned before he could answer and made my escape.

His eyes burned into my back as I exited the room.

· · · ● · ● · · ·

I woke up violently. My hand wrapped around Patty's throat. She was smiling like a lunatic.

I narrowed my eyes at her and barked, "I could have snapped your neck," as I snatched my hand back.

Patty laughed, slapping my shoulder when I sat up from the bed. "You didn't even squeeze. I wasn't worried. Besides, who doesn't like a little foreplay in the morning?"

I snorted at her and waved away her attempts to help me stand. I came to my feet with a groan, careful not to crack my head on the top bed. The bunks were short and uncomfortable for me. Better than the grate floor, but only marginally.

I'd had dreams of sex and tentacles and Mount Doom. His language really sounded like something straight out of Tolkien's books. It was haunting me in my sleep.

"Are the others awake?" I asked, looking around at the empty beds in the room.

"Yeah, everyone's getting breakfast. Or lunch? I have no idea what time it is. Not having day and night is going to mess up my circadian rhythm."

My friend Patty, always thinking of the real issues.

"Well, keep them there. I'm going to go get General At'ens," I said, walking out of the room towards the flight deck.

The doors were locked like he said they would be so I banged my fist on them.

"It's me, Jack. Ready to meet the family?"

The door slid open, and I was again treated with an up close view of his mouth-watering chest. The bioluminescent lines that ran over his shoulders and down his chest drew my eyes like a beacon. His scent flooded my nose and I had to jump back to avoid pressing my face into him again.

"I did not know they were your kin," he said with a tilt of his head, his horns just barely missing the doorframe.

I would never get used to the chest vibrating timber of his voice, or its effect on me. But it did the trick of pulling my gaze from his body to his face. His four glowing eyes were laughing at me. They narrowed slightly like when someone smiled even if he couldn't, with his mouth being a seam between the upper and lower parts of his face.

"They aren't. I was joking," I said, dryly.

He had to duck to come through the door, and stand in the hallway. He looked at me. I looked at him. Gazing, really. Ogling.

"Are we not going?" he asked, amused.

Busted.

I felt heat spread across my face and I turned to avoid his gaze, marching down the hall towards the dining room. The laughter and murmured buzz of many voices drifted towards us. I held my hand up to stop him when we were at the door, but he walked right into my hand, my palm pressing against the heat of his armored stomach. I stared at my hand for a second before slowly running it up to his chest. He was so warm even through the armor, which was smooth to the touch. I wanted to run my hands all over him. He leaned into my caress and I snapped my eyes to his face.

I hadn't thought the hard half mask of his face could show amusement when I first met him, but it was there, his glowing yellow eyes laughing at me... again. The heat blooming on my face spread. I'd never blushed in my life and he'd got me red-faced twice in one minute. I pulled my hand away and curled it into a fist against my thigh.

"Wait here," I ground out through clenched teeth. I entered the room, and the hum of conversation stopped.

I waved at everyone. "Hey guys. Um, so I'm gonna just come right out and say it." I paused for effect. "I let the alien prisoner out of his cage last night," I explained in a rush.

There were gasps and then outraged shouts overlapping each other until I couldn't understand a damn thing they were saying.

"Enough!" Callie bellowed, coming to her feet hard enough to make the table she'd been sitting at jerk across the floor a few inches, and the women fell silent.

She should have been a drill instructor and skipped being a pilot. That was impressive.

Callie turned to me, one dark eyebrow raised. "Well? Can he help?"

"I can fly the ship, yes," the General said from behind me.

There were shrieks and scrambling bodies as the girls jumped over tables and chairs to hit the wall farthest away from him.

I turned to fix him with a glare. "I told you to wait!"

He cocked his head at me and chuckled. "I apologize. I did not mean to cause alarm." He looked at the women pressed against the wall and raised his hands in a calming gesture. "Be at ease, I mean you no harm. I am General At'ens of Stellios," he said, his voice a soothing rumble of distant thunder. He placed his clawed hand on his chest and gave a small bow. The shrieking stopped.

Like a rescue worker coaxing feral cats.

And he laughed! If his voice was haunting my sleep, that low chuckle was going to be a poltergeist, just ruining my rest for the next half of eternity.

His tone had the desired effect. The ladies stopped cowering, and a few even slowly walked back to their seats.

Holy shit.

He was charming.

How about that?

Being abducted was a shock, but seeing this alien 'walking nightmare' charm a room full of frightened women was going to give me a stroke.

"Please, sit," he said gently, gesturing to the vacated chairs that hadn't been reclaimed yet. The last of the women took their seats and watched him with wary, hopeful expressions. A few were even gazing at him with curiosity.

I might go on another killing spree.

It was irrational and possessive, and there was only one way to stop it.

"I have sent distress messages to my ship. Once we reach the appropriate distance for a transitional jump, we will be within direct communication range and will be retrieved. I will personally make sure you are returned to your home planet. You have my vow," he said and bowed again.

Excited chatter spread throughout the mess hall. A few brave girls asked questions about how long it would take to get to the jump point and how long after that to get back to Earth. The General answered each one like they were the most important questions he'd ever heard. He even took the time to work out our Earth time to give accurate answers. How adorable.

It set my teeth on edge.

I didn't even hear the answers, so focused on not letting my possessive streak make me wolf out and eat some poor girl that I missed the entire conversation.

I was jealous.

Big, ugly, green jealousy. Over an alien male that was probably just doing his military duty of protecting and serving.

I groaned and buried my head in my hands. There really wasn't much of a point in denying it any further at this point.

This male—so different and strange—from a whole other fucking universe, was my mate.

My mate was an alien. A super freaky alien too. He couldn't be just some human looking dude with green skin. Oh no, mine had to have tentacles and multiple tails!

How do I get an alien interested in me? He has a cock, so he has to have sex, right?

Did I just come out and ask?

Yes, Mr. Alien General, sir. Do you have sexual relations with total strangers on an alien ship after being abducted or does inter-species dating offend you?

I cringed. What an embarrassing situation to be in.

I looked up at my mate in time to see one of the bolder girls, the cleaning organizer, Brittany? Jessica? Whatever the hell her name was, place her dirty, nameless hand on my General's arm.

A bone chilling growl burst out of my mouth like a bomb, echoing off the walls in the room.

Everyone froze.

The General looked at me, then down at the hand of Brittany/Jessica on his arm and then back at me.

I'd come to my feet, my skin rippling.

He looked back down at his arm and removed her hand gently. He took a step away from her and towards me. The growling stopped. I hadn't even known it had been continuous until the silence. It had been instinctual and out of my conscious control.

"Maybe no one touch him," Callie said, her brown eyes shooting me a wary look.

Make that three times I'd blushed in my life.

"Tiffany, why don't you come sit down with me? We can ask General At'ens about the food processor later," Sam said to the overly friendly, touchy-feely woman that had her hand on my alien.

I cleared my throat and grimaced. "Sorry guys. I don't know what that was."

Lies.

Callie snorted in disbelief.

Patty touched my arm and steered me to a seat at a table on the far side of the room, away from the others.

Everyone awkwardly got back to eating and talking amongst themselves again.

Eyeing me like I had three heads, Patty skirted the table and sat down across from me. She put her elbows on the tabletop and leaned forward, blue eyes glittering at me in amusement. "So what was that?"

I rubbed my hands down my face and sighed. "Territorial mating behavior. It'll go away after we bang it out."

Patty nodded and grinned at me. "So you want to fuck the alien? Damn girl, you work fast. Got over that fear real quick when you got an eye full of his big dick, huh? Oh, you think I hadn't noticed? Hard to miss with it lit up like a holiday candle and swinging around in the open air."

I didn't punch her in the face, but it was a struggle. "Don't look at his dick," I said, glaring at her.

Patty's peals of laughter swirled around me, lifting me out of my embarrassment. I smiled, then chuckled, and then I laughed right along with her. We laughed so hard, tears streamed down my face and I had to banged my fist on the table, fighting for breath.

It took forever for us to calm down.

We grinned at each other when we could breathe again and warmth spread through my chest. I was really glad Patty was here.

"Thanks, Patty. I needed that."

She brushed a tangled lock of brown hair out of her face before reaching across the table to grip my hand. "Yeah, me too." She wiggled her eyebrows. "Your alien hasn't stopped staring at you."

I glanced over my shoulder and spotted the General waiting by the door with his arms crossed over his chest, well away from the other women. His lights were off and his tails swished lazily around him. Tentacles waving behind him like they were caught in a breeze. He caught me looking and cocked his head, bioluminescence lighting faintly.

I turned back to Patty and made a face. "What do I even say? Hi, I'm pretty sure you're my once in a lifetime mate and I really want you to fuck me?"

Patty nodded her head sagely. "Yeah, that sounds about right. Why beat around the bush or keep it all bottled up? The worst he can say is no."

I pinched the bridge of my nose between my fingers and sighed. "I mean, that would be pretty bad, Patty. Did you miss the 'once in a lifetime' part?

He could say no, sure. But he could also say hell no, you disgust me, alien female!" I whisper-hissed the last part, pulling my hand from hers and curling it into a fist.

"I'm already pretty conflicted about being ready and willing to get down with an alien. Being ready, and willing, and being rejected? Brutal, dude."

"Would you just go talk to him? He's waiting so patiently and everything! It's adorable! I ship you guys so hard!" Patty said as she got up from the table and abandoned me to go sit with Sam and Callie. Both of them were eyeballing me like I was crazy. I flipped them the bird and laughter erupted from the group.

I may love them.

Alright. Don't be a sack.

I sucked in a breath and stood. He was still waiting for me by the door. When I approached, he glowed a little brighter. Please be a positive sign.

I stopped in front of him and gestured out the door. "Can I speak with you? Privately? We could go to the bridge or whatever and talk."

He chuffed and shook his head slightly, his primary eyes narrowing slightly before he wrapped his hands around my biceps and pulled me into him, bending his head to bring it closer to mine. Being my mate was going to give him neck problems.

I put my hands on his chest and tilted my head back to watch him.

He opened his mouth to speak—alarm klaxons blared. The ship shuddered, gave one hard jerk, and the lights went out.

Six

Orange lights flashed. The roar of the engines could be heard even over the alarms, and the ship was listing to the left.

We'd been knocked off our feet with the initial jerk. There'd been some nasty bruises and one woman had cracked her head on a table pretty severely. The General had taken control of the chaos, gotten people to their feet, and kept us all calm. He hadn't let me drift more than a foot from him the whole time. One tentacle or claw was always reaching out to touch me every moment or so.

I had totally let it go to my head.

Now everyone was crowded in the bridge while the General typed at the console monitor, his face grim.

He met my eyes. "The engines are overheating and have shut down. The stabilizing systems are offline! We are drifting into the planet's gravitational field," he shouted over the roar.

I hadn't looked out the window since yesterday. It had just been black space then.

Now a planet dominated the view. It was burnt orange and did not look inviting. We were being pulled into it? Fear once again coated the inside of my mouth with a sour taste.

Callie cupped her hands around her mouth. "What the hell happened?"

The General stepped back from the console, tentacles twisting around behind him. "Let's find out!" He turned to the engine room door behind him, his tails writhing and tentacles gripping the edges of the open door. He'd opened the biometric locks with an override on the captain's console.

I turned to the girl next to me and shouted into her ear. "Get everyone back into their rooms! We are going to figure this out! I'll come get you later!"

She nodded and started yelling, gesturing for the others to follow her. Only Callie, Sam, and Patty stayed.

I nodded to them and followed my mate into the hallway. The ship was shaking and the tilt was more severe now, making the descent down the stairs difficult, so I had to grab his arm for balance down the stairs. I had Patty's arm gripped in mine to keep her upright. She had Sam's, and Sam had Callie's, like a chain of teamwork. If I wasn't freaking out, it would have made me all fuzzy inside.

We came to the huge blast doors that were also biometric. They were already open. Did he open them from the console like the other door?

When we entered the engine room, all the coolant was gone. The engines were steaming, the heat in the room took my breath away. We could go no further than the door. It would blister our skin for sure.

The roaring here was deafening. I looked at Patty—she was pouring sweat and shouting, her mouth was moving but I couldn't hear anything over the engines. She pointed her finger, and I followed it. At the huge computer was the engineer shark. Our Designated Survivor. Guess that answered the question about the open door. He was red and badly blistered all over. His clothes were smoking.

I'd forgotten all about him. How the hell had he gotten out of the hold? I was just as bad at security as the sharks.

He was pulling wires and tossing them into the boil of the engines below us.

When he noticed us, I swear he smiled. Right before he pitched himself over the railing and died.

The General pushed us back up a flight of stairs to the first landing and went back into the oven. He looked over the ruined computer. His lights flared brightly, and he jerked the computer off its hooks to toss it into the heat below. He curled his claws, threw his head back, and roared. The muffled power of it could be heard even over the engines.

He stalked back to us, skin steaming. He wrapped a burning hot tentacle around each of us, and picked us up. My skin was on fire where his tentacle touched the bare skin of my stomach. Hopefully, the others were better off wearing full coverage shirts because he was wasting no time. He curled us close to his back like women-sized backpacks and bolted up the stairs. I recognized the doors and hallways as we raced past, he was taking us to the cargo hold.

He didn't set us down until we were back in the hold with our cages.

"What are we doing here? What's going on?" I shouted at his back. My hand was shaking when I raised it up to touch him. I curled it into a fist before I contacted his back and pressed it into my stomach. He was ripping paneling and wires out of the wall until the door slammed shut, locking us inside.

"What are you doing?" Callie demanded. She had her arms around Sam and was glaring at the General.

He ignored us both and pulled up another panel from the floor that revealed a huge yellow lever. He jerked it up at the same time his tentacles wrapped around all of us again. The hold jolted violently, an explosion rocked the ship, and then we were falling.

• • • ● • ● • • •

Searing pain in my side woke me. I lifted my hips to roll, but something pinned my legs. I couldn't see. My eyes were open, but I couldn't see. My breath sawed in and out of me in panicked rushes and I cried out, but only managed a croaked moan. I tentatively touched my side and my hand came away wet. I was bleeding, blind, and pinned to the floor. Where were the others? Patty and Sam, Callie and my General? Someone coughed and gagged.

"Hello? Is anyone else alive?" A hoarse voice called out.

"I'm here!" Patty's voice sounded from far away.

"Oh Jesus, Patty. Come help me!"

I heard grunting and feet scraping against the floor. Cool hands touched my face.

"Oh shit. Oh fuck, fuck. Jack? Jack!" Patty was crying and yelling at me, her hands patting all over the top half of my body.

I swallowed dust, and what felt like nails. "I'm—I'm alive."

Someone else was sobbing in the distance. Then Patty sighed in relief and moved away from me. The weight from my legs lifted. A crash sounded beside me and then I was lifted, too. The movement was torture.

I was set down after a short distance and water was dumped over my face and into my mouth, hands wiping away at me. Bright light stabbed through my eyelids, and my eyes watered against the glare until a shadow blocked it. I blinked furiously to clear my eyes of tears. The General was leaning over me, his four eyes wide, the yellow slit pupils dilated. His hard faceplate was cracked badly under his right eyes, yellow blood running from the wound. He pressed his forehead against mine and breathed.

"You lived," he said, with so much relief in his voice that it wavered.

I cupped the undamaged side of his face in my palm. We stayed like that for a long moment, just breathing each other in.

I gently pulled his face from mine. "Are the others okay?" I asked.

He sat back. "The three you kept with you are alive. One is badly wounded. I think her leg is broken and she may be bleeding inside. The other two females are not seriously injured. The one called Sam has a head injury, likely a concussion. I put them only a short distance from you. The nanos will make them sleep, to heal. You have a large wound. I fear it is from my claws gripping you during the crash. I am very sorry." His voice was rough, choked, like the guilt was making it difficult to speak.

I reached for him, and he gripped my hand tightly. "I'll heal, I promise. I don't have nanos, but I heal fast. See? It's not even bleeding anymore." I shifted to show him the already half healed tear in my side. "Don't apologize for saving my life. I'm okay. I'm alive, and so are my friends, because of you." I placed my other hand on top of his to sandwich it between my palms. "Thank you," I said, my voice wobbly.

"I only saved three of your friends, Jack. The others died in the crash," he said.

A knot in my throat tightened. I suspected they hadn't made it. All those women. They'd been so hopeful about going home, their nightmare was almost over. The light at the end of the tunnel had been so close!

It wasn't fair. I hadn't even taken the time to learn their names. I'd sent them to their rooms to stay safe, and told them we'd figure it out. Guilt and grief settled over me like an oppressive cloud, the weight trying to crush me under it. The tears burning my eyes spilled over and ran down my cheeks. Once I started crying, I couldn't stop. My side ached with each breath but I couldn't stop. The General gently gathered me in his lap and held me while I bawled my eyes out. Patty came to sit beside us, reached for my hand and cried with me. He pulled her to his side and wrapped his other arm around her in comfort. Seeing it made me cry harder. We sat together like this for a long time, until my tears dried and my side stopped aching.

I buried my face in his chest. His armor was warm and felt just like skin. His heartbeat was a double rhythm much slower than mine. It was soothing.

"Is At'ens your first name?" I asked, to distract myself from the guilt weighing me down.

He shifted and wrapped his arm around me more securely, careful not to knock Patty over. She was asleep against him, still holding my hand.

"It is my family name. The name of my House. My given name is Ohem." His chest rumbled like a sub-woofer speaker when he talked.

"Nice to meet you, Ohem," I said, stroking his arm with my free hand. His armor felt like smooth, hot rubber molded over stone. It was weird that it wasn't hard like metal. It emitted his body heat like a furnace and I was sweating in his arms from the close contact. It didn't help that the air was hot and dry, too.

I lifted my head from his chest and looked around. We were on the bank of a lake, in a valley surrounded by red mountains on three sides. The smoldering remains of half an alien shipping container was partially buried in the sand against the red stone wall of an enormous cliff about a mile away from us.

That explained the ceiling height disparities. We'd been in a roll out container for easy loading and unloading. No need to even take us out of our cages. More efficient than I would have given the shark's credit for, seeing as how they had been so lax on most everything else.

There was a ragged furrow torn into the ground leading away from the crash where we must have slid until finally coming to a stop. My eyes traced the smoking path of destruction beyond the mouth of the valley, across a vast desert plain. Heat waves obscured the horizon and what was left of the rest of the crash.

How had we survived?

We were leaning up against a cluster of boulders right on the water's edge. The lake water was muddy brown and still. There were no trees or plant life at all, just rocks and sand.

It was in the shadow of one boulder that I finally noticed Callie and Sam. They were laid side by side. I carefully slid myself off of Ohem's lap and stood. He was trapped by a sleeping Patty, but made moves to follow. I motioned with my hand for him to stay put. She needed to rest. My side had already healed, so I was fine, but who knows what kind of internal injuries Patty might have and not know it. I didn't want her to wake up before she was ready.

I walked the few steps, falling to my knees at Callie's side to look her over. Callie's leg was bound to a jagged piece of metal with wire. Her black clothes were torn and bloody, and her face was a mess of bruised skin. Her brown skin looked nearly gray and a black bruise on her stomach was stark against the skin visible through a big tear in her shirt. I checked her pulse and sighed in relief when I found it steady and strong, if slower than normal. She was in a coma, like Ohem said.

I moved to inspect Sam and to check her breathing and pulse. Sam had a shallow gash across her temple, and her short blond hair had blood in it. She might have some serious head trauma. Ohem had said they'd heal. I trusted his word, but we had no way to get them fluids other than pouring water down their throats. I looked back at Ohem. He had his arm wrapped securely over Patty's shoulders, her head resting on his side, and he was watching me. The sight didn't stir the possessive anger this time. Patty was only seeking comfort and I would be damned if I let the unfinished mating bond ruin that.

We would have been dead without him. He'd carried us all out of the wreck, splinted Callie's broken leg, and held us while we cried. Any doubts or hang-ups about being mated to an alien had burned up in the crash.

"What are we going to do now?" I said, coming back to tuck myself into his side.

He took a deep breath. "We are still in the same sector as we were when I sent word to my people. They will find us. What worries me is surviving long enough to be rescued."

I leaned away from him to meet his eyes.

"What do you mean? We have water, and I'm sure this dust bowl of a planet has got some sort of life on it. We're breathing the air right now, so that means it'll have life, right?" He nodded yes. "So we hunt for food and stay close to the crash site so it'll be easier for them to find us."

He brought his hand up from where he'd wrapped it around my waist to run the back of his fingers along my cheek, shaking his head. "My brave *ursang*." He lifted a tangled lock of my hair and rubbed it between two fingers. "We have more to fear than the struggles of surviving this planet. Did you not wonder how smugglers as incompetent and weak as the Vrax could capture one such as me?"

I snorted. "Yeah, they didn't seem like they were up to the task."

Though one did escape and blow up the ship.

"So, how'd you end up on their ship?" I snuggled back into his body, not caring about how hot it was making me. It felt good to be close to him. A mating bond made you ache to be close to your mate. It was much worse before it was completed. It would eventually push me beyond my capabilities to deny it, but for now, I was content to just be in his arms.

He wrapped his arm around me and paused, like he was gathering himself. "I was ambushed outside the orbital station of the Unity planet, Axsia. I was called there by an informant's promise of proof that Councilor Fennes Vero had found archaeological artifacts that were supposedly destroyed thousands of years ago. Artifacts belonging to the Unity's ancient enemy. An enemy with technology even more advanced than we have even now. A scourge upon the universe. My ancestor, At'ens the Liberator, oversaw the complete destruction of anything to do with the enemy. Whole worlds were destroyed." His voice dipped lower in what I thought might be sadness.

His grip tightened for a moment before he gave himself a little shake and let out a deep breath. "Vero has been quietly looking for artifacts and plotting war for decades now and the Unity has turned a blind eye to it. He has amassed weapons, soldiers, and allies in the criminal underbelly of many planets, yet still they do nothing!" He growled out between clenched teeth.

I pet his chest to soothe him. That growl did things to me, and I was trying very hard to ignore it. We had just crashed, my friends were injured, and he was telling me a story!

The mating bond did not care about any of that and was waking back up. It was pushing against the wall of my whirling emotions like a pacing tiger, just waiting for its chance to pounce.

"I was shot from a great distance with a sedative. I awoke on board the Vrax ship. I don't know why they didn't just kill me. It would have been the intelligent thing to do." His hand drifted up my back, slid under my hair to grip the back of my neck. He pulled me away from his chest and made me look at him. "But then I would not have found you. I don't think you understand the miracle it is that you exist. Or that it was me that found you. It is as if it was fated."

I was really confused right now. It must have shown on my face because Ohem laughed. A genuine laugh. It startled Patty awake. She glared at us and sat up. I winced and mouthed, "Sorry".

"What are you, Jack? Where are you from?" he asked, pulling his arm away from Patty to twist towards me, using both hands to cup my face.

I put my hands over his and in a really, really confused tone of voice, I answered, "I'm a Rijitera from New Mexico in the United States of America. Earth."

"And what is a Rijitera?" he murmured.

"Um, a shapeshifter?" I answered with a question because now I didn't know. He had me second guessing what the hell I was and where I was born.

He bent to press his forehead against mine. "The Rijitera, my *ursang*, were our ancient enemy."

Seven

Back the fuck up.

My people were from Earth. We'd been there just as long as humans. There were hundreds of myths in every culture mentioning us.

I pulled his hands from my face and got up to pace. "You said your ancestors wiped them out. Maybe we're distant cousins like monkeys are to people." There was no way my people were aliens.

No way.

We'd have had stories about it or something. No one had ever mentioned being some ancient alien race that came to Earth. No one. Not even my Memaw, who remembered everything and let everyone know about it. She wouldn't be able to sit on a bomb like that and keep it a secret. I'd traveled all over the world and met many of my kind in other countries, and none of them had said anything. Oh god, the nausea was coming back. I pressed a hand to my stomach to stave it off. Maybe the sharks didn't agree with me.

He stood and grabbed my arm, stopping my pacing and made me face him.

"They were destroyed, yes. We pulled apart their home planet and burned their technology. Destroyed their cities and temples on planets they'd conquered, erased anything they had made. We put them into our history recordings, where we thought they belonged and tried to forget, and yet here you are. Some must have escaped the purging. I have never come across a human before. Your Earth must truly be on the far reaches of the universe. It would have made an excellent hiding place. With their empire and armies destroyed, they would have needed somewhere no one would know them. To start over."

Patty was looking between us, her face scrunched up in confusion. She cocked her head to the side and raised her hand like she was in class. "If Jack's supposed people were so advanced and so savage, why didn't they use their shit to conquer Earth? I've seen this woman trussed up in a jail cell more times than I can count. Doesn't seem like the behavior of a superior race to me."

I looked at her with narrowed eyes, mock offended. "Hey! I was innocent," I said, and we grinned at each other before she returned her attention back to Ohem.

"All I'm saying is that if her people had been the locust of the universe, why isn't Earth some intergalactic empire right now? They've had thousands of years to set shit up. I've met Jack's mom, and while she's one scary bitch, she's not some warmongering super villain," Patty continued, pointing at Ohem.

He was glowing faintly now, and I couldn't tell if he was irritated by being questioned or if he just loved a good historical debate. While he was talking, I got the impression my mate was a huge history nerd. I guess if my ancestor had been a galaxy saving hero, I'd be pretty into history too.

"Perhaps the survivors were only civilians and not soldiers. Maybe they simply wanted peace after years of war, to fade into the background and live their lives. I do not know. I do know you are the same as the Rijitera pictured in the archival databases. My family has kept most of the records of the wars, including paintings and video recordings. There are thousands of hours of records. I have studied them extensively. You are the same. I knew the moment I observed you through the glass of my prison. I thought it was a trick of my mind. My nightmares come to life."

Oh geez, thanks a lot. That made me feel all warm and fuzzy inside. I pulled my arm from his grasp and put my hands on my hips.

"I'm in my human form right now. You said you've never seen a human before. Did the Rijitera in your histories have a human form? Bet they freaking didn't. So I'm not the same," I said, and I crossed my arms. Queen Denial, your name is mine.

He shook his head, amusement making his eyes glow brighter. He was faintly pulsing his lights, and he mimicked my stance with his arms crossed over his chest.

"They had genetically engineered themselves to take the best genes from any they mated with. They would birth a Rijitera no matter the species of the mate, with attributes from the mate that would strengthen them. What do you suppose would happen when they mated with humans repeatedly? Or perhaps they learned to shift their forms to blend in and hide. Maybe they brought enough technology with them to make the change possible. I would enjoy going to your planet and finding out. The Rijitera loved to make monuments and leave behind records of their deeds. I am positive there will be something that tells the history of their landing on Earth," he said, and the excitement in his voice was adorable.

My mate was a huge nerd. The big scary war General wanted to go on an archaeological dig. There were a lot of archaeological sites on Earth that scientists couldn't explain. He might be right. My stomach dropped.

Crap.

I was an alien.

Just roll with it.

I frowned and went back to pacing. "Why wouldn't we remember, though? We kept the name of our race, but nothing else? You said they were really into recording about themselves, but none of us know anything about who we are or where we come from."

I mean, we'd been egotistical maniacs that liked to war across space, so maybe that wasn't a bad thing.

"Maybe they didn't want to remember. Start over fresh, ya know? I mean, it worked. No one even knows your people are real. Your kind blended in and faded into myth. You're probably descended from some poor farmers or something that just wanted to be left alone," Patty said from her seat next to the rock. She was watching us with a look of intense fascination on her face. She looked hard at Ohem. "You mentioned breaking their planet and a purge? What does that mean, exactly?"

His lights dimmed and went out. They'd been getting brighter and brighter the more we talked and the more excited he got about the subject. Now he dropped his hands down by his side and his entire demeanor changed to one of shame.

He pulled in a deep breath and let it out slowly. "We had been fighting them for years. They would conquer a planet with ease. Their soldiers were savage and very hard to kill. They had weapons and warships that were far beyond us. We, as individual planets, were being slaughtered and conquered one by one." His tails flicked back and forth with his agitation and his tentacles rose behind him. He didn't like this part of his history. That much was clear.

"Six planets came together and formed an alliance we called the Unity. We pooled our military and resources and pushed them back. It was the bloodiest, longest war in known history. Of the six original Unity planets, only two still survive today. The Rijitera destroyed the others."

My people had been genocidal tyrants. Great. My stomach was tied in knots at hearing all this. I stepped closer to him and took his hand. He held on tight enough to make my bones creak.

"We kept pushing and fighting despite our terrible losses. The rage of the Unity was great. We wanted revenge for our dead and destroyed worlds. For our lost people. The Rijitera showed no mercy, so we gave them none in return. When my ancestor At'ens led the armies onto their home world, he razed it to ashes. The Rijiteran Imperial family were slaughtered in the streets of their capital. At'ens then had their planet torn apart, their outer colonies burned and their fleeing people hunted down and killed. We left none alive."

Patty gasped, covering her mouth with her hand. "Damn, that's brutal."

He sighed and nodded. "The history available to the public speaks of our Unity and victory over a greater foe. It does not shed light on the atrocities committed after we won. Atrocities committed by my own House. We are lauded as royalty for At'ens valiant charge against the Rijiteran's home planet. For his victory. It speaks nothing of his actions after the war was over. My House was the ones who hunted down fleeing Rijiteran people. Be they warriors or farmers. Rich or poor. They all fell to the claws of my kin. We hunted them for many years until none were left. We destroyed any of their records we found, until their history was destroyed. We wanted them to be wiped from existence, with nothing left but our one-sided account of who they were. Our records of triumph. My family is the only one to keep truer accounts of the war crimes committed. By the end, we had become our enemy, surpassing them in cruelty."

He pulled me into his embrace and held me. I was confused about what to feel.

They were my people, but it was a little like being related to Genghis Khan. You knew you were descended from an asshole and a conquer, but it was so far in the past that it didn't really affect you. He obviously carried a lot of shame for the actions of his ancestors. I was sad and a little angry that my people had been destroyed. Our history anyway. There were a lot of us on Earth. It sucked to know I wouldn't ever fully understand who we really were. All the stories and culture were gone. I'd never know my people's language or religion.

They'd been conquerors and tyrants, but that couldn't have been all they were. They mated and had children. They'd had lives outside of war.

We lived on, though. That counted for something. We'd come to Earth and hadn't repeated the same mistakes. We hadn't rebuilt our empire and struck back. We'd just lived. We were a volatile and violent group, but we were also pranksters and fun loving. We loved our family and friends fiercely. We were loyal and steadfast. We never backed down from a fight or preyed on the weak. We were good people.

That was our culture.

I rubbed my nose into his skin, breathing him in. I kissed him in the center of his chest and looked up at him. "Hey. You're not your ancestors and neither am I. They both did some fucked up shit and that shouldn't be forgotten, but we don't have to feel guilt for things that happened thousands of years ago. We're living right now. How we act now is what matters. Are you going to go to Earth and eradicate my people there?" I asked him.

He jerked. "Of course not," he said, offended.

I smiled and shrugged my shoulders. "And I'm not going out to conquer planets. I'm going to survive this one and get to know my mate."

He got really still. His lights glowing brighter and brighter until he was lit up like a glow stick.

"Your mate?" he breathed, his voice deepening even more.

Oh, Right. I hadn't had the chance to have that talk with him yet and all the touchy-feely moments with him made me forget I hadn't said anything. We'd done a good job of distracting ourselves with all the talk about my people.

My heart kicked into high gear and I swallowed hard. "Um, how does your kind feel about interspecies dating?" I said around a nervous laugh. He'd been holding me sure, but how the hell would I know what him touching me meant? Maybe his kind were just huggers?

Patty's shouted laughter saved me from myself. She was literally rolling around on the ground, howling.

I didn't think it was that funny, but I couldn't even glare at her. I was blushing furiously while Ohem just stared at me.

He slid his hands down my arms slowly, until he had my hands held loosely in his. He brought them up to his face and rubbed the smooth skin of his lower jaw over my fingers. His eyes never left my face. "My people encourage marriage with different species. It is celebrated when two people come together. My family would be overjoyed at the union of old enemies. It would lay the past to rest. Yes. I am honored to be chosen. You humble me, *ursang*."

His lights were flashing and pulsing in an intricate pattern, and I was starting to understand what all the different glow ups meant. This one was joy.

What would they do when he was aroused?

I was going to make it my mission in life to find out.

"So you aren't weirded out by my appearance or by my instincts choosing you and only you?" I asked, my stomach doing somersaults inside me.

Ohem chittered. "You do not look so different from many species I have met. You are well formed and strong. I find you beautiful. Powerful. I knew the moment you came to feed me inside my prison that I wanted you. I was worried you would be too afraid to accept my advances, but you stared so intently at my body on the Vrax ship, wanting me. I could smell you," he said, his voice a low growl. His fingers brushed my cheek, and I shuddered at the tone of his voice, half mesmerized. "My people know when we have met the one we are meant to spend our life with. In a way, we have our own instinct."

Patty squealed and clapped. "My ship has sailed!"

Lunatic.

I jumped and wrapped my arms around his neck and hugged him. His arms wrapped around my waist, holding me against his body tightly, pressing his face into my neck. I wished we were alone right now. Aside from ancestral revelations, sex was a pretty good distraction from grief. Reminded you that you were alive while pushing the seriousness of your situation to the background, if only for a little while.

I needed to be getting on a first name basis with his dick. For the distraction.

"I wish I could have you," he muttered into my neck, sending a goosebumps wave across my body.

"When you say 'have' do you mean–"

"I would have my cock buried deep inside you if we did not have an audience," he interrupted with a low, dark chuckle. "Or perhaps you don't mind being watched?" His voice was practically a purr, and the wet heat of his tongue gliding across the skin of my neck sent a lightening bolt of pure pleasure to my clit, and I seriously considered just fucking him in front of Patty. She'd probably cheer and give pointers.

His tongue continued its path up my neck to circle around my ear. It was textured and rough against my skin and I moaned, my sex clenching and needy.

Yeah... I didn't care about the audience. I just wanted him inside me.

"Ah, I can smell you, my *ursang*. So sweet. Will you taste as sweet, I wonder? Will my Rijitera beg for her pleasure?" His voice rumbled around me in amusement.

Hot *damn*.

I was opening my mouth to tell him I'd do whatever he wanted if he'd just fuck me, when a groan sounded from beside us. It was a pained groan, not a sexy one, and it pulled me out of my lust-filled haze.

Ohem pressed his face hard into my neck and growled in frustration.

I panted out a little laugh and patted his shoulder. "I know," I said and wriggled out of his grasp.

Sam was sitting up and clutching her head. I crouched down in front of her and gripped her shoulder to steady her.

"What happened?" she croaked, looking around in confusion.

"The nano bugs put you out to heal your concussion, we think," I said.

She grunted and squinted at me. "Hey, you seem better."

I smiled sheepishly. "I heal fast."

"Lucky," she said and stood. I reached out to help her up, steadying her again when she swayed.

"Fuck. I feel like shit." She looked around and spotted Ohem. She gave him a little wave and turned to check on Callie.

"Is she going to be okay?" she asked, looking down at her.

Sam's gash was healed, and the bruises were gone. She was still filthy and covered in blood, but it looks like the nanos did their job.

"The nanos healed you, so I imagine they will do their job with her, too," I said, pointing to the thin scar on her temple that had been a bloody gash a few hours ago. "She's probably going to be out a while longer. She was hurt the worst."

Callie's face was already cleared of the bruises, and her stomach was a mottled yellow instead of the stark black it was when she was pulled from the crash.

"Where's Patty?" Sam asked, still looking down at Callie.

I looked around and couldn't find Patty. She must have moved to give us some privacy.

"She is walking to the remains of the storage cell," Ohem said. He was standing right behind us. He was so quiet that Sam and I both jumped when he spoke.

He was still lit up like a Christmas tree and looking at me like he'd like to eat me.

The feeling was very mutual. My face must have relayed my thoughts because he growled roughly and turned to stalk off towards the wreck.

I grinned at his back. He wanted me! Wanted me badly! I shimmied a little dance. Sam eyed me like I'd lost my mind.

"What's happening? Why'd the General look like he was going to rip you apart?" she asked, eyeing me suspiciously.

I wiggled my eyebrows, grinning.

Her eyes widened, and she made a face halfway between disgust and curiosity. "Oh god! Did you sleep with him?"

"Not yet. If I had, he wouldn't look so full of aggression," I said, laughing. "No, I told him he was my mate, he accepted me, and we were three seconds from fucking against that boulder before you woke up and cock-blocked me."

She grimaced. "Oh man, sorry about that. But congrats on the whole mate thing." She raised her hand for a high five and I slapped her palm with mine.

We smiled at each other, and Sam laughed under her breath. "It's been a crazy few days, huh?" She was looking around, taking in the desert, the muddy lake, and following the path of the crash with her gaze.

Her smile faded as she looked at the blackened remains of the container. "The others are dead, aren't they?" she asked quietly.

I met her solemn blue eyes with mine, reached for her hand, and nodded. She'd known the others better than me. Had known their names.

She sucked in a shuddering breath and blew it out on a sob.

I pulled her into a hug, stroking her short hair and murmuring nonsense to her while she cried into my chest. Her tears soaking into the tattered remains of my makeshift tube top that had somehow survived the crash. Ohem and Patty were dragging things out of the wreck in the distance. Ohem glanced back at me and turned to speak to Patty. She looked up, spotted me holding a crying Sam, and jogged back towards us.

When she got to us, she wrapped her arms around Sam's back, sandwiching her between us.

We stood there like that until Sam's sobs quieted to shuddering breaths.

She gave me a hard squeeze, stepping away from me, wiping her eyes with the back of both hands, and then gave Patty a hard hug too, laughing a little when Patty grunted dramatically.

"I'm sorry for crying all over you, Jack. It's just so unfair. There was a girl, Cleo, that was supposed to be getting married in a few months. She was so nervous and excited to go home, wondering what she was going to tell her fiance about where she'd been all this time. And Tiffany had kids. Two little girls. They will never see their mom again." Her voice choked up, more tears ran down her cheeks, and she wiped them away. "Why'd they have to die?" She shuffled over to Callie to sit next to her, brushing Callie's hair away from her face.

Patty watched her, worry lines forming between her brows. She flicked her eyes up at me, reaching a hand out to touch my shoulder. "She'll be okay, eventually. We all will."

She went to sit with Sam to hold vigil over Callie while she slept. Her arm wrapped around Sam's shoulder.

I frowned at them, and turned to find Ohem, who was right beside me, making me jolt again in surprise. I cursed under my breath, shaking my head at him and giving him my best glare before asking the question I should have asked earlier.

"Will we be okay? We got caught up in the history lesson and I forgot to ask if someone was going to come hunting for you when the ship didn't show up with you all caged and helpless, and full of lady cargo."

Ohem looked up at the sky and then back at me. "It is likely that we will be hunted, yes. I am valuable for something or they would have just killed me. And rare females from an unknown planet are worth a lot of credits. The ship had dozens of tracking devices on it for any contingency. They will know we are on this planet."

Fuck. Why couldn't we just crash land and live like Cast-Away and be left alone with only a volleyball to worry about, but oh no. We had to have some politician hellbent for war and probably some nasty bounty hunter types gunning for us.

Ohem laid his big hand on my shoulder. "We need to get food. We can stay vigilant, but we need to worry about our immediate needs now. One of us should hunt and the other stay behind to guard the others," he said. "Would you like to hunt or stay here with your friends?"

A hunt sounded like heaven.

I glanced up at his face. "I'll take the hunt." He nodded and went to stand guard over my friends.

Eight

Running in my shifted form was always a thrill. The savage freedom of a wild thing on the loose. The form of my feet made me swift and light. I could run on all four, my arms were long enough, but it was faster to sprint upright.

I'd been loping across the desert for an hour, but I hadn't seen a single animal or even a sign of an animal. Just endless dirt. Not even a blade of grass.

Another issue was the sun... there were *two*. Not side by side, but on opposite ends of the planet, so it would never get dark here. I was beginning to wonder if there were any animals at all. It was a miracle there was water at all, and that we had landed right next to it. Freaking divine intervention is what it was. Or the universe's sick joke.

Screw you, Universe!

I stopped at a tall rock outcropping, my breath coming in pants that stirred up the dirt on the surface. I crouched and sprung halfway up the rock, claws scoring the stone, and then pulled myself up to the peak. I scanned the horizon for something, anything, that might point to food.

Desert, desert, oh look at that. More desert.

Why couldn't we have landed in a jungle?

We would not starve here. To survive being abducted, liberated, crashed landed, and then fucking die of starvation? No way in hell. The heavy weight of responsibility settled on my shoulders, and the pressure in my chest flared, becoming crushing as the worry ate me from the inside.

Throwing my head back, I let loose a howl of defiance at the universe. The sound spread out and faded into the desert.

Something bellowed back. I snapped my head to the right, in the direction the noise had come from. There in the distance, against the horizon, was movement. It bellowed again, like the sounds of an elephant and a cow got mixed up and blasted out of a cannon.

I jumped down from the rocks and trotted towards the bellowing, staying low and quiet. It was harder running in this direction, my legs feeling the strain a little more. I was going up a gradual incline. I realized we had crashed in a valley within a valley, and the lake we were at probably used to be a lot bigger, but had dried until only the very middle remained. It might have even been an ocean at one time, judging from how vast the desert was. No wonder I hadn't been able to see anything on the horizon.

I picked up speed, still staying silent. I ran for twenty minutes before the land above us came into view. It was still a desert, but there were what looked like trees or plants spread out in the distance, following along the base of another mountain range. Milling about those plants were animals. Big, scaly, lizard-camel things. They didn't actually look anything like either of those animals, but it's the closest thing I could compare them to. Four-legged, red scaled, with long necks and whip-like tails. They had a big hump on their back that was covered in bony spikes with flat heads that spread out like a hammerhead shark. They were a weird looking animal, but it wouldn't be the first time I'd eaten something weird. Probably wouldn't be the last either.

There were a dozen of them, tearing the skin off the thick green trunks of spiny trees. They shambled from tree to tree, grunting and snuffling.

Jackpot.

I creeped to the west of them, alongside their flank. I wanted to come from the north, through the trees, so they ran into the desert and not deeper into the canyons.

I dropped to all fours and kept my belly close to the ground, moving swiftly until I was in the treeline, along the mountainside. The tree's spines were thin and needle sharp, like cat-claw cactus from back home. The canopy consisted of thin yellow leaves as long as me that drooped and made the trees look like they were wearing bad wigs, casting spider-shaped shadows on the ground.

I weaved through the trees and stalked closer to the lizard-camels. They smelled awful, like spoiled milk left out in the sun, and they were easily the size of a large horse. I crouched and waited for one of them to amble close. Digging the claws of my feet into the soil, I sprang, landing on the shoulder of the unlucky creature that moved right past my hiding place. It bellowed and thrashed, trying to shake me off. The others scattered, leaving their herd mate to defend itself. It ran, but was slow and I was tearing into its neck before it could get far. Deep purple blood sprayed, and the thing stumbled to its knees, then collapsed, its breaths shallow before going still. I stood, looking at my kill with satisfaction, it had been quick and clean. Now I just had to drag its carcass all the way back to the lake.

I needed to lighten the load, so all those pesky internal organs would have to go. Whatever should I do with them? I smiled... and ate.

It may smell funky, but it tasted just fine to me. Its flesh was a lighter purple than its blood and it left a weird aftertaste, but overall it tasted how meat was supposed to. I saved the heart and what looks like the liver for Ohem. It was the best mating gift I could give for now.

Drained of its blood and most of its insides, the lizard-camel was light enough to carry back without being a colossal pain in the ass. I'd have to break a bunch of the spines off its hump too, so they wouldn't stab me when it came time to sling it over my back for the trip back to the others.

With that done and my belly full, it was time to explore a bit. I glanced around, ears flicking back and forth, listening for any predators that might try for my kill. It was silent. The herd of lizard-camels had moved far enough away that I couldn't hear them anymore.

I rose to my feet and wandered through the trees, following the smell of moisture and green things. Near to my kill, I found a narrow canyon that delved deeper into the mountain. It was shady and cool and there were other plants growing inside the walls of the canyon, moss like grass in the shadier parts closer to the wall and some red bell-shaped flowers dotting the ground. The canyon itself was no wider than twenty feet, but tall, reaching high above me; the walls narrowing and curving inward towards each other until they almost formed a complete roof, with only a three or four-foot gap. The sunlight cast a narrow line of golden light on the canyon floor.

I could smell water the deeper I ventured, and took note of the moss spreading further up the walls. I flicked my ears forwards, hearing the rush and spray of water against rock. I started jogging, my heart pounding, until the walls curved slightly to the right and opened up.

I walked straight into paradise.

A single spouted waterfall cascaded from the canyon wall into tiered pools of turquoise water lapping at a smooth rock beach half covered in soft moss. I walked over to the flat stone beach and stared in wonder. Excitement and relief made my heart pound harder.

Forget what I said earlier. Thank you, Universe!

I stepped into the water, it was cool, not frigid like I expected, and bent, scooping water into my cupped hands to pour it into my open mouth. It was the best water I'd ever tasted. I sank to my knees and dunked my head in, drinking deeply. So fresh. How long had it been since I'd had fresh water? Forever? Forever and a day? The lake water I'd choked down had tasted like hot sludge.

I came up for air, jumped to my feet and backed up to get a running start, and cannon balled in. It was perfect. I sank to the bottom and then kicked to the surface, letting loose a brief howl of pure elation that echoed off the canyon walls.

I swam around for a moment and then crawled back out, shaking the water from my fur and looking up at the top of the canyon and around. It was wider here and let in more light that shined onto the pools of water, but left the rest of the ground shaded. The walls made a closed circle, so we'd be boxed in if trouble came, but maybe Ohem and I could stack some trees or something against the opening to bar the way in. We could make it work.

I had to get them! Hopefully, Callie was healed enough to travel.

I sprinted all the way back to my kill, hefted it over my shoulder and then ran back to the oasis. Tearing strips off it to fill their bellies for the journey, I then stashed the rest of it on a ledge above one pool to keep it cool and away from anything that might want to eat it.

I took one last look at the oasis before tearing off as fast as I could back towards my friends to bring them some good news for a change.

• • • ● • ● • ● • •

I howled long and loud when the lake came into view with three shapes standing together by the water's edge. They turned in my direction when they heard it. I howled again, joy coloring the sound as it faded in the air. I'd been sprinting for an hour and the fur on my sides was wet with sweat by the time I stopped in front of Ohem, who was shining brightly at my return.

I panted rapidly for a full minute before I changed back. I bent over, hands on my knees, and panted some more, trying to catch my breath. Ohem moved to my side and rubbed my back. He was trying to be soothing, but his touch was painfully arousing, sending shivers down my spine. Being touched by a mate was a new and pleasurably frustrating experience.

Even small touches felt electric. I groaned in my throat and Ohem's hand stilled. He stepped back, his scent deepening in a way I hadn't noticed before. He was suffering, too. He took a deep breath, pulling in my scent, and let it out in a deep, rumbling growl.

Sam and Patty came to stand next to Ohem, looking at us with amusement.

Still panting, I held out the thick strips of meat I'd brought with me, and shook them when no one made any moves to take them from me. Ohem chuckled and lifted them from my hand. "The hunt was a success then?" he asked, amusement and arousal thickening his voice.

I nodded, still unable to speak.

When I could breathe, I sucked in a deep breath, then squealed like a little girl and did a happy dance right there.

Patty started laughing, Sam joined her and Ohem's eyes flared bright as he watched my body move. I was naked, my breasts bouncing with my movements and Ohem was transfixed.

"What is it, girl? Did Timmy fall down the well?" Patty asked, grinning at me, bent at the waist and slapping her knees.

I shot her the bird, laughing and still shimming my hips. My mate growled under his breath, muttering curses. I'd have to dance for him in private one day when we were alone.

I stopped torturing him and quit dancing. I looked between all of them, pressing my palms together, fingers against my lips. I pointed my pressed hands at them. "I found something." I took a breath, pausing for a moment to let the excitement build. "I found a freaking oasis," I said. "I killed a lizard-camel, and it's waiting for us there. Is Callie good to travel? It's not that far. We should still be able to see any ships that come to the rescue," I said in a rush and looked over at Callie's sleeping form and back at the others, eyebrows raised in question.

Patty scrunched her face up. "Lizard-camel?"

I threw my hands up. "Did you not hear what I said? Oasis. Food. Is Callie okay to travel? We should leave soon."

Ohem had taken the food to a pile of metal scraps they must have gathered while I was gone, placing the meat on a flat metal fragment, and slicing it into pieces with his claws. He looked up from his task. "Callie's leg is mended, however, her internal injuries are keeping her in the healing coma. We should not move her. Carrying her will only make the healing take longer," he said and went back to cutting.

Patty handed me my clothes, and I held the scraps of black cloth in my hands, thinking.

We needed to get out of the sun and to fresher water. Moving her might do more damage, but not getting her to cleaner water might kill her in the long run, too.

Ohem handed Sam pieces of raw meat. She held the purplish flesh in her hand, her face twisting in disgust. "Ugh. Wish we could find some wood for a fire. Eating raw alien meat can't be good for you."

Patty popped some into her mouth. "It's better than starving to death. Just eat it," she said, speaking while she chewed. She swallowed and popped another piece into her mouth. "It's not that bad, chewy and a little tough, but not that bad."

Sam grimaced and ate, looking sick the whole time. She kept it down and ate another piece. "We better get rescued soon. I don't want any nasty parasites from eating raw meat."

Ohem opened his maw and dropped in the meat before looking at Sam. "Your nanos should kill any parasites before you have to worry about it. Eat. You will need to keep up your strength. You don't want to starve to death. The nanos will keep you alive for far longer than you would wish. In the end, you would pray for death."

Sam paled. "You are just a ray of sunshine, aren't you?" she said dryly, but kept eating. "This is weird right?"

I tilted my head at her, a minor flash of anxiety flaring in my mind. "What's weird?"

She shrugged and gestured with her hand to Ohem and then all around us. "This. All of this. Eating this weird meat, after crash landing on an alien planet, with an alien. I feel like I should be freaking out right now, but I'm almost numb. Thankful to be alive, but numb."

Patty shifted closer to Sam, draping an arm over her shoulder. "I'm sure there is a scientific term for it but it's survivor mode. You stop freaking out at things. It's almost like you can't be afraid anymore; the worst has already happened. Now you are just at base survival. It won't ever completely go away, but it will get better. Trust me."

I stared at Patty, and she caught me watching her. I hated that she already understood what it was. She shrugged and gave me a sad smile.

Sam sighed, brushing a blonde curl off her forehead. "Yeah, I guess that makes sense. Just worries me that I'm so calm. I'm sure it will all hit me at some point and I'll be a mess."

"We'll be okay," Patty said and squeezed Sam again before focusing back on her food.

We fell silent except for the sounds of chewing. Well, we chewed. Ohem just threw meat into his mouth and swallowed.

It gave me intense satisfaction to watch him eat something I hunted. I was eager to get back and hand him the good stuff I'd saved. The small amount I'd brought with me was nowhere near enough to satisfy someone as large as him. It was giving me anxiety, thinking he might still be hungry.

I shifted from one foot to the other. "There is more at the oasis."

He glanced at me, his four yellow eyes narrowing in amusement and the lines on his body glowing brighter. "This is enough for now, *ursang*. I can satisfy other hungers later," he purred.

My core clenched at the sound and I closed my eyes. Stupid damn mating frenzy. It had no respect for the very serious situation we were in. It really didn't care if you wanted to get your friends to relative safety or not. It wanted to bone and bone now. His dark chuckle swirled around me, pressing against my skin and flaring my desire higher. If we didn't have sex soon, I was going to lose my mind.

"Soon," Ohem whispered into my ear.

I hadn't heard him move. My eyes flashed open, and I leaned my head back against his chest to look up at him. He moved his hand across my stomach and up, passing over my naked breast, brushing my nipple lightly with his palm, and wrapped his hand around my throat. His other hand gripped my hip and pulled me firmly against him. His fingers brushed through my pubic hair and were dangerously close to my clit. He used his fingers at my throat to tilt my head further back and lowered his head, the plates and exposed skin of his mouth pressing against mine. His tongue flicked against my lips and I opened for him. He rushed in, his rough tongue stroking mine. It wasn't quite a proper kiss, with his lack of lips and all, but it didn't matter. The effect was fire, burning me alive.

I moaned against his mouth and pressed harder into his face, my hand coming up to grip the back of his neck, the ridges on his spine digging into my palm.

His fingers at my hip brushed past my clit and slid through the slick folds of my pussy. I whimpered, gripping his forearm in my free hand, and tilted my hips forward, trying to grind into his palm. He tightened his grip on my neck and then oddly shaped hands clasped my hips, holding me still. Two more hands palmed my breasts, squeezing and lifting. *His tentacles.* I moaned again into his mouth, his answering growl rattling my teeth. He pressed two fingers into my aching center and pumped them in and out of me slowly. I may die. I couldn't ride his hand with him holding me still and he was going so slow!

I groaned in frustration and he chuckled again in that Mount Doom voice of his, the dark, *evil* tones sinking into my bones.

Hot liquid moved against the skin of my back and then his naked cock was pressing into my lower back. It was searing and hard and I ground backwards into him. He growled again, lifting me with his tentacles when I heard someone take a shuddering breath behind us.

"Um, do you mind us watching or is this a 'you forgot we were here' kind of situation?" Sam asked, her voice shaky.

Patty shushed her.

I froze and opened my eyes. Ohem's eyes were open, burning into mine. His yellow pupils were blown wide, covering the slightly darker yellow of his sclera. He pulled his tongue from my mouth and lifted his head, his teeth bared in a silent snarl.

"Ohem," I whimpered. I tightened my hand around his neck and then dropped it slowly. He pressed his hand harder into me and then withdrew his fingers. He set me back down on my feet, tentacles releasing their hold on my hips and breasts. He squeezed my throat once, twice, and then let go, stepping back from me. I turned to face him, taking him in. He was breathing heavily, shoulders heaving. His lights flared like the sun and pulsed with agitation, tails twisting over themselves. His cock was hard, straining upwards, the spiraling dots shining around its thick girth stopping at the frilled tip. It was beautiful, impossibly large, and I wanted to sob.

I shook all over, so turned on that wetness was dripping down my thighs and my nipples were painfully hard points.

We'd almost fucked in front of Sam and Patty. I didn't care about that so much right now, but we had shit to do. Like get Callie to the oasis. The mating frenzy was making us lose focus.

We stared at each other, panting and growling. My nails lengthened into claws and my muscles swelled. My teeth ached, wanting to sink into his flesh, marking him.

Sam cleared her throat. "Sorry to interrupt. I just thought maybe I should say something before you got really carried away." Her brown eyes were glazed and dilated. She'd been enjoying the show, but had still stopped us. How thoughtful.

She sucked.

Patty was fanning her flushed face and grinning. "I told her to let y'all work it out of your system," she said, leering at us.

I huffed out a laugh and raised a shaky hand to my face. "Yeah. Thanks for stopping us." I shook my head and dropped my hand. "We have too many things to do to be taking a break to have sex. Sorry," I said.

Patty waved my apology away. "Don't apologize. That was better than any porn I've ever seen," she said, sighing dreamily.

Sam was blushing, but her eyes were trailing down my body and then Ohem's. "Yeah, that was intense," she whispered, her voice hoarse. I didn't feel any possessive jealousy by her eyeing him. I liked Sam. She wasn't a threat.

I flicked my eyes to Ohem. He'd let his armor flow back over his body, his cock hidden from sight. I wanted to mourn that fact. Holding a funeral for it and everything.

I growled and went to get my clothes from the ground where I'd dropped them and put them on.

Ohem watched me dress. His eyes narrowed to thin lines, then turned and stalked off towards the wreck. I watched him go, following the wide set of his shoulders, down his back to his twisting tails. His tentacles were waving wildly around him. It was turning me on so much that he was so frustrated. It made me feel a little better about my suffering. At least I wasn't alone in it. I ground my teeth until they hurt and set to figuring out how to take care of Callie.

Nine

OHEM ENDED UP FINDING the perfect solution.

He'd ripped a six foot long strip of metal off the hull of the container in pure frustration, discovered it would work as a stretcher, and dragged it back to camp. It was four feet wide and had several thick cables on the underside that we could use to drag it along with Callie resting on the top. We placed the metal sled as close to Callie's body as we could get it, and then carefully shifted her onto it.

Sam and Patty ripped the long sleeves off their tops and wrapped them around their feet to protect them from the hot desert ground. Ohem bent some metal with his hands and then hammered it with a rock, shaping it into a crude, misshapen bucket we filled with water from the lake. It leaked, so we tore strips from my pants and stuffed them inside to plug any weak points.

With Ohem pulling the sled, and me carrying the heavy water bucket, we started walking. The twin suns cooked us from above, making the slow progression miserable for the women. We had to make frequent stops to let them rest and drink the muddy water, forcing some of it down Callie's throat.

Our skin was burning under the suns and my lips were cracking, just to heal and then crack again. It was annoying as hell. The sweat gathering under my boobs was making me chafe and driving me mad.

Patty ended up tearing off her pant legs below the knee and making head coverings for her and Sam. She tore another strip of fabric from around her waist and wrapped it around Callie's face, leaving only her nose uncovered.

Sam collapsed first. I dunked her head covering into the water, re-wrapped it around her head and face, and then draped her over my shoulder in a fireman's carry. I picked the water bucket back up in one arm and wrapped the other around Sam's legs.

We walked for another hour before Patty collapsed, too. Ohem wrapped one of his tentacles around her and curled her into his back and I poured what was left of the water over her head before setting the bucket next to Callie's hip so I could shift my hold on Sam to bridal style to make her more comfortable.

We went much faster carrying the women, but it was still miserable. By the time the trees could be seen, I was ready to collapse myself.

I led the way past my killing ground and into the canyon mouth. The shade was a welcomed relief, my skin was on fire from a wicked sunburn, but it was healing as we walked, and I knew the others would be miserable until their nanos caught up.

When we came around the bend into the oasis, I walked straight to the pool and sat down in it. I placed Sam on my lap, an arm against her back to keep her upper body out of the water. Dirt and filth clouded the water around us and I lowered my arm, easing her upper body closer to the water so I could dip her head to rinse her hair and splash her sunburned face. She groaned, her eyes flickering open. I grinned down at her and kept washing her hair, letting my nails scrape her scalp. She waved the arm not tucked against my stomach in the water lazily.

"That feels amazing," she murmured, closing her eyes again.

A splash to my right made me turn to see Ohem lowering a disoriented Patty into the water next to me. I stopped scrubbing Sam's hair so I could reach and steady Patty with a hand to her back. She sighed and leaned her head against my shoulder. Her eyes were still a little dazed, and we sat there while Ohem situated Callie in a cool spot in the shade.

He picked up the bucket, went to the water's edge to fill it, and walked back to splash a little over Callie to cool her before lifting her head to coax water into her mouth. When he was done, he sat the bucket next to her sled and then turned to dive headfirst into our pool with almost no splash. The water was crystal clear, giving us an unobstructed view of him gliding around like the Loch Ness Monster. He moved like an alligator, using his tails to push himself along.

He swam in circles underwater before surfacing a few feet in front of us.

"Ten points," Patty said, holding up her fist like she had a sign in hand.

Sam laughed and sat up in my lap. She stood, wobbled for a second, and dove in next to Ohem, surfacing quickly and backstroking around the large pool.

I looked at Patty. "Are you steady enough to swim?"

She shrugged and went to stand. She would have fallen over if I hadn't stood with her and kept my hand on her back. I snorted out a laugh, scooped her up in my arms, and jumped. She shrieked, her arms circling around my neck in a death grip. We hit the water with an enormous splash. Patty sputtered when our heads broke the surface, laughing and coughing. She wriggled out of my arms and turned to float on her back, smiling up at the sky. I kept a sharp eye on them in case one fainted.

The pool we swam in was the largest of the many here, clear blue water that deepened into a black hole below us. The waterfall crashed into a shallower pool three tiers above, with each pool pouring into the next, until they flowed into ours from all sides. The sounds of the waterfall mixed with our laughter echoed all around us.

It was a much needed moment of fun. We swam, splashing each other, jumping from the high pools, and playing. Forgetting for a moment that we were stranded and possibly being hunted.

Ohem swam close around me, sliding his hands across my stomach and up my back. He pulled me into him and I wrapped my arms around his neck, my legs around his waist.

He swam us backwards out of the middle where it was deep, until the water was only chest high. He ran his hands up my thighs and palmed my ass. I ground my core into his stomach. He still had his armor covering himself or he could have been balls deep right now. I was bitterly disappointed by that fact.

Patty swam past us and walked out of the water, looking back and smiling. "We're gonna go collect some spines and leaves from the trees. See if we can't get a fire going to cook that meat you have stashed. We'll be back in an hour or two," she said, winking at me. Sam followed her out of the water and together they left the oasis. Leaving us alone but for an unconscious Callie. We were alone. I blinked at Ohem. A slow smile spread across my face.

We were alone!

I wasted no time. I ground myself harder against Ohem and wrapped my hand around one horn to pull his head down to mine so I could press my mouth to his. He groaned and slipped his tongue between my lips.

His armor dissolved into the torque, his hot, naked skin against mine, slick and wet. He walked out of the pool and laid me down on the smooth, wet stone at the water's edge. He broke away from the kiss and leaned back, grabbing me around my knees and slowly pulled my legs apart. He growled at the torn black pants covering my sex and used his tentacles to hook the waistband and peel them off of me. His hands pulled the banded cloth from around my breasts and over my head. He tossed it aside and pulled my legs open again. He stared at my bared pussy, eyes narrow slits, bioluminescence glowing bright. I moaned and lifted my hips in offering.

"Ohem, touch me." I was desperate at this point and he was only staring at me.

His quiet chuckle shot through me like a bolt of lightning. "Giving orders, Rijitera? I think not."

Oh god.

I writhed in his grasp, but he waited like a patient hunter.

"Please! Please, Ohem," I said, half sobbing, half growling at him.

"You beg so prettily, Rijitera," he said, sweeping his hand down my stomach in a whispered caress. "Again."

"Ohem, Please!"

I didn't know who this submissive creature was, didn't recognize the mewling, needy voice that had spoken. I loved her, though, whoever she was. Her pleading worked.

The first rough rasp of his tongue through my pussy had me shrieking, my hands reaching for his horns to drag him closer so I could grind my wet core into his face. He snarled and gripped the top of my thighs, pulling me harder against him, licking and spearing his tongue into me, fucking me with it, twirling it around my clit before thrusting it back inside me. My inner walls clenched around his tongue, trying to keep him inside, but he pulled it out of me and I moaned at the loss, only to gasp when it wrapped around my clit and rolled it.

So it was dexterous. Good to know.

Something large nudged my opening. It pressed into me slowly and opened like fingers from a fist. I groaned at the sensation and looked down at Ohem between my legs. It was his tentacle. He was using his tentacle to fuck me.

There was a God.

He thrust it hard into me, opening the fingers and scraping them against my walls on the downstroke, closing them to thrust forward again. Over and over. His tongue still working my clit.

The orgasm barreled towards me like a freight train, the power of it building higher and higher with every thrust of his tentacle inside me.

"Yes! Harder, Ohem. Don't stop!" I was giving commands, but Ohem didn't stop to chastise me. He drove his tentacle harder into me, flattened his rough tongue over my clit, and growled loudly. The vibrations thundered through my sex and the storm hit me.

Liquid fire spread from my core, engulfing me, *consuming* me. Burning pleasure erupted inside me. I wailed, back bowing, grinding my pussy into his face.

And I had worried about him eating me.

Ohem let me ride it out for a few seconds before he tugged his horns from my grasp and pulled his tentacle from inside me. I was sputtering in protest when he jerked upright, wrapped his hands around my hips, and thrust his cock inside me while pulling me into the thrust, forcing his cock through the spasming walls and spiking another orgasm from me before the first one had ended. Our hips met with a slap, the burn from his invasion adding pleasure/pain to my release.

He grunted and pulled almost completely out before brutally thrusting back inside. I screamed and thrashed, half trying to get away, half trying to meet his thrusts by raising my hips, but his hands held me firm, controlling my movements. He snarled viciously, his tentacle snapping out and wrapping around my wrists to pin my arms above my head with bruising force. He thrust again and again, plunging deeper and deeper in a steady, punishing rhythm. Hammering into me without mercy. He was huge above me, a black nightmare between my legs, teeth bared and eyes blazing.

"Come for me, Rijitera. Scream for me again," he growled out between clenched teeth.

The orgasm took me violently, the pleasure whiting out my vision. My body pulled taut like a bowstring pushed to its limit, a scream tearing out of my throat.

Ohem's thrusts became harder and erratic. I felt his cock swell impossibly larger, and he pressed hard inside me, grinding our pelvises together, and roared. His seed coated the walls of my spasming pussy, scalding hot inside me. It fed my release to the point of losing consciousness, and my instinct flared into overdrive.

Pure aggression flooded my system, a need to complete the bond so primal that the strength Ohem had sapped in his relentless fucking came roaring back, and I threw myself forwards, wrenching my wrists from his grasp, my claws digging into his chest to pull him down to me, and I sunk my fangs into the hard muscle between neck and shoulder, right under the torque.

His blood flooded into my mouth, hot and sweet. He roared again, another hot spurt of his come filling me. His hand came up to cup the back of my head, pressing my face harder into him. I snarled into the bite and came again, my legs wrapping around his waist, holding him inside me. The force of my orgasm made my bite savage and deep. We stayed locked like that, riding out our pleasure until it gradually faded, leaving me dazed and drained.

My muscles were weak and shaking when I let my legs go limp, falling from his waist to rest over his thighs. I retracted my claws from his chest, unlocked my jaw and licked the wound of my mating mark. Ohem shuddered against me, his hand still cradling my head. He curled around me, his other arm snaking around my waist to hold me, his tentacles hooking under my knees to pull my legs tighter around him.

I finished cleaning the mark and sighed. I rested my cheek on his chest and closed my eyes. Ohem shifted and stood, keeping me pressed into him, his cock still firmly lodged inside me. He walked over to the wall and slid down it to sit with his back against it.

"Rest, Jack," he murmured into my hair. And I did just that.

• • • • ● • ● • • •

Low voices woke me.

I was pleasantly warm. The smooth skin against my naked body was like silk, slick and soft, and I snuggled harder into Ohem. He was no longer inside me, but pressed between us, a hot hard bar digging into the muscles of my stomach. We'd mated twice more before I fell asleep for real, and I felt empty without him inside. I pressed harder into him, grinding myself into his erection, and he chuckled quietly, the sound mostly trapped inside his throat and vibrating in his chest.

"The others are back," he warned me, his hand sliding down my back to cup my ass to hold me still.

"And? Let them watch," I grumbled into his chest.

He chuffed with amusement. "What happened to my possessive Rijiteran *ursang*? There was a time when looking at or touching me incited your ire."

I wriggled a little in embarrassment at the memory of my irrational behavior on the ship. "It was the incomplete mating bond. That wasn't me," I mumbled.

He chuckled louder. "And is it complete now?" he asked, scraping his claws along my spine. Goosebumps broke out over my skin and I shivered. "Yes, you wear my mark." I pushed my upper body off his chest with my hands and met his eyes. "So what does *ursang* mean? My translator isn't telling me," I said, pointing to the metal in my ear.

"Ah. It would not. The language is dead. It is the Rijiteran word for warrior, or strong one," he said, tucking my hair behind my ear.

He called me a warrior. His warrior. How freaking cute was that? Best pet name ever.

"Do you know any more of my ancestor's language?" I asked him, curious.

He shook his head. "Much of it was destroyed. I know only a few words. *Ursang* was used the most often and survived into the archives. I am sorry," he said, cupping my cheek.

I turned my face and kissed his palm. "It's okay. It's not your fault."

I traced my fingers along the bioluminescent lines along his collarbone and down his chest.

"What do you call these?"

"They are called Izi. It is an old Orixas word for inner fire."

I leaned forward and traced a glowing line running down his chest with my tongue. It glowed brighter. I smiled and lifted my head to look at him from under my lashes. "Does it glow with your emotions, like when you're aroused?" I murmured and licked him again.

He sucked in a hissing breath. His cock twitched against my belly. "Yes," he rumbled. "I can control them when I need to, but it is better to let them do as they will. One shouldn't stifle their Izi unless they are stalking prey or enemies."

"Hmm, no. We shouldn't smother fire," I said and trailed my tongue up his chest to my mating mark. It had healed into a nice raised scar. There was something in our saliva that kept it from healing smoothly with our own kind, and I was pleased to see it worked on him, despite his nanos.

I sucked hard on the mark, making him groan low in his throat. I reached between us to wrap my hand around his cock. I pumped from base to tip, feeling the raised bumps and fingering the frills around the head. They formed a solid inch line circling the tip of his cock, stiff rubbery mini tentacles that provided the most delicious stimulation inside of me. I slid my hand down again, cupping his balls, kneading them in my palm, watching the precum bead from his slit.

Sam and Patty's voices murmured quietly to our left, where Callie was laying. The crackle of a fire and the smell of meat cooking added an almost romantic feel to the oasis.

Dinner and a show.

Once the mating was complete, my people had never minded mating wherever the need struck them, regardless if there was an audience or even if there were other participants.

I lifted myself up with my thighs gripping the side of his hips, my knees unable to touch the ground while straddling him. I grasped his cock and fit the head against my opening before sinking down, groaning at the feeling of him sliding deep, stretching me to the point of pain.

Ohem growled and lifted me with his hands on my ass, his claws pricking my skin, and slammed me back down onto his thick cock, thrusting up into me at the same time. I watched where he entered me, moaning and panting. Lifted and being pulled back down, him powering into me, faster and harder, until the sounds of flesh slapping flesh and our grunts and snarls echoed off the walls. One of his tentacles snaked around to pinch my clit, rolling it between its smooth, stiff digits. He lifted me over him and kept me there, pounding into me from below. He lowered his head and pressed his mouth to mine, thrusting his tongue between my lips, twirling and teasing it against mine. I opened my mouth wider and tilted my head, closing my eyes, allowing the kiss to deepen, my arms thrown around his neck for balance.

The orgasm moved through me slowly, spreading out from my core in a wave, crushing me under a weight of pure euphoria. My ragged wail was muffled by his mouth pressed to mine.

Ohem pulled his tongue from my mouth to lightly bite my shoulder, surging up a final time, and roaring into my skin as he came.

I sagged against him, spent and boneless.

I heard slow clapping from our forgotten audience. "Son of a bitch, that was hot. Spank bank material for days," Patty said, her voice husky.

I laughed, turning my head to look at her. They were sitting around a small fire, meat being burned to a crisp, forgotten on skewers made from the spines of the lizard-camel held over the fire by two more spines, split at the top and stabbed into the ground.

Sam was smiling lazily at us, face flushed and a little embarrassed.

Sorry, not sorry.

Ohem rumbled a laugh and lifted me off of him to place me on my feet, his seed leaking down my thighs when I stood. I wobbled my way over to the water on jelly legs and waded into it to scrub my skin, between my thighs and dunk my head under the water to rinse my hair. I needed to cut it. It had been medium length and straight before the abduction, but now it was matted.

I lifted my head out of the water, and Ohem was next to me. I jumped and gave a little shriek. *I was going to get him a freaking bell.* He really could sneak up on a girl. He was lucky he had that body to distract me from being irritated. I watched the water run down his black skin, marveling at him. My mate truly was a monster, in the best ways. All that lethal strength was mine. It made me positively giddy.

He had some of the skin from a tree in his hand. "Sam says to use this to wash. She says it is like a plant you have in your home world, an aloe vera, and will soothe your tangled hair."

"Oh, sweet," I said and took the skin from him. I peeled it apart and scooped the jellied insides out and rubbed them in my hair. I finger-comb it into the tangles, but they were dense, almost dread-like and it was a slow process.

Ohem came up behind me and took the skin from me. "Allow me to assist. Please, sit."

I sat in the shallow water and he lowered himself behind me, bracketing me between his thighs, and began working the jelly into my knots, using his claws to cut away the parts that couldn't be saved. He used his tentacles to work over my entire head in conjunction with his hands. It was relaxing, and such a domestic mate chore that I couldn't help but smile and close my eyes, basking in the feeling of intense contentment.

Who'd have thought I'd get abducted by aliens and find my mate on the same ship? It was such a crazy story. I couldn't wait to tell our kids about it one day.

I frowned. Could we even have kids?

I placed my hand on Ohem's thigh and tilted my head back against his chest. "Can we have children? Are we compatible, I mean."

My heart jolted when he went still, his hands frozen in my hair. I twisted and looked back at him.

He nodded his head slowly. "Yes. The Rijitera can mate and bear young with most species. It was what they engineered themselves for. To have young with strong mates so that their species would grow to have many special traits." His voice was rough, almost unsteady.

He touched my cheek with his fingertips. "Do–," he paused and took a breath, "Do you want children?" he asked, his voice subdued, but there was an underlying hopeful edge to it. My Big Bad wanted kids.

I wanted to fuck with him and say something outrageous like kids were goblins and I hated them, but his face was so adorable and hesitant and hopeful that I just couldn't. It would be like kicking a puppy. *An evil-looking puppy that would eat your leg for the audacity.*

I smiled at him instead and went with the truth. "Yeah. I want kids one day. I've got an IUD. It's a type of birth control, so we'd have to take it out if we want to eventually get pregnant."

His Izi flickered, flared bright, and then Ohem was crushing me in a hug that punched the breath from my lungs and made my ribs ache. I grunted, and he released me, cupping my face with his hands. "I am so very glad to have met you, Jack. I am honored more than I can say to be your mate. I will spend my life making sure you and any children we have are loved and happy. I fear I may spoil you." He was so genuine and solemn.

Ah, hell. He was making falling in love with him too easy. Not that I minded, he was my mate. It was going to happen fast regardless, but him being such a sweet, honorable, total *sex god* was making shit move at light speed.

Get it? Cause we're in space.

I grinned and straddled him, wrapping my arms around his neck. "Spoil away, General. I like tacky t-shirts, coffee in all its forms, and sex. Lots of sex. As a matter of fact, you should fuck me at least three times a day or else I'll wilt like a neglected flower. I'm sure of it," I said with mock gravity, nodding my head *very* seriously.

Ohem threw his head back and laughed. It was a thunderous sound. All deep and booming, like a volcano eruption. It was my new favorite sound. My new purpose in life was going to be making him roar in pleasure and laugh like that all the time. It was a good thing I was both a sexy warrior lady and funny as shit.

Humble too.

So humble.

His laughter faded around us and Ohem squeezed my ass, his cock rubbing against my sex. "I will fulfill all your needs, my *ursang*. That I can promise you," he said, eyes glittering with amusement and his voice a husky rasp against my skin.

"Come on, you two. Quit flirting and come eat. If you fuck in front of Sam again, she's gonna develop a complex," Patty said from her spot by the fire.

Ohem shook his head in amusement and used his hands at my waist to shift me around to face away from him again so he could continue combing his claws through my hair. It was weird being handled like I was a small lady. No man had ever lifted me so easily, not even the males of my kind. Our females were usually larger than them. Another box checked on the long list of shit my mate does that turned me on.

He finished my hair quickly and helped me to my feet. His armor rushed around his body, covering all that naked skin and I tried, and failed, not to whine about it.

I found my clothes folded next to the fire, scrubbed clean and dried. I pulled them on, wincing at the tattered shape of the top. It was on its last leg. It still covered all the important bits and kept the girls from bouncing around, but there were holes and tears all over it. Still, being dressed and clean, with freshly combed hair, felt like the highest of luxuries. My hair was shorter, Ohem having had to cut pieces off, about chin length and ragged edged, but it was clean and soft. Miracle of miracles.

Ohem folded himself in a seated position and wrapped his hand around mine to tug me into his lap.

Patty looked at me with wide eyes and pouted. "I want one. Find me an alien lover that has a big cock too, Jack," she demanded, wagging her eyebrows at me.

"What are friends for if not for making sure their friend's future boyfriends are hung? It'll be on the alien application lists I make for you. Must Have Huge Dick," I said, spreading my hands out like I was reading from a banner.

"You say the sweetest things to me," Patty purred, batting her eyelashes.

Sam couldn't meet my eyes. She was blushing furiously and fidgeting.

"Enjoy the show, Doctor?" I asked her in a velvety tone.

She blushed harder and laughed, her hands going to her cheeks. "I've never even watched porn before and you've ruined it for me forever," she confessed in a whisper.

Patty narrowed her eyes at her. "Never watched porn? What are you? A nun?"

Sam's blush spread down her neck and chest and she cleared her throat, "Something like that."

Oh no.

Patty gasped, her hand going to her mouth to stifle a laugh. "Oh my god, you're a virgin, aren't you?"

Sam groaned and covered her face with her hands.

Patty laughed uproariously, hugging Sam to her. "Oh my god, Jack. She's never had sex and her first pornographic experience is a werewolf fucking an alien right in front of her. She's ruined for life. Nothing will ever compare!" She cracked up harder, shaking Sam.

Ohem shifted beneath me, uncomfortable with the situation.

"You're welcome," I howled, rolling to the floor clutching my stomach. Patty crawled to me, throwing herself over my back, crying with laughter.

Ohem murmuring apologies to Sam, probably making her even more embarrassed, and I laughed harder.

"What's so funny?" a dry, scratchy voice asked, barely heard over the laughter. Callie had finally woken up.

Ten

"Callie!" Sam jumped to her feet and dashed around us to kneel by Callie's makeshift metal stretcher.

Patty rolled off me, crawling to Callie, and I grabbed the bucket and filled it with water, bringing it back to press the lip to Callie's mouth while Ohem helped prop her up.

I let her sip it, making her pause in between each sip to make sure she didn't drink too much and throw it all back up.

She pushed the bucket away from her with her hand and sat the rest of the way up without help.

"Oh man, I feel like crap," she groaned, hunching over her legs.

Ohem stepped around us and crouched by her feet. "May I?" he asked, gesturing to her leg that had been broken.

Callie nodded her head yes and sat up straight. I kept my hand hovering behind her just in case.

Ohem unwrapped the metal splint and set it aside. He grabbed her foot and lifted her leg, gently rotating it one way and then the other, pushing her leg up, making her bend her knee. "Do you feel any discomfort?" he asked, putting her leg back down.

"No, it feels fine."

Ohem nodded. "Do you feel any pain in your abdomen?"

Callie shook her head. "Nah, I feel fine. Just thirsty, and hungry, and my head is all fuzzy." She looked around at the oasis, her face scrunched in confusion. "Where the hell are we? What happened?"

We filled her in on the crash, the lost women, the potential threat from the Councilor guy and whatever thugs he had working for him, and finally on what we'd learned about the Rijitera and my mating to Ohem. She'd cried for the women, the rest of us holding her. She'd known all their names. Everything else she'd taken in stride. She was tough, or maybe like Sam, she just couldn't muster the energy to be shocked anymore.

We had gathered around the fire after she bathed for over an hour in the pool, scrubbing the jelly from the tree skin into her hair and all over her body. Sam took her clothes and scrubbed them clean for her while she bathed and hung them next to the fire so they'd dry out for when Callie was done luxuriating in the cool water.

Ohem had finished butchering the lizard-camel, freaking the girls out when he'd opened his mouth wide, the seams of his mouth farther back on his face than was natural, and ate the heart and liver I'd saved for him.

Whole.

He'd thanked me for the gift, nuzzling my neck.

I'd been fidgety that they weren't fresh and made a mental note to hunt for him again, soon.

Callie dressed and then sat down with us, and proceeded to eat enough meat for three people. When she had a nice food baby, she wiped her mouth with the back of her hand.

She took the aloe vera type skin from the spiny trees that Patty handed her and started rubbing it into the burned skin of her nose, hands, and feet. The other women were slathering more over their sunburned skin. I'd never been so thankful for my rapid healing as I was watching them wince and hiss while applying it.

Callie sighed when she finished, tossing the tree skin aside to meet my eyes with a small smile. "So, how do you feel about being from an ancient alien civilization?"

"I don't know. I don't feel like an alien. I'm from Earth. I grew up in a small town in the southwest. I went to a freaking public school, for Christ's sake. My mom's a long-haul trucker! Aside from being a Rijitera and shifting into a huge wolf monster, I'm totally normal," I said, and the girls laughed softly. I shrugged my shoulders. "It was a shock, sure, but after all the shit we've been through? Hell. Ohem could have told me God was a unicorn that breathed fire and shit rainbows and I'd have rolled with it."

Callie barked out a laugh. "Yeah, it doesn't seem like much would shock you for long." She grew serious and held my gaze for a long moment. "I haven't thanked you for what you did on the ship." She sucked in a breath and blew it out slowly. "So, thank you, Jack. Really. I know things didn't exactly end the way we wanted, but thank you for saving us and for helping keep us alive." She looked to Ohem, who I was again perched on. "Thank you, too. For getting us off the ship and everything after."

Ohem tipped his head at her. "It was my pleasure, Callie of Earth. I would do it again. I only wished I could have saved the others. It will be a regret I carry with me for the rest of my life," he said, his deep voice somber. I stroked his forearm that lay across my stomach, leaning back against him. He squeezed me in silent thanks for the comfort I offered.

"It wasn't your fault. You did what you could. It was that shark asshole and whoever was paying to have us delivered," Patty said, giving him a kind smile.

"I thank you for your words, Patty. You are a good friend," Ohem said, reaching out to her to touch her shoulder lightly. She patted his fingers and swallowed hard.

We sat in a comfortable silence. Ohem's arms curled around me tightly, my head resting against his chest. Sam and Patty stared into the fire, Sam's head on Patty's shoulder with Patty resting her head on Sam's hair. Callie had Sam's hand clasped in hers, her head on Patty's other shoulder, her gaze on the water.

What a group we were. Survivors. Friends. Lovers.

Fuck those shark aliens for abducting us, but I was thankful, too. Thankful that I'd met Ohem and my friends.

"What's your last name, Callie? Where are you from?" I asked her, wanting to know them better. We hadn't really had a suitable moment to introduce ourselves before. Cages made for terrible first meeting places.

She flicked her gaze to mine, lifting her head from Patty to sit up straight. She smiled at me. "Ramirez. My mama is from Mexico and fell in love with a black boy from Los Angeles. I was raised and lived in LA my whole life. Went to a nice private school my dad worked double shifts to pay for. He was a nurse. It's how he and my mom met. She came in with a broken wrist. She'd been bucked off her horse at the finals of a cutting horse show. She was still wearing her cowboy hat and Dad said it was love at first sight. He still gets all hot and bothered by my mom in her hat."

She smiled warmly. "He retired last year. They travel all over for mom's shows." She was getting teary-eyed talking about her parents, and took a shaky breath. "Ugh, sorry," she said, laughing and wiping at her eyes. "They're probably losing their minds about my disappearance. We're really close," she sighed sadly and continued, "I went to the Air Force Academy, got stationed at Nellis. I'm twenty-six years old and I'm an only child. No boyfriend at the moment. Oh, and I was abducted by aliens," she said, and chuckles erupted across the space.

I turned to Sam. "And you, Sam? Tell us about Dr. Samantha Johnson." I gave her my best seductive look. It was pretty potent, I'd been told. I enjoyed teasing her way too much. I'd always loved the shy girls.

She blushed and cleared her throat, sitting up and scooting a little away from Patty. "Um, well, I was born in New York, but we moved to Seattle when I was eight. There was a special school for gifted children there." She looked around, embarrassed.

"Well, go on, don't be shy." I winked at her.

She smiled and shook her head. "My mom is a florist. Divorced. My dad left when I was two or three and I don't remember him. I graduated high school at fifteen and my mom really wanted me to be a surgeon, but I was always interested in crime and solving them. My mom didn't want me to be a cop, so I met her in the middle and became a medical examiner. I didn't have time to date between school and then my job. I'm twenty-four and I was also abducted by aliens," she said, laughing.

We were having an AA meeting. Alien Abductees.

I looked at Patty, asking her silently if she wanted to talk about herself. Her story wasn't a happy one, and many people judged her harshly for the things she'd done to survive.

She smiled thinly at me and lifted a bony shoulder. "My full name is Patricia Dells. I'm twenty-five. I was born in Chicago. I was raised there by my father, who was an alcoholic. When life got too bad living with him, I left. Lived on the streets at sixteen and got into a dangerous crowd. Got into drugs," she hesitated for a second, "Got into prostitution." She held up a hand as if to stop any apologies for her hard life. "It wasn't all bad. I met some nice guys and even enjoyed my work, mostly. I wasn't being forced by some pimp with a cane, but I had a terrible addiction to heroin. I eventually got tired of the cold and wanted to get away from the city. To get clean and start somewhere fresh. I bounced around state to state until I got trapped in New Mexico with a bad boyfriend. It was when he was hitting me on the corner of our street that I met our Amazon." She grinned at me and I grinned back. My smile was sharp and predatory. "Out of a dark alleyway comes this gigantic woman. She was pissed and had the meanest face I'd ever seen."

I snickered when she flared her eyes, enjoying the drama she injected into the story. "She grabbed my boyfriend, shook him hard, and said to him if he enjoys hitting women, he should try to hit her. He called her a stupid bitch." She rolled her eyes. "He wasn't very smart. She snapped his neck like a twig and tossed him down the alley like it was nothing, and then looked at me and smiled. Introduced herself as Jack, all casual, like she didn't just kill a man with her bare hands. Said if I ever needed help to call her, and then disappeared back into the alley. I ran into her after that pretty often in jail. She was always getting busted for fighting. She looked out for me on the streets, helped me find housing and rehab, and she was a pretty good friend. She didn't judge me for who or what I was. I did secretly think of her as 'Jack the Giant' in my head, though." She gave me another smile, this one watery. I was feeling a little choked up myself. My throat was tight.

"I always called you Patty the Prostitute in my head. With love," I joked, sniffing away the tears.

She laughed, flipping me off.

"I'd been clean for two years by the time I was abducted. Now that big ass scary woman is my best friend."

Don't cry. Don't you cry.

I stuffed my tears deep inside. Patty eyed me, blinking away her own tears.

"It's really nice to meet you all," Sam said, with watery eyes too.

Callie swiped her face, and we laughed at each other.

Ohem had stayed quiet, taking in all the information and letting us talk.

Callie glanced at him and shook her finger. "Don't think you're getting out of our sharing and caring circle. Tell us all about our favorite General."

Ohem's Izi glowed brighter with amusement, his deep chuckle vibrating from his chest into my back. He bowed his head. "I would be honored to be included in your circle. I am Ohem Pax At'ens. My age is one hundred and twenty in what I understand of your Earth's year. My planet is much closer to our star, so the rotational orbit is shorter. Our 'year' is only about two hundred days. Our planet's spin on its axis is similar to yours, with only an hour or two difference. So I am closer to two-hundred and forty-three years of age on Stellios."

"How long do your kind live?" Sam interrupted, shocked.

I wanted to know, too. My kind lived for about four-hundred years, give or take.

Ohem chuffed in amusement. "We can live indefinitely. There are aging treatments in the nanos that all in the Unity are provided. You were given the same, albeit a much cruder and painful method was used," he said, pretty damn casually and matter of fact for telling three humans they were essentially immortal now. I was going to need some of those anti-aging treatments if I wanted to live as long as my mate. Something to worry about later.

Callie choked on air, coughing and gasping, while Patty slapped her back, looking at me in shock.

"What! We won't age now? Holy shit," Sam asked, eyes wide in her suddenly pale face.

Ohem flickered his Izi in a calming pattern. "The nanos can be removed if you wish," he said gently.

Sam breathed in relief, her shoulders drooping. "Thank god. I wouldn't want to go back to Earth and watch everyone I know die."

Ohem cocked his head at her, and his Izi faded. "Will you not stay? Can you go back to your planet knowing what you do and live a normal life? It is not against the law to bring the family of Unity citizens to live with them, even if they live on an uncontacted planet. It would be my honor to include you in my House as new citizens of the Unity if you should choose to stay. It would be a simple thing to find your planet and bring your kin with you," he said, placing his left fist over his chest.

We all looked at him in stunned silence.

I fell in love with him fiercely at that moment. Cannon balling off the precipice I'd been teetering on. No regrets.

"What would we even do on an alien planet? My whole life and career are on Earth," Callie said, balking at the idea.

"You said you were military and a pilot? We have our own flying combat crafts. It would be nothing to get you into a Fleet accelerated training course. I am not above using my position to make this happen," he said and turned to Sam. "We have crimes that need the knowledge of medical professionals in solving them. You are a very smart female. I have no doubt that you could learn all you would need to become a doctor of the Unity. I would help you all in whatever field you choose. My mate loves you, and as she is now my family, so are you. I also consider you friends."

The women were looking at my mate with soft eyes.

"Damn. That was the sweetest thing ever. I'm staying. I want a sweet alien man too. I'm not going to find that on Earth," Patty said. "Also, you couldn't make me leave Jack." She winked at me and I blew her a kiss.

Callie blew out a breath. "I mean, I'll think about it. Flying in space would be cool. I'd have to talk to my parent's. I couldn't stay if they didn't want to come."

Sam was staring at Ohem with wonder and a little excitement. "I could learn advanced medicine? Like alien medicine and solving alien crime?" she asked. He nodded his head at her, and she smiled wide, eyes shining. "I might stay. I don't know. It's a lot to think about." She gave her head a shake and waved at him. "I'm sorry, we interrupted you! You were telling us about yourself! Please continue." The rest of us nodded our heads in agreement and murmured for him to continue as well.

Ohem chuckled, his Izi brightening. "Very well. As I was saying, I am the First General of the Unity Command Fleet. I was born and raised in House At'ens on the First Unity planet Stellios. My mother is the Matriarch of our clan and my father is a retired Councilor of Stellios. My elder brother took up his mantle as Councilor. He is a good leader and I am very fond of him. He was instrumental in my pursuit of a military career and has always been my biggest supporter. I have two younger sisters, who are wild, fierce soldiers, and the youngest of our family is my brother Kahn, who is only ten. Once I reached the minimum age of thirty-five years for service, I went to the Fleet. I have served as General for these last fifty years. I was a fleet officer before that for roughly sixty years. I have served all of my military career onboard the Solus Geshgid, a Dread class starship that I now command. I was abducted by smugglers on the hunt for my enemy and saved by aliens," he smiled his stiff smile and his Izi flickered at us.

"I'd save you anytime, Big Bad," I said and kissed his jaw.

He squeezed my thigh lightly, his head cocked to the side. "And what of you, Rijitera? What is your story?"

"Yeah! We want a werewolf campfire story," Patty piped in.

I flicked my eyes to her and glared. "It's Rijitera, *Patricia*."

Patty gasped in outrage, her hand clutching imaginary pearls. "How dare you. The insult!"

I snickered and reached over to flick her leg. She smacked my hand and hissed at me.

"Children, children. We were about to get a story?" Callie said.

I stuck my tongue out at Patty and she stuck hers out in answer.

Rolling my eyes at her, I shifted against Ohem, finding a comfy position before starting. "Not much to tell. I'm twenty-eight. My full name is Jacqueline Ramsey, I was born and raised in the southwest. My mom is the head of my clan. She's terrifying and awesome. Patty can attest, she's met her," I nod to Patty.

"Can confirm. She's terrifying," Patty said, shuddering in remembered fear. My mom was intense that way.

"She owns and runs a trucking company. Most of my clan works for her, myself included. I don't have any siblings, but I have a shit ton of cousins. My mom has ten sisters. They all had a million kids." I shrugged. "That's pretty much it. I like to fight. I like movies and video games. I have a mate now and here we are."

Sam scoots closer to me. "How many were—Rijitera—are there?" She corrected herself before calling me a werewolf. She was just too precious for this world.

I looked up at the overhang, mentally counting. "Uh, at the last conclave, they reported our numbers had grown to about a million." I met Sam's eyes. "We have yearly conclaves so clans can mingle and whatnot. It's kinda like the highland games. Couple thousand of us show up and we have a huge party with games and shit. Every country has their own conclaves and everyone is invited. It's kind of a thing to travel and go to all the different ones. I've been to conclaves in America, obviously, but also Mexico, the UK, Australia, South Korea, one year in China that *got wild*, Spain, and my last one was in India. Rijitera are really family focused and they consider any of our kind family. Most of the clan heads know each other and their kids, so I'm pretty familiar with them. There are about thirty-five clans, all in all. Each clan has about thirty-thousand members. Clan heads are like mayors or governors. Only its hereditary and the clan heads are always female."

Whew. Word vomit. I hadn't had to explain our clan workings in years. My mom used to make me help teach all this in the schools with the little kids. I liked kids. We all did. I gazed up at Ohem. Yeah. I wanted his babies one day. He'd be an adorable father.

"That's so cool. You belong to a huge spread out family. Sounds amazing," Sam said, dreamily.

Yeah. I guess I did. I hadn't ever thought of it like that. But yeah, Rijitera were crazy loyal to our people.

"You guys belong to that family now. I'm officially adopting you into my clan," I declared.

Callie smirked at me and crossed her arms. "Do we need to be bitten under a full moon"

"Ha. Ha. She's got jokes."

Patty laughed and covered a yawn with her hand. It was contagious, spreading to the rest of us.

"Storytime is over, kiddos. Time for bed," Callie said, getting up to grab the bucket to get water so she could douse the fire. We had the rocks and the piece of metal they'd used to start it earlier, so there was no need to keep it burning. Plus, we definitely didn't need it for warmth. Even in the oasis, it was pretty toasty. She poured water on the fire and found a nice mossy spot to lie on, her arm curled under her head. Sam and Patty went to join her. Ohem stood in one smooth motion, taking me with him. He laid me down a short distance from them on a patch of moss and settled down behind me, his big body spooning me, tails and tentacles winding around various parts of my body until I was snuggled tightly against him. Heaven on Earth. Well, heaven on this hellhole of a planet.

"Sleep well, Jack," Ohem murmured into my hair.

I smiled to myself and closed my eyes.

• • • ● • ● • • •

We lounged around the pools for the next few days, eating smoked meat, and having a relatively good time. Sam had figured out a way to make a smoker by piling rocks together and laying the bony spines of the lizard-camel over smaller stones to make a grill grate. She placed cut up spikes and leaves from the trees and had them under the bone grate, smoking away. It would help preserve the meat and not make the girls sick. Though Ohem pointed out they wouldn't die with their nanos working to kill any bacteria, we still didn't want to risk it. I desperately wished we had salt, but the smokey flavor was still pretty good. I may enjoy my meat raw from time to time, but I was a civilized, not-quite-human human being.

Ohem and I snuck away to have sex under the trees every few hours, not wanting a repeat performance now that Ohem was deeply uncomfortable being intimate in front of an "innocent". Sam looked both offended and disappointed, which had cracked Patty and I up to no end. Callie had to be filled in on what had happened and looked positively scandalized, which sent me and Patty into another tailspin of laughter.

We didn't wander far from the oasis for those days until we ran out of meat.

Which led to mine and Ohem's first argument, about who was going hunting. He felt as though it was his duty to provide for me, but I had a biological imperative to provide for him. Instinct trumps duty, every time. I may have growled and stomped my foot until he'd relented, but that was beside the point. Either way, I won hunting rights and left him to watch the girls.

I had to track the damn lizard-camels for miles to the east. They'd run forever. I must have left a nasty impression on them.

I finally found them at the mouth of another oasis, about twenty miles from ours. This mountain range must be riddled with hidden canyons filled with water. No wonder all the vegetation stuck to the base of the mountainside. Which also meant that the lake we'd been drinking out of was probably toxic since nothing grew around it. It's a damn good thing the girls had the superbug, and we'd left quickly.

I trotted around the lizard-camels on all fours, moving swiftly to cut them off. I'd just taken one down and had started to gut it when the whine of a ship stopped me cold. The sound of my heart stuttering and the blood rushing in my ears drowned out the ship's noise.

A gray ship had dropped out of the sky in the distance, heading to our crash site, flying parallel to the mountains. I dragged my kill under the cover of the trees and watched it. No doubt Ohem had heard it, too. I had to get back. I needed to know if that was friend or foe. If it was friends, happy day. But if it was enemies? I needed to kill them all. They'd captured my mate, never mind that I hadn't known him at the time. It was still revenge worthy. They would be here to retake my family. Never. Gonna. Happen.

I tore through the trees to the oasis, fear driving me to run as fast I could. The distance stretched out before me like a never ending hallway. Though I covered the distance in ten minutes, it felt like hours. When I barreled through the canyon and into the oasis, Ohem was waiting and caught me up in his arms, the breath whooshing out of me at the sudden stop.

I shifted back and looked over his shoulder, sagging in relief when three pairs of confused eyes met mine. They were safe. For now.

"Did you hear it?" I asked when Ohem set me back on my feet.

Izi going dim, he nodded. "Yes. I went to see. It is not my crew," he said. He looked at me and I knew what he was about to say. My heart dropped into my stomach, a cold sweat breaking out over my skin.

He watched me solemnly, his Izi flicking on and off rapidly, sadness in all four of his eyes. He slid his hand around the back of my neck, bending to place his forehead against mine. "I must go." One of his tails wound around my calf. "One of us must stay to guard the others. I need to see if it is Vero. I need to get answers."

It went against every instinct I had to let him go alone. He was my mate. I wanted to tear and shred all who threatened him. I wanted to eat their hearts and howl my victories to the sky in warning to any others who would dare touch what was mine.

I understood that what he was saying was logical. He knew the enemy, and I didn't. Sure, I could go out there and kill them all, but then they would be too dead to answer questions. While logically I knew this was the right choice, my instincts fought hard against it.

I couldn't let him go! I'd just found him. I wrapped my hand around his forearm and took a deep breath through my nose, pulling as much of his scent into me as I could. I drowned myself in it.

I was shaking, barely in control when I released my clenched teeth enough to grind out, "Okay. Okay, go." It was the most difficult thing I'd ever done.

I needed to trust him, trust that he would survive and come back to me.

He pulled his face away from mine, his grip on my neck tightening almost painfully, forcing me to look him in the eyes. "I love you, My Rijiteran *ursang*. You have been my salvation, from the very first moment of our meeting until the end of eternity. I will come back to you. You are stronger than any force that could keep me from you," he whispered, wiping tears from my cheeks and then he was gone.

One moment he was in front of me and then next it was empty air, with only the lingering scent of him remaining. I locked my muscles to keep me from going after him, my breathing hoarse and fast. Hands touched me from all sides, and I looked down to see my friends stood around me, eyes solemn, tears tracking down their faces. Patty stepped in front of me to wrap her arms around my waist, holding me tightly against her. Sam and Callie followed suit, surrounding me in love and support. I rested my hand against the back of Patty's head and soaked them in. I couldn't leave them alone, couldn't risk them being captured. The two protective instincts warred in my heart, trying to pull me apart.

I had no idea how long it would take Ohem to reach the crash site. I didn't know how fast he truly was. It took me a few hours, but I'd been running to bring joy, not to kill my enemies and save my people. He could be there in an hour with that type of motivation. He didn't heal as fast as me, though. The cut on his face took hours to mend. What if he was badly injured? Who would protect him while he healed? Who would protect the girls from the smugglers if I went to get him? I was trapped. Trapped by my word to Ohem that I would stay, trapped by my need to guard Patty, Sam, and Callie.

"He's a big bad alien. He'll be fine," Patty reassured me. Her head was below my boobs, her cheek pressed into my sternum, and I couldn't see her without tilting my head forward. It made a sliver of humor sneak past the despair. I could do this. We just needed to wait. I'd give him a few hours, he moved fast, faster than me, and had a reason that would push him to test his limits.

Please, God. I don't pray often, but please. Let him get his answers and come back to me. If he can't get answers, let him kill them quickly and then come back to me.

I needed him. Rijitera didn't survive well when their mates died. Most killed themselves and the ones who lived, lived a half-life, a husk of a person, or went mad and had to be put down.

"Jack?" Callie's stern voice called me. She might have been calling my name for a while, I'd been staring at nothing, lost in my thoughts.

I looked to my right and down, where her head rested against my arm, her tight black curls soft against my skin. She hugged me hard and stepped back. "We're here for you. What do you need?" she asked softly, her brown eyes filled with a steady kind of determination. It did a lot to reassure me.

I took in a shaky breath. "Just sit with me. We need to listen for any approaching enemies and for any sounds of gunshots. Hopefully, they have guns that shoot bullets so it can be heard from here," I said and went to lean against the mouth of the canyon wall that opened into the oasis. If anything came through the trees, I'd hear them before they entered the canyon. I'd also be able to hear any sounds of a battle. The corridor of the canyon created a deep echo, amplifying outside sounds.

The girl's settled in next to me, and we waited.

• • • ● • ● • • •

I don't know what alerted me. A feeling of intense unease, a sixth sense that my mate was in desperate trouble. I jerked away from the wall where I'd been leaning for the past two hours. I knew exactly how long it had been since Ohem left. I had been fucking counting the seconds in my head. My skin pulled tight and my blood was roaring in my ears.

I turned to the others and caught Patty's eyes searing into me, she'd been watching me closely the whole time.

She came to me, giving me a small push. "Go, Jack. We'll be okay. We'll hide behind the waterfall until you get back. They won't come, and if they do, we'll fight." She stepped into me quickly, gave me a fierce hug and then pushed me away again.

"Go."

I shifted instantly and went.

The canyon was a blur, the trees passing in a blink; then I was moving across the desert at what had to be light speed, my feet barely touching the ground. My heart was crashing in my chest, Ohem was in trouble, and I had to get to him fast. I *had* to.

I made it to the crash site in an hour.

I ran up to the furrow from the crash and slowed. The gray ship had landed next to the lake, close to the boulders we'd sheltered by. I dropped to all fours and slid along the ground. It was all flat ground here with no cover, so I jumped into the furrow, falling a good eight feet to the bottom, and moved towards the wreck. There were the sounds of hissing voices and fighting. Ohem snarled, and then a warping crack, the smell of ozone in the air, similar to a lighting strike and then Ohem went silent.

Cold rushed over my body, everything became crystal clear, like I was seeing things in the future before they happened. I was standing slightly behind the remains of the shipping container without even realizing I'd moved. It gave me a perfect view of my mate's back and the aliens surrounding him. A hot churning started in my heart, spreading the harder I stared at the scene.

In the center of thirteen red armored soldiers of the same species, kneeled Ohem, they all wore faceless helmets and were pointing strange looking weapons at him. Ohem's head was still uncovered, and he was bloody. Around him lay six dead soldiers, their bodies torn into pieces. He'd been slaughtering them, why'd he stop?

There was an unarmored male of the same species as Ohem standing directly in front of him. They just stared at each other. Ohem's Izi were strobing in a way that expressed shock and confusion and the male was smiling in that stiff way Ohem did, his Izi glowing softly. What the hell was going on? I shifted further behind the container, ensuring they couldn't see me. I was stretching my claws to grab the edge of the torn ceiling to pull myself to the roof when Ohem spoke, his voice anguished and sharp with betrayal.

"Brother."

Eleven

His brother.

Fuck.

That's how they'd gotten him to surrender. His brother had strolled off that ship and probably called out to him, shocking him into immobility. It would do the same to me if someone in my clan had shown up.

Jesus. *His brother.*

"What have you done?" Ohem demanded, his Izi dark now.

To my people, betrayal by blood was the highest offense. It didn't happen often, but when it did, it was always a death sentence. That kind of rot couldn't be allowed to fester and infect anyone else. We cut it out swiftly. I would gladly purge Ohem's brother to save him the pain of killing his own kin. I crouched and pressed against the black metal, readying myself. Ohem's head tilted to the side and his Izi flared briefly. He'd scented me or heard me. *Don't give me away, love. Just keep him talking.* Ohem stiffened as if he'd heard my thoughts and returned his full attention to his brother.

The brother circled Ohem slowly, tsking and shaking his head in disappointment. "I had given explicit instructions that you were not to be harmed. You were never supposed to know, Ohem. I had arranged for you to be taken to a mining encampment on Crosos. The moon is very isolated. You would have heard no news until I came to rescue you. It would have already been done by then. You would have only known me to be a hero of the Unity and your rescuer." He placed his hand on Ohem's shoulder and my mate flinched. "I am deeply sorry it has come to this. I hadn't wanted to come myself, but your ship was closing in and you were getting too close to Vero. I couldn't leave it to anyone else. A job well done is done by your own hand, you understand?"

Don't you do it, you bastard. Don't do it!

Ohem's brother raised a small handgun looking weapon and pressed it to the side of my mate's head. Time froze.

• • • ● • ● • • •

An unholy roar erupted in the valley. The soldiers screamed in terror and ducked, their weapons pointing wildly in every direction, but no one fired, too panicked to think.

A nightmare landed in their midst. The screaming intensified, soldiers shooting blue fire at the beast that had started slaughtering them. The fire did nothing. Only enraged it more.

It cleaved meat from bone. Tore limbs from wailing bodies. The creature turned towards the still kneeling Ohem, the brother was scrambling away in terror. It screamed in rage and attacked, but two soldiers stepped in its path, shooting their blue fire at the creature's face. It cut them down like a scythe through wheat. The brother was moving, a black blur heading for the open ramp of his ship. The monster could not let him escape. It needed to feast on his flesh. Wash itself in his blood. The brother needed to know agony before he died, for daring to threaten that which belonged to the creature. Soldiers blocked its path, sacrificing themselves so their leader could escape. The monster moved fast, disappearing and reappearing in a blink, butchering the soldiers.

The brother's ship was closing its ramp, lifting off the ground, its engines sending scorching hot air billowing across the valley. Its weapons whined and fired, blue flame engulfing the monster. The brother breathed a sigh of relief from his seat in the cockpit as the plasma shot hit the monster.

He screamed in renewed terror when the creature jumped through the flames, roaring its rage, deafening them, even inside the ship. It cleared the fifty feet of space between itself and the ship, claws scoring the hull but not gaining purchase. The creature howled in rage as it fell back to the ground, watching as its prey escaped.

The creature turned to see the carnage it had wrought. Bodies and blood covered the valley floor; a single black figure still kneeling on the ground.

"Jack," the mate whispered, and the creature remembered.

I was towering over Ohem. Even when he stood, I was looking down at him. At least three feet separated his head from mine.

I was confused, my mind was on fire. Ohem reached up and ran his hand down my chest.

"Jack," he said again.

He caught my naked body when I fell from the shift.

• • • • • • • • • •

I awoke in Ohem's arms, my body one large sore, like I'd been run over by a train. Every muscle and bone hurt. I'd shifted into something *huge*, something impossible. I'd lost myself to the shift... that had never happened before. To anyone in any of the clans on Earth.

I moved my eyes to Ohem's. "What happened?" I needed it said aloud. I felt like I had gone insane and hallucinated the whole thing.

He stroked my hair, glowing a sad faded yellow. "My brother Rakis, Councilor of Stellios, is working for Vero. Maybe even driving him. They mean to start a war. You saw him try to kill me. You killed them all, Jack. You were ferocious." There was pride in his voice.

I gaped at him. Ferocious? I'd been huge! *Unhinged.*

"I think," he said slowly, "somewhere in your line, one of your ancestors mated with a Y'ani."

I stared at him, eyes wide. "What is that?" I couldn't help but feel trepidation. I was used to being a monster, but whatever the fuck I had turned into made my normal monster look like a damn poodle.

"Y'ani were enormous creatures that inhabited the harsh frozen planets known to be incredibly dangerous. They would enter a type of trance. A killing rage the likes of which has never been seen since. They died out naturally in direct relation to the great difficulty they had in reproducing. It would seem that one of your ancestors mated with one before that happened." He gathered me close to his chest, and pressed his hard mouth into my hair. His voice was pensive. "You were twice your normal size and mass, Jack. Plasma shots had no effect on you. I was about to die, shot by my brother."

I flinched at the memory. I'd almost watched my mate be murdered. I would have nightmares of that moment for the rest of my life.

"It triggered your enhanced shift and the trance. You saved my life. Again. It would seem I am becoming quite the troublesome mate."

Was he nuts? He'd have been just fine on his own had his *own brother* not distracted him and then tried to kill him. His brother was responsible for his capture and imprisonment on the smugglers' ship.

That was so messed up.

I was going to kill that motherfucker so hard. I was going to eat him alive, starting at the bottom so it lasted longer. Rip out his heart and lay it at Ohem's feet. I took a few breaths through my nose to calm my growing rage and leaned away from him so I could place my hands on either side of his face. I needed to look into his eyes and make sure he understood.

"You will never be troublesome, Ohem. *I love you.* The circumstances of our meeting and my berserker shift have absolutely not been your fault. Never doubt your worth to me. Whatever challenges you face, whatever the danger, I will be there fighting beside you. Fighting for you. No battle is too great, no enemy that I wouldn't face down for you. I am a Rijiteran *ursang* and I stand with you. Forever." I kissed his jaw, then his hard cheek. He turned his head and pressed his mouth to mine. I opened to him and his tongue stroked inside. The kiss was gentle, sweet. I kissed him back, reassuring myself that he was here with me. I'd come so close to losing him.

I had never been this angry in my life, wrath was swirling inside me like a storm, a hurricane about to make landfall and kill everything in its path. I wanted revenge for the pain my mate was feeling. I needed to right this wrong. My body swelled, trying to change again. Searing agony stabbed me from all over, my body going rigid and then limp. Ohem grunted and held me tighter. It would seem like I wouldn't be shifting anytime soon. He broke away from the kiss and stood. "I love you too, Jack. You are right, we face this together. I am hurting and angry, but with you beside me, we will conquer all." There was my scary, fierce mate. The alien General rose and walked with sure strides back towards the oasis.

I glared into the sky as he walked. My mate's arms held me securely while I quietly seethed. *I'll find you, Rakis. You will never run far enough to escape me. You will never have enough power to stand against me. No matter how large your armies are or how advanced your weapons, I will cut you down.*

• • • ● • ● • • •

The girls were still behind the waterfall when Ohem carried me into the oasis.

"It's us. It's safe," I shouted to be heard over the waterfall. Patty emerged first. She jumped into the deep pool and swam to us.

"What happened?" she asked, pushing her hair out of her face, glancing between us.

Ohem put me on my feet, keeping a firm hold around my waist in case my legs gave out. My body still ached, even after the three hours it had taken him to walk across the desert. He had taken extra care, but every footfall made my bones feel like they were going to abandon ship. It was taking a long time to heal whatever trauma the berserker shift had caused. Naming it after crazed Viking warriors seemed appropriate. I stumble-walked over to the wall and Ohem helped me slide down to sit. He crouched beside me and started rubbing the muscles of my legs. I tilted my head against the wall and groaned, half in pain and half in pleasure. I was so damn sore. My freaking bones hurt so badly.

"Ohem's brother is behind his capture. He showed up to kill him," I said with my eyes still closed.

Patty sucked in a shocked breath and I heard her move to stand by my mate, probably to lay a hand on him in sympathy. Aggression flooded my system, my eyes flew open, and a rattling growl burst from between bared fangs. Patty froze. She raised her hands and slowly backed away from Ohem.

Ohem moved closer to me and gathered me back into his arms to place me on his lap. I took several deep breaths, trying to calm down and not kill my friend. When I could look at her without wanting to tear her throat out, I gave her a wane smile. "I'm sorry. Maybe don't touch him for a while. He almost died and I'm a little sensitive right now. Probably don't stand too close to him either."

Patty gave me a reassuring smile. "It's okay, I understand."

I sighed in relief and relaxed against Ohem's chest. I didn't know that this feeling would ever go away. I was probably going to be a huge territorial pain in the ass for the rest of our lives. Not ideal. Maybe they had trauma counseling on Stellios because I was so going to have PTSD from this.

"Forgive her. She is dealing with more than just my brush with death."

I really wish he wouldn't talk about almost dying so casually. It was stressing me out. He waited until Sam and Callie stood next to Patty to explain my episode of pure unadulterated rage and the shift into a giant Rijiteran killing machine.

Callie turned wide eyes to me. "Are you okay?" she asked, concern making the line between her eyebrows stand out.

Sam made a move to approach me and Patty put a hand out to stop her, shaking her head when Sam looked at her in question. "She's feeling territorial and protective. We should hang back from Ohem for a while. She might hurt us by accident and then hate herself after."

I gave Patty a grateful smile. Sam nodded in understanding and took a step back, wrapping her arms around herself. Oily guilt swarmed under my skin like wasps. They shouldn't have to watch themselves around me, it wasn't fair to them.

I lifted my shoulders to shrug and winced in pain. "I'm sore. Everything feels like it's been stretched out," I grimaced. "I don't know how long it's going to take me to heal."

I needed to heal quickly. I doubted very much that the good Councilor was going to just give up and leave us be. If I was a betting woman, I'd say we should expect more soldiers with bigger guns coming soon. Ohem's ship better get here before then. We could use the help. I stilled and glanced up at Ohem's face. What if his men couldn't be trusted? How many people of the Unity were corrupt? How far did this go? And why the hell did they want a war? Why hunt down old artifacts? I voiced these concerns to my mate, and he growled deep in his chest.

"My ship and her crew can be trusted. That I know. We are rarely on Stellios and I have trained almost all the officers on my ship. Why do they want to cause a war?" He shook his head and sighed. "It would generate credits and allow a grab for more power. In times of war, the Unity may raise taxes exponentially. They may pass laws without citizen votes if it pertains to the war and the common good. Rakis has long been keen on expanding the Unity's reach. He would claim it was for the good of all and for protecting our way of life, but the council always voted against it. If we were at war and the expansion happened because of annexed worlds? He would need no votes." His arms tightened subtly around me.

To be betrayed by your own sibling and then realizing their motive was something as petty and predictable as riches and power? Disgusting.

"Stellios is the strongest, and most influential planet of the Unity. Our vote holds more weight. Others look to us for guidance. Rakis is from a famous, well-respected family. He could get away with much before citizens noticed any wrongdoings. The trust in the At'ens House is almost absolute," he said grimly, no doubt thinking that he had trusted his brother explicitly too. Why wouldn't you trust your family? The whole situation was fucked. Sideways.

Sam started pacing, her hands waving in the air as she talked. "But why use Rijiteran artifacts? Do you know what they were looking for?"

"I have my suspicions, but nothing is sound. There have been rumors of some type of weapon. My brother had access to our archives, he must have found something and set Vero on the hunt to locate it. All Rijiteran weapons were devastating. Nothing good will come of this," he said.

"Add it to the list of shit we have to sort out when we get off this planet," I said wearily. I just needed to rest my eyes for a moment. Just five minutes. I was about to tell them we needed to set up a watch, but lost the battle with unconsciousness.

• • • ● • ● • • •

The rumble whine of another ship dropping into our air space woke me with a jolt. I'd been having a nightmare. I'd been too late to save Ohem, and his brother had pulled the trigger and I'd watched him die. Sam, Patty, and Callie were being loaded into cages on Rakis's ship, calling out to me to save them.

I was on my feet as quickly as possible, senses dulled and started to shift, blinding agony burning through me as my body tried to reject the change. I clenched my teeth and forced it. I was burning alive from the inside out.

It took forever, and I was panting by the finish. I was my normal size, thank god. I don't know that I'd survive going full berserker-rage-demon so soon after the first time. My body was all kinds of jacked up, trembling so bad that I stumbled a few steps before I sank to one knee. My head weighed a thousand pounds when I lifted it to look around me. The girls were all standing in various frozen stages of rushing towards me. I blinked and gave them a very weak, toothy smile.

Patty moved first, gripping my arm. "Jesus, Jack. Are you okay? That was horrible to watch. Your bones looked like they were breaking. Maybe don't shift for a while after this."

Where was Ohem? I gathered myself and stood. It was an act of sheer will to keep my feet under me.

Callie grabbed my other arm to keep me steady. "Ohem is in the canyon, watching. He heard it too."

Adrenaline surged, and I could walk into the canyon, but every step hurt.

"Be careful, Jack," Patty called to me. I gave a brief yip in response, not loud enough to be heard by anyone but them and marched forward with clenched teeth.

Ohem was standing in the canyon's opening, under the trees. He glanced back at me and then did a double take and came rushing to my side. "What is wrong, Jack?" he asked, running his hands over my shoulders.

"Hurts. It hurts to shift. Weak," I said, trying to make my words understandable.

He curled his arm around my waist and took my weight. I wrapped my arm around his neck and let him take it, my legs muscles burning with fatigue. Ohem half dragged me to where he'd been standing and pointed at the ship flying slowly across the open desert.

"They are searching. It's not my crew, but I recognize the ship. It is the Vrax. The smugglers are here looking for their cargo. No doubt my brother has sent them to confirm that I am dead."

I looked at him in confusion.

He chuckled. "He doesn't know that I was the monster's mate. He in all likelihood assumes I have been torn to pieces along with his soldiers."

So he sent some smugglers to check it out. No doubt he hadn't told them of the dangerous creature lurking about. What an asshole.

I frowned. "You think he recognized I was a Rijitera?"

He paused for a moment and then shook his head. "I do not know, perhaps not. The public history of them always depicts them in armor. The recordings and paintings in our family archives are locked in a separate vault from the written accounts. I don't know that he even knows what a Rijitera looks like."

I guess it didn't really matter, but I liked the element of surprise. Guess I'd have to be extra murdery when I ran into him next time to make up for the potential loss of secrecy.

The ship was making slow loops around the desert, hovering over where the crash site was. When it landed and disappeared from our sight, my heart stuttered. I'd have to leave the girls. No way was I ever letting Ohem out of my sight again. I looked up at him to find his eyes on me.

"Are you well enough?" he asked.

I'd never be injured enough to let him go into a fight alone.

I nodded. "I'm fine. Let's go kill these assholes."

His Izi flared brightly for a moment before he started towards the crash site, moving fast. I followed; every step torture. My muscles screamed and my bones were like shattered glass under my skin. Still, I followed and swallowed down any sounds of pain. Ohem was watching me. I gave him a wolf's smile and picked up my pace, not wanting him to order me back. He'd fail miserably, but I didn't want to fight with him right now.

The trek across the desert took longer than normal. Ohem had gradually slowed his pace, forcing me to slow to match it. It had allowed my body time to warm up, and the pain had lessened some. He knew. He'd known he wouldn't have been able to make me leave him to fight alone, so he'd been subtly going easy. Sneaky bastard.

God, I loved him.

The blocky matte black ship of the Vrax was on the ground when we made it to the crash site, its engines still powered up, and there were eight shark assholes patrolling the site of the massacre. My hackles rose at the sight, I hated this fucking lake. It would forever feature in my night terrors. Being back here was doing weird, not friendly things to my mind, almost like a panic attack.

Ohem's hand on my shoulder made me look at him. He did that calming, slow flashing pattern with his Izi and damn if it didn't work. I nodded at him to let him know I had myself under control.

"I am alive, *ursang*," he whispered.

I did a little jump and licked his chin. "I know. Love you," I growled at him and advanced. Ohem followed me and together we walked out onto the lakeside.

The shark aliens didn't notice us. Shocker. They really were the worst aliens imaginable. Why anyone would hire them was beyond me. I snorted and lifted my muzzle and let loose an eerie Hunting Howl. The sharks whirled to point their shitty, bullet filled guns at us and the fight was on. I darted forward, shoving the pain that caused me aside, and snatched the gun out of the hands of the shark closest to me...or at least that was my intention. His arm just sorta ripped off right along with the gun.

I stared at the arm in my hand and then back at the screaming, thrashing shark on the ground, holding his bloody stump with his other hand. I mean, yeah, I was strong enough to pull someone's arm off, but I hadn't been trying for that. Huh, how about that? Seems like the berserker demon shift had left some side effects besides the pain. Effortless arm ripping capabilities. I could live with that.

I crushed the armless shark under my foot and used his arm to brain his buddy. My new victim's head exploded, blood and bone sprayed all over his comrade next to him.

Oh yeah, baby.

I'd gotten stronger. I'd have to have a scientific discussion with my mate later about why that might be. I flashed my fangs in a grin and started weaving in and out of the sharks, slashing and biting, ripping them apart. I never lost sight of where Ohem was, acutely aware of him on the field at all times. I was paranoid now and wasn't allowing myself to drift too far away from him, just in case. The paranoia was helping me ignore the internal screaming my body was doing from the pain I'd shoved deep down. I kept watching him in my peripheral vision and it was magnificent to behold.

He was beautiful, fluid and savage. I was witnessing a being perfectly adapted for killing find joy in his purpose. He moved gracefully, with no wasted movements, slashing with his black claws, his Izi blazing and taking on an ominous light. He punched through chests and crushed heads, ripped bodies in half. Where I snarled and growled, he was absolutely silent. He really was a Terrible Terror. A creature out of our worst nightmares and he was all mine! I practically vibrated with pride. Ohem caught me admiring him and I swear he stood taller, his muscles flexing a little more and he killed with greater enthusiasm. Would it be taboo to fuck on blood-soaked ground?

I tore the head off the last shark, and was striding towards my mate, my movements predatory, when the ship shot me. It threw me forwards enough that I stumbled and nearly fell. My pain reminded me it hadn't been shoved deep enough, just muted in the fight's adrenaline, and it flared again in a sunspot of pure agony. I whined, and righted myself, shaking from the effort, and turned to give the ship a snarl. It was struck by something and exploded, the force of it knocking me back into Ohem's waiting arms. We slid backwards several feet and stopped. The ship was nearly broken in half, a vast hole blown into its side by whatever had hit it.

Two sleek black shapes roared over our heads, their engines blasting us with heat. The new ships were arrow shaped and nimble, turning sharply and coming to hover over their handiwork.

They were just the super advanced, futuristic planes I'd been led to believe aliens would have. There was a yellow symbol on the bottom of the alien ships, right under the pointed nose, swirling lines around two spears.

Ohem was laughing, that loud happy sound that made me want to jump him.

I turned my head to look at him over my shoulder. "What are you laughing at?" I asked him, curious and a little nervous.

He chuckled and stepped back from me, but kept a steadying hand on my shoulder, and put his left fist over his chest and roared.

He was super stoked. Must be his crew. I was getting excited too until a deep voice bellowed from the ship's intercom systems.

"Step away from the General or we will open fire."

I looked around at the bodies and then at Ohem. Ah, shit. They thought I was with the sharks and an enemy. The sound of the ship's guns powering up confirmed it. I groaned and rubbed my hands over my snout. I really didn't feel like putting up with this right now.

Ohem stepped in front of me and splayed his arms wide. "She is *mine*! You will stand down your weapons and land," he snarled at them. He didn't yell, so I'm guessing they had cameras that zoomed or something. I'd think that was cool later, after a great night's sleep and maybe some painkillers. I was more impressed that they immediately followed his orders. No, 'but sirs', no hesitation at all. Just Ohem ordering and them obeying. Damn. Why was that hot? I was tired, in pain, and I was still probably, *definitely*, down to fuck him. There should be a concern there, but I couldn't find it.

The ships landed at the mouth of the valley, right next to the crash ditch. The ramps at the back of the arrow opened and three aliens from each ship walked out. They were all armored in the same red metal as Ohem, but not all of them were the same species. I shouldn't be so surprised since he'd already explained the whole Unified planets thing, but I was. One soldier had four legs and it had six—count 'em—*six* arms. What a time to be alive.

They approached quickly and formed a line. Left fist over chest salutes and then they stood rigid, waiting for Ohem.

He stalked around them twice before coming to stand in front of them again, and then twisted around to hold his hand out to me, so I placed my bloody claws into his. We both looked like extras from a horror movie, covered in blood and gore. What a great first impression.

I couldn't see their eyes, the helmets were the same as Rakis's forces but, all the aliens' heads followed my movements. It was kinda creepy, the helmets being faceless, with grooves that ran vertically over the helmet's surface, lit faintly with yellow lights like Ohem's Izi.

"This is Jack. My wife. *My mate*. She rescued me from smugglers and betrayal. There are three other human females hidden in an oasis near here. We must retrieve them before we leave this planet." He paused and stared hard at them. They stood straighter. "We have much to discuss. Block all communications and tracking from the Unity. I want the Solus to be completely undetectable. Relay that to Commander Rema immediately. I need one of your links."

One soldier lifted his hand to press something on his helmet and a small ball popped out of the side. He handed it to Ohem who thanked him softly. "Send a transport ship when I send the coordinates." He paused again and glanced at me. "And have them bring clothes for Jack."

He missed nothing, I'd shredded my clothes when I'd panic shifted to rescue him. He'd remembered to get me more, even after all the crazy shit that had happened. How did he manage that? I shook my head and gave him my best thankful smile that this form could manage.

"Dismissed." He saluted them with his fist to his chest and they repeated the action back to him. They then did the same to me. It threw me off for a second, but I repeated it back to them, which seemed to prompt them into turning as one, splitting off to march towards their ships and enter their respective crafts, and powered up. It wasn't until they took off with a blast of heat and sound that Ohem pressed the ball to his neck above his torque.

It freaking *burrowed* into his skin and lit up. It split under his skin, one half traveling up towards his ear and the other staying in his neck. It was freaky as hell. I was glad for my ear marble. That stayed mostly external and adapted to my changing forms, no burrowing required.

"Change back. I know you are in pain. I will carry you," he said.

He didn't have to tell me twice. I *hurt*. I gritted my teeth against the horrible scream that wanted to tear up out of my throat from the pain that flared when I shifted back to my human body. I slumped and Ohem caught me smoothly in his arms.

"Do not shift again until I can have you examined on the Solus."

He took off at an easy run towards our girls. I couldn't wait to tell Patty and the others that we were saved! They better have soap on board Ohem's ship. I'd cry if they didn't. God, I missed coffee too. So much. Sweet nectar of the gods. A hot cup of coffee would go a long way in making me feel better.

My skin hurt. It hurt to breathe, and as smoothly as Ohem moved, it was still jarring me. That berserker shift did a number on me. Added strength didn't mean jackshit if I couldn't function.

· · · ● · ● ● · ·

By the time we made it to the oasis, I was ready to meet my maker. I'd managed not to scream and cry or demand Ohem put me out of my misery like a three-legged dog, but it had been a close thing.

The girls were again hiding behind the waterfall, and Ohem called them out. I just didn't have the strength to yell right now. That trip had sucked.

"You okay?" Sam asked. She hadn't approached us, which was a relief. I still didn't want anyone to touch Ohem, but if she'd laid a hand on me in comfort, I'd have passed out.

"I feel like I've been pushed through a meat grinder. Twice," I mumbled to her. She hummed in sympathy but kept her distance.

"My ship is in orbit. I have already sent details of our location to the transport crew and they will be here in two minutes."

I worried Callie might pass out in relief, all the tension leaving her body in a rush after we shared the news. Patty looked nervous, her teeth biting into her lip, and Sam just had a dazed expression on her face, like she couldn't believe it was almost over.

I just wanted whatever medical doohickey they'd better have on an advanced alien ship to make me feel good. I swear to god if Ohem's ship isn't up to sci-fi standards, I would riot. There better not be any fucking green buttons that open doors. Or mops.

I was still ranting in my head when we emerged from the trees in time to see another sleek black ship landing about two hundred yards in front of us, its engine stirring up the dust in big swirls. The side opened and aliens in red cloth shirts and pants jumped out to assist. These looked like they should be underwater somewhere, with blue-green scales and long frilled tails. They had two legs and two arms, but long betta fin like hair. It was waving around like a betta tail underwater.

They were pretty aliens, with human looking lips and eyes. No nose though and they had fish hole ears too, but no gills that I could see, and they didn't have webbed hands. Their feet were encased in red leather boots, so I couldn't tell if they were webbed or not. Callie, Patty, and Sam had all stopped and stared until one alien trilled uncomfortably. It spurred the ladies into motion and they allowed the two helpful betta aliens to strap them in very rubbery black bucket seats inside the shuttle. The fabric of the seats looked like they were made of rubber lava rock. There were six chairs, three on either side of a wide aisle.

It was weird and alien, and I was here for it. Finally! I had a good feeling about Ohem's big ship. This was just a transport ship, and it looked absolutely nothing like anything found on Earth, so the big ship had to be something crazy to see.

Ohem sat on the lava rock chair with me still in his arms. I caught the betta aliens eyeing me with curiosity. I was in my human form and naked, but if I'd been able to, I'd have shifted to really give them something to look at. Instead, I bared my sharp teeth and growled at them. One trilled loudly and almost fell over its co-pilot. Patty snickered from her seat in front of me. One of them came and cautiously handed me a red bundle of clothes and Ohem helped me pull them on. I had been dubious when I'd shaken them out and noticed how small they were, but to my surprise, they stretched and fit perfectly. They stuck uncomfortably to my skin from all the blood on my body, but they fit. Ohem scooped me up into his arms again as soon as I was dressed and re-situated me on his lap.

"Stop terrifying my crew," Ohem said, sounding both amused and exasperated, but I could tell he was satisfied that I was clothed when his shoulders relaxed.

I smiled up into his face. "That's gonna cost you, General. My compliance will have to be bought."

His Izi had been glowing a nice neutral yellow, and they flared to that aroused brightness that I liked. "After you see the med bay, I will take pleasure in reminding you who is the alpha in this relationship," he growled softly into my ear.

I shivered and gave his smooth jaw a lick. He tasted like fish blood. *Hmm. Should have licked him clean when I'd had the chance.*

A solid black door dropped over the opening and enclosed us in darkness for a few seconds before yellow lights flared to life in the ceiling.

The loud but smooth take off stopped me from answering him. The black shielding pulled back from the door like Tetris in reverse and revealed a large window. I watched with the others as we rose above the desert. The path of the crash could be seen from this height. We'd really slid a long way. We must have clipped one of the mountain tops, as it was damaged and there were burn marks on the rock of its shattered peak. We rose over the mountain range, and I gasped. On the other side, impassable from the desert by the solid wall of the mountains, was the remains of the Vrax ship. It was shattered into pieces and burned to a crisp. The final resting place of the human women stolen from their homes and families.

I'd make sure we wrote all their names down, Callie and Sam remembered them all, and made some type of memorial that could make its way back to Earth and to their families.

Twelve

The transport ship was fast, it only took ten minutes before the planet could be seen in its entirety, a horrible orange ball of hatred and contempt for life. I wouldn't be sad to see the last of it. Then there was the black void of space. I hated space. What I didn't hate though, was the damn monstrosity that was Ohem's ship. The Solus Geshgid was absolutely gigantic. An obsidian arrowhead at least five miles long and that was just me taking a wildly inaccurate guess. It was also bristling with guns, with huge two pronged cannon type things attached above the bow with so many other weapons that I gave up counting.

"The Solus Geshgid, fondly called Solus by her crew. The finest, largest warship in our Fleet. Her shielding is impregnable and her proton canons can break planets. She is Stellios's pride. I have had the honor of being her captain for many years," Ohem explained to us. We were all gaping at the sheer scale of the thing. The closer we got, the more like an insect I felt. Or like a single cell organism trying to hitch a ride on a blue whale.

A light shone in an open hatch large enough for our transport to float inside. It flew down a tube and slowed to glide into a claw that hooked around the craft and pulled us into a cargo bay... a cargo bay roughly the size of Manhattan. It was also just as busy. There were so many beings and machines flying around and walking on the labyrinth of floating walkways at least a mile above the floor that it was overwhelming to take in. On the ground level were ships and vehicles of mystery origins. It was a city... and this was also probably only a single cargo bay of many spread throughout the ship. Damn. I would never find my way around. I was going to get lost, and they'd have to send out search parties that Patty would never let me live down.

The claw docked us on the ground level in a bay with a bunch of alien writing on it and the door hissed open. Ohem stood and carried me out. The girls followed behind him, staring in wide-eyed wonder at the sights. It was loud, with metal screeching and people talking. Small ships and gliders zipping around in the air, people working and yelling. Pure chaos.

Waiting on the tarmac type floor outside our parking bay was the most beautiful male I had ever seen, and I was very partial to horned aliens with tentacles and black shiny skin with big teeth. But this guy was hot. Like, if an elf and an orc had a four armed baby that grew up to surpass its parents in hotness and then grew freaking wings, that's what this dude would look like. Motherfucker was shredded. Warrior stacked and racked. His luxurious black hair hung in neat braids to his waist and he had pointy ears. Elves existed! I was getting drunk later to celebrate. *So drunk*. Me and Patty were going to fan girl over the winged elf together, judging by the way she was eye fucking him right now. *Slow your role, Patty. He hasn't passed the dick measuring test yet. He could have a small peen and then where would you be?*

Though, he looked like he was packing a cannon in those tight red pants, so I had confidence in his passing grade. He had four arms. Four! The possibilities were endless.

He stepped up in front of Ohem. He was tall, not as tall as Ohem, my mate was a freak of nature, but taller than me. Seven feet tall and bulletproof, baby. I discreetly looked over Ohem's shoulder at Patty and caught her eye. I grinned at her and wagged my eyebrows. She smacked her lips and raised her hand to fan her face.

I looked back and caught Ohem staring at me, eyes narrowed to slits.

Oops. Busted.

I kissed his chin. No more looking at the elf if I wanted him to live long enough for Patty to seduce him.

Ohem growled under his breath and looked at the elf, who was staring at us in wary confusion. Poor guy. He had no idea what he was in for.

"This is Commander Rema. My second. He is in charge of the Solus in my absence." Ohem introduces Patty and the girls to Rema. Patty blows him a kiss and I swear to god, the elf blushed. *Blushed*. Patty looked positively predatory. He didn't stand a chance.

Ohem gazed down at me and then back at Rema. "This is my mate, Jack. We will discuss her more in my cabin, with the dampeners on. For now, I need to take her to the medical bay. The other women need to be examined as well."

Yes. Painkillers, stat.

Rema nodded stiffly and led the way down the wide tarmac. There was a floating flat craft bobbing about a foot off the ground, with three rows of bench seats made of the same lava rock material as the ones on the transport ship. Rema stepped to the side and held out his arm, indicating we were to proceed onto the craft. Ohem stepped on and quickly took the first bench seat. The girls sat down in the middle, except for Patty. When Rema sat on the third bench at the rear, draping his wings behind the seat, she sashayed her barely clothed ass onto the craft and sat right next to him, her thigh pressed firmly against his. He stiffened and looked up at Ohem with a helpless expression, but Ohem was facing forward and didn't see it. I did though. I had been watching him over Ohem's shoulder. I met Rema's eyes and winked and his pearly skin turned a lovely pink color. Patty grinned at me, and I couldn't help but laugh at her antics.

"Rema is a Neldre. It is the females who initiate courtship. By sitting so close to him, Patty is showing she wants to court him... for marriage," Ohem said dryly.

I blink at him, giving my best effort at innocence. "She's only sitting next to him."

"If you look at him like that again, I may have to remind you to whom you belong," he growled out, the sound low and dangerous. It sent a shiver of pleasure down my spine that left heat in its wake. It helped ease some of the pain I was feeling.

I pressed my face to his chest, smiling against his armor and shook my head. "I won't. But you can remind me, anyway," I said and kissed his chest. He stroked my thigh in response and if I'd had the energy, I'd have squirmed in his lap.

The craft moved forward smoothly and sped along the wide lane. It took us thirty minutes to cross just a portion of the cargo bay to the huge double doors that stood open at one end. We passed through the door and entered a tunnel, other crafts moving past us, carrying crates and vehicles back and forth through the tunnel. It reminded me of those underground highways I'd driven through during my travels in Europe.

We stopped next to a platform that had a cylindrical metal door only a few feet from the bay doors. Ohem stood, carrying me to the door that slid open silently at our approach. It was some type of elevator, big enough for twenty people. We all piled in, with Rema bringing up the rear and the door closed immediately behind him. I was confused when they opened a minute later. I hadn't felt us move at all. Rema led us out and down a well-lit corridor with smooth, black floors and walls that cast our reflections back at us. What the hell kind of elevator had that been? Did we just fucking *teleport?* There'd been no whoosh or particle beams.

We passed various glass doors and I peeked over Ohem's shoulder and spied aliens working in labs. One had a spider guy firing an enormous weapon at an alien mannequin, blue flames erupted where the mannequin had been, casting a glow out into the corridor. The rooms must be sound-proofed because no sounds escaped. I strained to see the aftermath, but we moved past it before I could see how the mannequin fared. Bummer.

Sam was staring in wide-eyed wonder into some of the laboratories as we passed, her mouth slightly open. Callie had to drag her along so they'd keep up with the rest of us. Patty had drifted behind Rema and was checking out his ass in those tight red cargo pants when his wings moved just right to give her glimpses of it as he walked. He was blushing again, but he was also smiling a little. I guess the initial shock of having a female come onto him so strongly was wearing off enough for him to enjoy the attention.

Ohem stepped through the door on the right and we followed him into another well lit black room that had medical equipment and lava rock beds. Ohem placed me on one of them and stepped back, his hand tracing along my body before he turned to start across the room towards Rema, and what I assumed was a doctor that had arrived through a glass door on the other side of the room. The lava rock mattress was warm and molded to my body, I sighed in relief and laid my head back on the square rubbery pillow.

"This place is wild, Jack," Patty said, coming to stand by my head.

I snorted at her and grinned. "You didn't see a goddamned thing. You were too busy looking at the locals."

Patty snickered and shrugged her shoulders in a 'it can't be helped' gesture. "He's just so pretty. I want the shiny elf man, Jack."

It was a good thing Rema was talking with Ohem and the doctor and couldn't hear our commentary, or he'd be getting flustered right now. Though, his ears were twitching and turning pink, so maybe he had.

"Did you see all the planes? Those were definitely fighters," Callie said. She and Sam were standing on the other side of my bed at my feet. Sam was gazing at all the medical stuff with longing and not paying attention to any of us.

Rema turned and came to stand next to the beds. He was trying to avoid looking at Patty, but his eyes kept flicking over to her while he talked.

"If you all would lie on the beds, the Healer would like to examine you," Rema said, his voice smooth and cultured. He gestured for Sam, Callie, and Patty to make their way towards the beds lining the wall. All the women laid down, and I heard sighs of appreciation. They really were the most comfortable beds ever. The heated feature was a pleasant touch since they didn't come with sheets or blankets of any kind.

The doctor approached with Ohem, coming to stand by my other side. The type of alien the doctor was didn't have a discernible gender. They also didn't have a mouth, nose, or eyes in its pointed head, with deep reddish pink skin that wasn't like anything I could compare it to, bumpy and smooth at the same time. The doctor had two primary arms that were long and thin and two smaller clasper-like arms that extended from its chest. They walked on two legs that twisted backwards and ended on two circular toes. I was beyond being freaked out by strange things at this point, so when they reached out their two fingered primary hands and placed the sucker cup fingertips against my temple I didn't flinch. Their touch was warm, and an unnatural wave of calm washed over me.

They glowed like a jellyfish when they spoke in a lyrical voice; the ear that didn't have my translator heard singing, like how a whale would communicate, only without a mouth.

"I am Inaeh. You may call me Healer if that is easier to pronounce in your tongue. Your body has taken very serious damage, Nin At'ens. I am going to heal you. You may feel mild discomfort," they said, and their jellyfish glow spread down their arm and onto me. It spread over my body and a strange tingling sensation started wherever the glow touched. It didn't hurt, but it was weird as hell. I looked at Ohem to find him watching me, my hand engulfed in his. The pain that had been constant since my berserker shift faded into an ache, and then it was gone entirely.

I smiled at him in shocked relief. "I feel better." I shifted my smile to the doctor and thanked them, too. Ohem's Izi lit up in a slow flowing pattern that started at his horns and drifted down his body.

He breathed a sigh. "Thank you, Inaeh," he said to the healer.

The alien pulled their glow back from my body. "It was my pleasure, General." They turned to me and bowed. "Nin At'ens."

They made their way over to the girls and checked them over, only having to glow over Callie. Her nanos must have still been healing her. We were very lucky she was alive.

When Healer left the room, Ohem pulled more red clothing from inside a compartment on the wall and handed them to the girls.

"Rema, would you show them where the changing rooms are?" Ohem asked. Rema nodded and led the girls through the glass door Healer had just left through.

Ohem picked me up the second they left the room and hitched me high on his stomach, my legs wrapping around him automatically. I hugged my arms around his thick neck. "Happy to be back?" I asked him. He didn't answer me, just pressed his mouth to mine, slipping his tongue past my lips to stroke inside. I hummed in appreciation and kissed him back, tightening my hold.

He broke the kiss to lick along my neck and around my ear. "I feared for you, Jack. I have never been so happy to see the medical labs in my long life. Are you truly better?" he asked, lifting his head to look into my eyes.

"Yes, Ohem. I'm good as new. I promise." He nodded and gave me a tight squeeze before setting me down.

I frowned at him in disappointment and he chuckled. "The others are coming back."

Sure enough, Rema opened the door a second later and led the girls back into the room. They were all dressed in the red outfits of most of the crew and myself. The red pants were snug and comfortable and the long sleeve shirt was a thick material that tightened across my chest and theirs to provide support for breasts. Was that by design or just happenstance? The girls had been given the same red leather flats that I had been. They were comfortable, like everything we'd been provided so far. I smiled at the girl's looks of satisfaction and relief at finally being properly clothed.

Patty had a satisfied, smug look on her face and Rema looked flushed. I gave her a questioning look, and she mouthed "later" at me.

Ohem stared at Rema with amused eyes and the elf blushed darker. The tips of his ears turning pink again. Oh yeah, Patty had made some type of move alright. I looked at Callie and Sam. Sam grinned at me while Callie rolled her eyes. Girl was a stick in the mud sometimes.

"Rema can show you to your rooms. I need to have Jack see one of our scientists for a few moments," Ohem said, and reached for my hand.

Sam chewed her lip and stepped forward, her curls falling across her face as she did. "Can I come? I'd really like to see the science department," she asked, blowing her hair out of her face with a puff of breath. Patty took a step up to stand beside her, and gave us puppy dog eyes. The two women were of similar size, with Sam maybe an inch taller than Patty's five foot frame, and the combined power of their adorable faces was too much to resist.

Ohem stared down at them, his eyes narrowing in amusement, and nodded. "Yes, you can come. I must warn you, it may be dull. I am giving Jack our armor and having some samples taken to help explain why her body is rejecting some of our technology. Don't think I hadn't noticed you scratching at your ear, *ursang*," he said.

I had? I hadn't even noticed, but now that he had so kindly pointed it out to me, my ear was a little itchy. Dang. I couldn't even have external tech? Learning Ohem's language the hard way was a sucky prospect. His mouth was shaped a lot different from mine and the language was guttural. I couldn't even roll my Rs for Spanish.

Ohem's fingers pinching my chin pulled me from my thoughts, and I looked up at him.

"We will discover something that works better for you, Jack. We also have ways of giving you information directly to your mind, though the process is painful and I would like to avoid it, as it can sometimes cause complications and confusion."

I shrugged. Bring it on.

"Well, we'd still like to come," Callie said, and Ohem sighed but nodded and led the way out of the medical room and back down the hallway to the room where the mannequin had been blown up. I was disappointed to see that it had been cleared away. The room bore no evidence at all of a live fire test. It was exactly how I pictured a science lab would look; lots of equipment and desks spread around in the large room with testing areas that resembled indoor firing ranges to the back.

The same spider alien that had been testing the weapon was still in the room. He turned from his work at a desk when we entered and gave Ohem the fist over chest salute and bowed his head to me. He had a friendly face if you ignored the six black eyes and the sharp teeth that he had bared in a welcoming smile. His upper body was almost entirely human, and he was a handsome male for one with spider parts, with dark skin and hair in many braids, with gold pieces woven into them. He had the typical eight legs of a spider and what looked like claspers that extended from the side where his spider half met the human skin of his upper body.

His spider body was almost the same deep brown as his skin and segmented with hard plates with brown fuzzy fibers on his legs that made me cringe when I looked at them. Sam was staring at him with shy curiosity, her eyes roaming over his body in a way that surprised me. Or maybe it shouldn't have, since she had enjoyed watching Ohem and me back on the shithole planet. Our little doctor was a closet freak, I would bet my life on it. The quiet ones always were. Someone just needed to coax it out of her.

The spider doctor shifted his bulk to the side and waved at the girls. "Hello," he bowed at the waist at us, "I'm Dr. Ghix. How may I help you?" he said. His language in my untranslated ear was all clicks and bird songs. How pretty for such a menacing looking alien.

Ohem saluted him back. "I ask if you'd perform some tests on my wife. Her body isn't taking our technology well." Ohem narrowed his eyes at the doctor. "What you learn about her in this room stays with you. Do I make myself clear?" he growled, his voice filled with menace.

Dr. Ghix saluted again and took a little shuffle step back, away from my mate. "Yes, of course, General."

Ohem sighed and rubbed his hand over his face. "Jack is a Rijitera."

The doctor didn't get scared, but he vibrated a little in place. I didn't think it was from fear. He had that 'holy shit, once in a lifetime discovery' look on his face that I sometimes saw on the history channel when archaeologists found a new tomb.

Ohem's eyes narrowed until they were glowing yellow slits. "You will be the only one taking samples. No talking about your findings with your peers. No talking to anyone about it. After you have the data you need, all samples are to be destroyed. Do you understand?" Ohem said, his tone sharp enough to cut.

Dr. Ghix jolted and snatched up his tablet, and moved closer to Ohem. "Of course! It is a genuine pleasure to meet you, Jack. I would never dishonor myself by sharing any information without your permission." He bowed, his front legs folding and the others splaying out so his head almost touched the floor. He popped back up and gave me a solemn look. "Please explain the symptoms, and we can take some samples of your blood and tissue to see what's going on inside your body." He looked at Sam and the girls and his smile widened. "Look around. Nothing can hurt you in this lab, so touch and test to your heart's desire," he said cheerfully.

It was the right thing to say.

Sam squealed and immediately went to a microscope at one of the desks. Patty and Callie gravitated towards the firing range. None of the weapons better be out or they'd be screwing around with them. I didn't have any ear protection and didn't feel like being deafened by the sound of gunfire in close quarters.

I turned when Dr. Ghix held out his hand to me. "Please, if you would let me take some blood for analysis," he said, and I extended my arm towards him, pulling up my sleeve. He waved a rod-shaped scanner over my forearm in a slow back-and-forth motion, humming when the scanner pinged and sat it down on the desk next to us. He picked up a white disk that looked like a hockey puck and pressed it to my forearm. I jumped when it pinched me and glared at the doctor. He smiled at me in apology and lifted the puck when it pinged at him.

"Sorry, I should have warned you about the sting." He placed the puck inside a slot in what looked like a white computer tower and then turned back to me. "Now, what are your symptoms?" he asked.

I remembered the nano super pill on the shark ship and made a face. "I puked my guts up when they tried to give me the pill of nanos on the Vrax ship. I was out for days recovering and I was weak when I woke up. Shaky, headache, cramps. Now the translator is itching," I said, pointing at my ear.

Ghix nodded and typed on his tablet. He placed it on the table next to the tower and picked up another puck. He met my eyes. "This is going to sting again. I'm taking tissue samples. It will take skin, muscle, and a piece of your nerve." I nodded for him to do it, and he placed the puck against my forearm. It pinched worse than the other and I barely managed not to jerk my arm away from it. The puck pinged, and the doctor placed it into the tower like the last one.

"What was the test earlier?" I asked to break up the silence we'd fallen into while waiting for the tower to do something with the pucks.

Dr. Ghix looked at me in confusion, so I pointed at the firing range on the other side of the room where Callie and Patty were poking around. He looked back and his face brightened in understanding. "Ah yes, I was testing a new cannon. We have plasma cannons for close proximity contact with overwhelming enemy forces, however, the blow back burns many of our troop support. I was trying to find a new delivery method to minimize the risks."

I smiled at him. "We call that danger close back where I'm from."

He returned my smile. "That's an excellent name for it! Yes. Danger close. I like that," he said, picking up his tablet to make a note.

I chuckled at him. "You'll have to ask Callie about all the other military jargon we have on Earth. You'd probably like a lot of it," I said, and pointed Callie out to the doctor and he made more notes on his tablet.

"Was your test successful?" I asked.

He shook his head. "No. There was still significant plasma fallout risk. Had I not been behind a shield, I would have been badly burned. It's less of a problem for the armored soldier as plasma burn through is low risk, but if there is unarmored support or civilians then they would be harmed or killed by the cannon. Close proximity cannons or CPCs are used fairly often during wartime, especially during this last war we took part in on the planet Xemia. It spilled over into their cities and the CPC was used against their forces inside buildings. Civilians died."

He gestured to Ohem, who stood at my side. "General At'ens tasked me with finding a solution."

I looked over at my mate, who met my gaze. "Civilian deaths are unacceptable to me. No matter the enemy. We aim to make our weapons target only enemy combatants and avoid the unarmed."

Knowing what I did about his ancestors' actions towards my people and his opinion about those actions, it didn't come as a surprise that he hated unnecessary death. He'd grown up learning about the atrocities committed by his own family. It was a wonder he hadn't become a doctor or something instead of a soldier.

The computer tower pinged at us and Dr. Ghix looked down at the tablet in his hand. He stared at his tablet in confusion, tapping and swiping at it for several minutes. His brows lowered more and more as he read the results of my test. A hollow boom broke the tension that had been building while Ohem and I waited for the doctor to tell us what the hell was wrong with me.

I turned towards the noise and found Patty with a gun in hand, looking back at us sheepishly. She was behind a shimmering blue barrier that separated the shooting range from the rest of the room, and it must have come down when she'd picked up the weapon as an automated protective measure because it hadn't been there before.

Callie started shooting another gun at the mannequin that rose from the floor at the end of the range, there was almost no sound other than hollow popping. Sam didn't even look up from whatever she was researching at her desk. Our little genius was no doubt in her version of heaven with all that information available to her. I grinned at Patty, gave her a thumbs up, and she went back to blowing pieces off her alien shaped target.

"You already have nanos in your system," Dr. Ghix said, and I turned away from the girls to give him my full attention. He was still looking at his tablet and tapping away at it. He looked up, his face was excited. "They are far more advanced than ours. I am going to have to run more tests to understand the extent of their capabilities, but I can tell you right now that these are absolutely revolutionary! It would take us years to reverse engineer them. It's no wonder they rejected our inferior technology."

He was almost manic as he shifted over to a desk and waved his hand in the air. A hologram screen appeared above the desk. Ohem and I moved to look at the data stream. I couldn't make any sense of what I was looking at, but Ohem had gone stiff with shock.

He touched the screen and moved data around. "Rijitera nanotechnology. It's no wonder you heal so fast," he whispered, more to himself than to me. He scrolled through the screen some more and muttered to himself. He looked at the doctor. "She has the old tech inside her."

I looked between them in confusion. "What does that mean?"

Ohem turned to fully face me and grabbed my hands. "You have the old Rijiteran systems inside you. Their nanos used to power everything of theirs. It was all biometrically locked to their species. They needed specialized nanos to power their weapons and armor. It gave them advanced reflexes and healing far beyond the capabilities of their already considerable natural baseline. It would seem yours are dormant. They work to adapt your body to environmental changes and heal damages, but all other functions are shut down."

I shook my head. "How'd I get them? I'd remember the pain from the injections if I'd gotten them when I was younger. I didn't even get my vaccines like normal Earth kids. I got no shots or pills growing up,"

Ohem chuffed. "You got them in utero, most likely. As did the rest of your kind. We do the same. Once a mother has nanos, her children will not have to get them later in life as they pass from mother to child during pregnancy. I imagine your people have had them for thousands of years from your ancestors before you. I don't know why I didn't think of that sooner." He shook his head in self depreciation. "It was an obvious answer to your rejections. You had me too occupied with mating to think clearly," he said, laughing.

I grinned and winked at him. "I'll never apologize for that."

I looked at the doctor who was watching us with a soft smile. "Can we activate the dormant parts? Maybe they will work as a translator too?"

He looked thoughtful at my question. "We don't even have the beginnings of a program advanced enough to give commands to the nanos," he said, shaking his head. "I'm afraid all I can do is speculate at this point. You would need to get your hands on a Rijiteran computer system to activate the more complicated settings these nanos no doubt have."

I sighed in disappointment. That sucked. Ghix touched my shoulder. "But we can give basic commands to our nanos with our minds in certain areas. Maybe you can try that? But wait so I can hook you up to a scan," he said, and he hurried to a desk and pulled out a small box and returned to my side. "I want to watch to see if they react." He pulled small glass circles out of the box and looked at me for permission. "May I?" he asked and I nodded my head.

He placed four circles on my face. Two at my temples and two on the center of my forehead, then two went behind my ears at the base of my skull. He put two on my chest under my collar bone over my shirt and the rest went along my spine, also over my shirt. He pulled up the hologram screen along the entire wall to our left and I watched as my body was scanned and put on the display.

My nervous system lit up with electric pulses. Ghix clicked his tablet a few times, and then the display showed a countless number of little dots all over my body. It looked like I had a galaxy inside me. They swirled through my bloodstream and throughout my nerves. Saturated my muscles and bones. They were everywhere.

"Now try to give them a command," Ohem said. I looked at both males in exasperation.

"How? I've lived with them my whole life and they've never given me super powers before now."

Dr. Ghix laughed, wagging his finger at me. "It's because you've lived with them your entire life that they've never been further activated. You never knew to try! They have only been performing base functions. Now think of a command, anything. We don't know what they can do, so we should try as many things as we can to get a working idea of what they are capable of," he said, his tablet at the ready. He pressed something on his tablet and the lights dimmed in the room. The girls came over and I filled them in on what was going on.

"Why don't you tell them something simple? Like, umm," Patty said and tapped her finger against her chin. She snapped her fingers and pointed at me. "Like tell them to give you x-ray vision."

"That's not simple," I said, dryly.

She shrugged and turned to watch the monitor. "Worth a shot."

Alright. A command. I can do that. I closed my eyes and concentrated on something simple. Maybe just telling them to wake up would work? I mean, Ghix said they were dormant.

Wake up. I waited for a few breaths, but nothing happened.

Dr. Ghix's gasp had my eyes flying open. On the screen, the nanos had exploded into action. Before they'd been passively floating along inside my body. Now they were swirling in complicated geometric patterns. I couldn't feel anything. I hadn't ever noticed them before, so it made sense that I wouldn't now. Still, it was kind of anticlimactic.

After about a minute, the nanos settled back into the passive state.

I looked at Dr. Ghix. "Well now—" Pain flared from the ear that held the translating marble, so hot that I started screaming and tried to claw it out. There was a terrible rushing sound all around me, drowning me in sensory overload that blended with the molten agony.

"Get it off! Get it off! Get it off!" I was screaming. Someone pinned me to the floor. Hands gripped my head to hold me still, cool fingers touched my ear and then the pain was gone. I stayed on the floor, panting and covered in sweat.

"Well, that sucked," I said. Someone huffed out a relieved laugh, and I was pulled to my feet by Ohem. I shook my head and sat down hard on the desk behind me. Ohem's Mordor speech caught my attention.

I looked at him and shook my head. "I can't understand you," I said in frustration. Just great. I was going to have to learn a whole new language never meant for human mouths. Ohem looked at the doctor, who glanced up and down from his tablet and nodded at my mate, who then continued to speak to me.

I looked at Patty. "What is he saying?"

She scowled at them. "He's saying random words to you. Like up, down, red, white. That kind of shit. The Doc says your nanos are in learning mode."

I looked up at the screen and they were still passive. I didn't know what Dr. Ghix was seeing, but it looked to be like my nanos were just doing their normal thing. Whatever that was.

"Water, earth, child, ship, soldier, love, hate," Ohem said.

I jerked my head towards him. "Hey, I understood that," I said in relief. Ohem's Izi flared briefly and settled into a steady glow.

"Thank the gods," he said, his shoulders dropping. He touched my cheek with two fingers, "It would seem your nano translator was activated, it learned my language in under thirty seconds, Jack. That's unimaginable."

Weird that the one thing I was really worried about was what the nano's picked up on. I didn't know how I should feel about that. Maybe they'd solve the whole 'my mate was an immortal' thing for me too.

"Yeah well, they really don't like inferior technology." I was a fast healer and all that, but the pain still sucked. "Maybe we skip trying any armor? I don't feel like having my skin try to burn right off my bones," I said, rubbing my ear.

Dr. Ghix moved to stand on the other side of me and started in with his pretty bird song. I started counting and almost exactly thirty seconds later, I could understand his words.

"I can understand, Doctor." I told him to get him to stop with the random colors he was throwing out. It was like I had learned their language the old-fashioned way. I understood what they were saying rather than a translator just turning it into English for me. I wonder if I could read their languages too? I asked the doctor, and he handed me his tablet. Sure enough, I could read the strange symbols on the screen.

I handed him his tablet back. "Yeah. I can read it."

His eyes widened, and he shook his head. "The Rijitera were technological geniuses. This is astounding! It takes many days to install languages directly to the mind and not always will the recipient be able to read. The process is usually painful and the side effects are high in probability. I am going to be studying these samples for years," he said, shuffling his many legs in his enthusiasm.

He clicked on his tablet and then looked up at the screen to zoom in on my brain. There were nanos clustered in sections of my brain that probably controlled language processing and speech. "You can probably write as well. Here, try on this," he said and handed me another larger tablet.

I took it and clicked the stylus from its base and wrote a simple message. "Hello, how are you?" I wanted to write in Ohem's language and I did, as if I'd always known it. The glyphs were the same as the ones spread all over the ship.

I handed the large tablet back to Ohem with shaky hands. He stared at the writing before handing it to the doctor. Ohem wrapped his arm around my shoulders, pulling me into him. I soaked up his support. It was a lot of new information to process. Just one bomb after another. Aliens are real. I'm also an alien. I'm not only an alien, but a super alien with super tech from an evil galaxy conquering species.

My super alien tech is light years in the future even while they themselves are from thousands of years in the past and they've been lurking in my body and those of my kind all this time. I needed a drink.

"What else can they do?" Sam asked the doctor. Her eyes flitted around the room, anywhere but Dr. Ghix's face. I made a mental note to tease her about it later.

Dr. Ghix looked at the monitor and then back at us. "I don't know. Most Rijitera history, as you know, has been wiped out. I'll keep researching the samples and get back to you with any results I find." Ohem chuffed and stood, pulling me to my feet with him and gave the doctor a little bow. "Thank you, Dr. Ghix. We will check in again later with you for more tests. For now, I have to get them into their rooms so we can all rest. It has been a very stressful few days for all of us," he said. It was the understatement of the century.

Dr. Ghix smiled at all of us. "Of course. Rest up well. We have much to do."

We said our goodbyes and filed out of the room. It had been an insane few days. So much had happened in only a short time that it was like I was trapped in the Matrix and had only now woken up. I was going to need so much sleep to process all this. They had better have blankets on our beds, heated gel mattresses or not, a girl needed a good blanket to snuggle when dealing with stress.

Thirteen

Rema was waiting for us in the hallway when we came out. I hadn't even noticed that he'd stayed behind. I was definitely too tired to function. He nodded his head at us and took up his place at the rear of our little pack.

"We can trust Ghix. He has helped me research my family's archives in the past," Ohem said, while we walked out of the med bay and down the corridor, back to the teleportation elevator. I only nodded. The doctor had that trustworthy puppy dog feel to him. I hadn't been worried.

"Does this teleport us to places?" I asked, instead of commenting on the good doctor, when the tube doors closed.

"No. It's a type of portal," Rema answered. His voice was deep and smooth, like a college philosophy professor. He looked like he'd be a professor. All sharp angles and serious nature. Patty was going to have to bring some fun into his life.

"How do you contain it?" Sam asked.

He looked down at her and smiled. "It uses a magnetic field to stabilize the tube."

They continued their physics discussion out of the portal and into a short hallway that ended with a big, plain metal door. We walked through the door, and Sam's voice trailed off as she gaped at the room we'd arrived in.

It was an opulent living room, with soft blue marble like floors and various lava rock couches and chairs placed around a massive cylindrical fireplace made of black glass, built like a center support column between the floor and the mirrored ceiling. Black fur rugs lay strewn under couches and around the floor for added warmth.

The whole sidewall past the seating area was one solid window that curved out into space. There were three curved back couches placed along the window so you could stare out into the void in comfort. A bar stretched the entire length of the right wall with colorful glass containers of various sizes and shapes shining from shelves above the bar. The reflective black walls showed our shocked faces and Ohem's laughing yellow eyes. Rema held his fist to his chest, nodding at us before backing out of the room.

"These are my private quarters. This is the social area. If you follow me, I will show you the rest."

We trailed after Ohem as he led us past the bar and down a short hallway with curved walls into a circular library filled to the brim with books or scrolls and more couches. There was another column shaped fireplace in the center of the room with another window for a back wall. I didn't like seeing out into space. It was creepy. Judging by the looks of wonder from the other ladies however, only I felt that way. Solely having glass separating me from the cold vacuum of space was kind of freaking me out.

Two more curved hallways forked off from the library and Ohem led us through the one to the left first, into a dining room. A long black table that came to sharp points at both ends dominated the room. There were tall black chairs lining the table, enough for forty people at least. Yellow lines and dots glowed on the table's surface and a multi-colored glass chandelier hung above it. The entire room was windows. It gave the impression you were standing in open space. It was a horrible room and I hated it with a fiery passion.

Ohem looked at my face and placed a hand on my back to steer me back into the library again and through the right hallway. They really had a thing for black shiny walls or the color black in general. There were bright pops of color here and there, but the overall look was sleek, modern, and very black.

This hallway was long with doors on either side, spaced out from each other by twenty feet. Ohem stopped at the first door on his right and it slid open, revealing a bedroom. It had another curved window that served as the back wall, with a large oval bed against the left wall and a sitting area against the window, complete with two couches and a coffee table. A small desk was directly across from the bed.

"This will be your room, Callie. That door leads to the bathing chamber," he said, pointing to the black door next to the desk. "The pool is voice activated. I had drying cloths, soaps, and more clothing delivered. There are more female things in the storage units. If you are missing anything, there is a comms unit on the desk, ask for Lilien and she will bring you anything you require," Ohem said, he stepped back so Callie could go in and explore.

She paused by the bed, running her hand over it and had to cover her mouth to muffle the ragged sob that had escaped her. She was getting emotional over the bed. I didn't blame her one bit, I was so damn tired.

"I will show the other's to their rooms. A meal will be brought to you in thirty minutes. Get some rest," he said. "The doors lock automatically when you are inside. Say 'open' when you want out and it will unlock for you."

Callie turned in a circle and collapsed on the bed. It had black velvet type blankets and actual pillows. "Oh god, guys. It's so comfy." She sat up and gave us a water smile. "See you in the morning. I'm gonna wash until I'm red and raw," she said, practically skipping to the bathroom. The door opened automatically, and she disappeared inside. We heard an excited squeal before her bedroom door closed behind us.

Ohem showed Sam and Patty to identical rooms further down the hall and they both gave me tight hugs before closing themselves inside.

We continued down the hall to a dead end at a black door that Ohem led me through. It was his room. A seating area with another fireplace was the first thing we stepped into, the space was inviting and warm, Ohem even had colors in here. Orange and red lava rock couches and deep blue pillows with white furs on the floors.

Ohem walked right past and up a short flight of stairs to another set of doors. We passed through them into his bedroom. The massive bed took up most of the space, and the room was done in shades of red clay and cream. He didn't stop to let me admire his floral artwork on the walls or his knickknacks spread over floating shelves, instead he pulled me into a bathroom the size of my entire house back home. It had a pool made of gray stone in the center, steam rising off the water. It was humid and warm.

He turned to me, his armor retracting into the torque, and started undressing me. I lifted my arms and legs at the appropriate time and when he had me naked he scooped me up into his arms and used the stone steps to walk into the water. He placed me on my feet when we were in the center of the pool and reached for some glass bottles that lined one side on stone shelves.

I closed my eyes and enjoyed the hot water. It felt like years since I'd had a hot bath. When Ohem's hands returned, I was languid and half asleep. He ran soapy hands over my body, washing and massaging, and had me step onto the stone benches that lined the wall of the pool so he could get my lower half clean and then turned and sat down on the bench, pulling me to sit sideways across his thighs.

He poured more soap from the bottle into my hair and ran his claws along my scalp. I tilted my head back and groaned. He chuckled, the deep sound bouncing off the walls of the bathroom and poured water over my hair, rinsing it clean and then sat me aside on the bench to soak while he washed himself.

I had my head resting against the lip of the pool and fell asleep, only startling awake when Ohem picked me up. He lifted me from the pool, only setting me down long enough to wrap me in a plush towel that covered me from neck to toes, and walked us back into the sitting area of his room.

There were covered trays on a table that hadn't been there before with two black lava chairs pulled out and waiting. Ohem sat me down in one and stood next to the table. The smell of whatever food was under the black domed dishes woke me up out of my daze, my stomach rumbling loudly.

He lifted the lids, and I almost cried. Red and purple meats, seasoned and grilled with sides of steamed colorful vegetables, leafy green salads and three different soups were laid out before me on gold plates. There was a red glass bottle beside two wavy blue glasses filled with ice.

Ohem took my plate and served me a large portion of everything and filled three smaller bowls with the soups. He poured the drink; it bubbled, and fog rose from the glass. He placed everything in front of me before serving himself and taking his seat.

"Eat, Jack," he said, picking up a two prong fork.

I lifted mine and Ohem didn't take his first bite until after I'd speared a neatly cut piece of meat and put it into my mouth. Flavors exploded on my tongue and I groaned in appreciation. The meat was tender, spicy with a tang, and melted like butter. I fell on my food like the savage animal I was. Everything was delicious and flavorful, nothing much matched anything from home, but it was tasty all the same. The drink was like carbonated wine and very sweet. When I'd all but licked my plate clean, Ohem stood and served me more until we'd eaten all there was and I had an uncomfortably full belly.

I sat back with a sigh and smiled at him. "That was amazing, thank you," I said in a yawn, covering my mouth with my hand.

Ohem's Izi glowed with pleasure and he pulled me into his arms again. "I'm glad you enjoyed your meal. It's time for sleep. We will conquer our enemies tomorrow, after you have properly rested," he said. That was rich coming from him. I don't think he'd slept the whole time we'd been stranded on that planet.

Ohem walked into the bedroom, straight to his bed and pulled back the blankets to tuck me into them. The bed was a dream, soft and warm. His fur blanket was softer than velvet. I snuggled deeper, already half asleep. Ohem slid in behind me and pulled me into his body, warming me further, one of his tails wrapping around my leg.

"I love you," he whispered to me before I drifted into one of the deepest sleeps I'd ever had in my life.

Fourteen

We were gathered in the common room, drinking what was very, *very* close to coffee. They even had cream and sugar. I could die happy now.

We'd all slept almost twenty-four hours, had long showers and were in fresh red clothing. I felt like a whole new person. Ohem had been gone when I'd woken up, but I remembered him murmuring to me about a meeting with Rema at some point, but I had been mostly asleep and couldn't remember everything he'd said. I had followed the sound of laughter and found the girls seated at a round table that must have been brought in while we slept. It had been laden with breakfast food and a black carafe full of our almost coffee.

"I can't believe they have coffee. It's a miracle. I feel like I died in that crash, and this is just a post-death hallucination," Patty said, taking a long sip from her mug, eyes closed in bliss.

The drink had a slight earthy aftertaste, making it not exactly the same, but it was close enough to keep me on this ship for eternity.

"The food is really close to Earth food, too. These are definitely eggs," Callie said, pointing her fork at her plate, "and they have toast. Just needs butter and this would be an all-American breakfast." She groaned in pleasure after taking a bite out of the thick slice of toast she had in her hand. Callie looked good, the dark circles under eyes were gone, and she'd found something to trim up her hair, the sides and back a neat fade now, with the black curls on the top only slightly longer than the sides.

"How'd everyone sleep?" I asked. There were enthusiastic responses from around the table and I smiled.

"They had toothpaste and brushes," Patty said, her eyes misty.

I had the same overly emotional response when I'd found mine. It had been a surprise to see them on the stone sinks, they'd been shaped odd but I'd known immediately what they were. I'd brushed my teeth until my gums bled.

"I can't wait to explore those labs some more. I was a little disappointed not to find any fancy medical healing pods, though," Sam said between bites of her breakfast. "There were more of the pink healers down the hall. I saw them in different rooms when we went to get changed. They all look exactly the same. It was a little unnerving."

Patty leaned forward, her hair swinging forward in a shiny clean curtain. "How do they see? Or speak? Did you see the big alien bird working on one of the vehicles in the hangar? It had been straight up, a bird. A gigantic bird working on a truck."

I shook my head. "I was too busy trying to figure out how the damn floating platform we were on knew where we wanted to go. No one was driving it and I didn't see any engines or anything. And the portals." I made a face. "I was big mad about the sharks having such shitty technology and now I have extreme alien tech and it's a little overwhelming."

Sam smiled, her soft brown eyes excited. "I know! There is so much to learn." She glanced around, suddenly serious. "I'm staying. For good, I mean."

A bright flare of relief lit up inside my chest and I looked at Callie.

She nodded her head, her face serious. "I'm still thinking about it, but I'm leaning more towards staying too. I still want to talk to my parents before I make my final decision, but I think I'll stay even if they don't come with me. I just want them to know I'm safe and that it was my decision to stay."

"I was already planning on staying, but the coffee officially sold me," Patty said.

I rolled my eyes at her. "Oh and the sexy winged orc-elf didn't factor in at all. Don't think I've forgotten you owe me a story."

Patty grinned and gave me a look so full of mischief that I worried about whether Rema could handle her. "I kissed him. Right on the mouth, tongue and all."

Sam and Callie cracked up at her 'cat got the cream' look.

I shook my head. "Ohem said that was a courtship thing. Are you going to court him for marriage?" I asked her seriously. Rema looked like a very serious male and he was my mate's second. I loved Patty, but I didn't want anyone to get hurt.

Patty's smile got wider. "I'll court him alright. He was so flustered and shy. It was adorable. He still kissed me back, though. After his initial shock, he kissed me back *enthusiastically*." She sat back in her chair, her eyes half closed.

Oh yeah, she was smug as hell. Screw it. They were adults. Let Patty get her some alien cock and be happy. She deserved it.

"Get it, girl," I told her.

She blew me a kiss and I pretended to catch it in the air to press over my heart and sighed, fluttering my eyes at her.

"You guys are ridiculous," Callie said, but she was smiling.

"You love us," Patty teased.

"We make your life complete," I sang to her.

"You were so empty before you met us."

"So empty and unfulfilled."

Callie snorted and tossed a bite sized muffin at me. I picked one out of the big bowl in the middle of the table and threw it back at her. Then Patty joined in on it. Sam laughed and watched, ducking flying muffins. Ohem walked in right as Patty stood up on her chair, hand cocked back to put some power into her throw, but she had to quickly tuck her hands over her head as we pelted her together.

"I leave you females for a single hour and it's war," he said in amusement.

We froze, staring at him. He had his arms crossed over his chest, his tentacles waving behind him, tails coiled around his feet. Patty started laughing first, and it was all downhill from there. Ohem shook his head and came to stand behind me, his hand on my shoulder while I calmed down.

I pointed at Callie. "She started it."

Callie hit me in the chest with another muffin. "I did not."

"See! She's abusing me, mate. Eat her," I said, throwing her muffin back at her.

Ohem plucked the muffin from the air and tossed it into his mouth. "I am glad to see you having a good time," he said, his eyes bright and laughing. "Did you sleep well?"

I grinned up at him. "Yeah, I did. Y'all's beds are out of this world." The girls groaned in unison. "Hey, That was a perfect pun. It had gravity."

Sam cringed. "Please stop."

Ohem chuckled and took a seat next to me. "I have made the announcement to the crew of your presence on the ship. I brought you all links so you can communicate with the ship's interface, myself or my crew if you need anything." He handed out round metal marbles to the girls. "Place them against the skin of your neck. It will enter your body. It is painless. You will only feel it moving."

I frowned. "I thought it connected to your vocal cords or something since I can see it blinking in your neck. I only saw it split into two pieces."

Ohem nodded. "Yes it does split into two parts, but inside is a small chip that will connect to your nerve stem. It allows imaging and projections. It also will allow you to see each other's locations. It has many functions, but those are the ones that will be most useful to you."

Patty was the first to press it to the skin of her neck. It burrowed and split off like I'd seen before. It still gave me the creeps.

Patty blinked at the space in front of her and gasped. "Holy shit, it has a map."

Sam and Callie followed Patty's lead and allowed the link to implant. Callie shuddered a little and held her hand over her neck where the link was already blinking. Sam just shrugged and went back to eating and watched Callie with an amused look on her face.

"You will be able to navigate the ship this way, it will open doors and power the transit portal. Just think about what you want to do and the link will perform its task."

Patty blinked again and looked at me. "How cool is that?" She frowned and looked at Ohem. "What about Jack? Her body rejected the nanos violently, so I don't think the link will stay in her body. Her nanos would probably try to eat it."

Ohem handed me a slim black wire. "It goes around your neck, we had it coated in a film to help minimize contact with your skin."

I shrugged and put it on. It snapped together with a click and tightened. He'd given me a black choker. I'd had a million of them when I'd gone through my scene phase in my teen years, it was very nostalgic.

Ohem handed me my choker's matching bracelet and I secured it around my right wrist.

He pressed the bracelet, and a 3D hologram map of the ship lit up above my wrist. He touched the hologram and zoomed in the same way you would on a touch screen. He zoomed in on our common area and it had three glowing yellow human shapes seated at a table, one yellow Ohem, and a red me.

"Locate Rema," he said. The hologram moved, a yellow line highlighting a path from us, through a maze of corridors along the ship, until it stopped at what was probably the bridge and on Rema's glowing shape.

"That is the coolest thing ever. Thank you." I touched the bracelet, and the hologram disappeared.

"You can communicate with us through the neck comm unit. You are welcome, Nin At'ens," he said, smiling with his Izi at me.

I frowned at Ohem, "Nin has a bunch of different translated meanings in my mind. What does it mean when you use it like that?" I asked.

Ohem nodded. "It means honored lady, or wife, when used as a title. If only called Nin, it would mean queen. The crew will treat you as my wife even before any formal ceremony. Are you agreeable to this?" he asked me, his voice a little unsure.

I laughed and shook my head at him. "Ohem, we're mated. As far as I'm concerned, we're already married. Though, my people don't really get married in the traditional sense. Mates are mates. We have a celebration after the mating is complete, but no preacher and no government paper is needed."

Ohem leaned over and down to rub his jaw against my hair and rumbled a joyful sound at me. "Then we will have a celebration. My people only state that they are joined in front of witnesses, and it is so. I have already done this, and you did not deny it, so we are married in their eyes."

It was official the second I sunk my teeth into his flesh, but I was kind of glad his people didn't do any grand scale thing. Plus, getting "officially" married in front of an enormous crowd of strangers without my mother there would suck. My mom was going to be pretty put out that she didn't get to do the whole 'I'll break your neck if you hurt my daughter' speech. Never mind that I didn't need any help with breaking necks. One didn't take away my mom's thunder if they wanted to live.

"We should have a private celebration, too. Just you and me... with no interruptions," I said to him, staring up and into his eyes so he'd understand exactly what I was saying. No fancy meals, no music. Just naked, writhing bodies on an actual bed. Or in his tub. Or on the sink. Heck, the floor was really nice with all those soft furs everywhere

Ohem flared brightly, his eyes narrowed to slits. "Yes. Tonight. A feast can wait. I can not," he said, his voice deep enough to vibrate the water in the glasses.

Callie cleared her throat awkwardly.

I turned to glare at her. "We're having a moment here."

She gave me a pleading look.

I rolled my eyes. "Okay, alright. We'll stop... for now."

Ohem chuckled and leaned away from me to sit upright in his seat again. "You should go explore. There are only a few places that are restricted, but that is only because they pose a danger to you. Jack and I are needed in a meeting with the officers to explain my brother and his involvement." He paused and met each of the girl's eyes before continuing. "We are safe on my ship. I trust most of her crew, but once we break the news of my brother's betrayal and of what my mate is, I would like you to keep your ears open while you explore. Be careful. Stay alert. We can never be too cautious. If you want a guard, I can assign one to you."

Patty perked up at this and got a sly look on her face.

Ohem caught it and pointed his clawed finger at her. "Not Rema, he is needed elsewhere." He laughed when Patty deflated against the back of her chair and pouted at him. Ohem sighed. "I suppose I can let him skip this meeting. He was already briefed about my brother and Jack."

Patty beamed at him and immediately got up from her seat and started to leave the room.

"Um Pat? You don't have shoes on," I said, shaking my head at her as she spun around and ran to her room to get the red leather flats we'd been issued. She jogged out of her room and waved at us over her shoulder as she left through the door.

Ohem chuckled and turned to me. "Rema told me about Patty kissing him. He is unsure, and a little intimidated by her, but finds her beautiful and fascinating. The females of his kind are solitary, shy creatures. To have one such as our Patty pursue him? He is in for a shock. I look forward to watching it happen."

"We've corrupted you." I laughed and stood, holding out my hand to Ohem. "Let's get this meeting over with." He took my hand and rose.

I turned as we were walking to the door to glance back at Sam and Callie, still seated at the table. "See you later?"

Sam raised her coffee glass and smiled at me. "Have fun. I'll be in the lab with Dr. Ghix. I want to see if I can help with your nano data."

"I'm going to go check out those black jets we saw in the hangar," Callie said, practically vibrating with anticipation.

I waved goodbye and followed Ohem out into the hall, tilting my head back to look up at him. "On a scale from one to ten, how fucked are we?" I asked. I was going to need serious chiropractic work done from all the staring up at him I was going to be doing for the rest of my life.

He chuffed and cocked his head at me. "What do you mean?"

I waved my hand in the air in front of me. "You know, how much trouble is this going to be? Telling your people their leader is an asshole and I'm the creature out of the worst part of their history books."

Ohem paused for a moment to pull me into the portal tube. "My officers are the best soldiers in the Unity. I hand picked and trained most of them. There are a few that I would like to watch, however. One has always given me trouble. The rest of the crew? While I am confident that most are loyal, it is impossible to know if all of them, down to the last sanitary worker, will be as trustworthy as I hope. It was something that Rema reminded me of when I spoke to him this morning. My second is rather skeptical of others. You and he are very much alike in that regard."

Good job, Rema, gotta look out for our General. He was entirely too trusting.

The portal opened, and Ohem pulled me into another long hallway. "We will be ready if the worst should happen."

We walked a long way down a hallway that ended in ornate, white double doors. The voices inside were loud.

"And what about the news of the Rijitera lurking in their halls? Are you sure we should even tell them what I am?"

Ohem shook his head, tightening his hand on mine. "They have been betrayed by their Councilor. I will not keep this secret from them, and I will not hide you away. No. Better to be forthcoming and honest from the start so that no one can accuse us of subterfuge later on when loyalties are tested. It will go well, Jack. Just be yourself and explain that you don't have any plans to conquer the universe; only me and I have already been won," he said, his Izi flashing with amusement.

He dropped my hand to push open the doors, and we walked into a large auditorium type room with raised seating with a stage at the bottom center of the room.

We made our way down the slanted middle aisle to the stage where Ohem turned to face the crowd. They had all risen to their feet when we entered and saluted silently. I looked at all the faces staring at us. There were fewer officers than I thought there would be on a spaceship this large, probably only three thousand. Maybe these were all really high ranked or something? They would all probably have meetings with their underlings who would then tell the majority of the foot soldiers and crew. At least, that's how I'd read the military worked, but what did I know?

Ohem took a breath before speaking, his voice carrying effortlessly across the cavernous room. "I won't waste your time or mine by giving a long convoluted story of the events. You already know the parts pertaining to my capture and my rescue by the female prisoners. These were explained in the brief sent to you by Commander Rema. What I am here to tell you today can only come from me as it has to do with my own House." He paused, making sure everyone was paying attention. "On the unnamed desert planet, my brother, Stellios Councilor Rakis At'ens, came to kill me."

He held up a hand to quiet the shocked, uneasy murmurs that erupted around the room. "He confessed to arranging my ambush and imprisonment on the Vrax vessel intending to keep me trapped on a mining moon. My brother is either working for Vero or is the force behind the Councilor of Axsia."

Stunned silence followed his words. Ohem sighed and bowed his head for a moment before continuing. "We know they are looking for, or have found, a Rijiteran artifact. A weapon. We have the coordinates of the planet that they were reported to be searching. Intel suggests they have left. We do not know with certainty if they found anything, so we will investigate the planet soon to find out if there are Rijiteran ruins left intact."

He turned and reached his hand out to me, and I placed mine into his claws, letting him pull me closer. He turned me to stand in front of him and placed his hands on my shoulders. "I met my wife on that Vrax ship. My brother's betrayal was not the only revelation during my time away from the Solus. I discovered a living Rijitera. My mate," he said and gave my shoulders a squeeze.

It was the scoff that drew my eye to a red alien seated in the front.

He gestured towards me and scoffed again. "Forgive me, General At'ens, but this female looks nothing like a Rijitera. They were monsters," he said in Ohem's language.

It must be the common tongue since most everyone spoke it. The sneer in his voice was hateful, and I made a mental note to keep an eye on him. He was being disrespectful to Ohem, and that didn't seem to align with Ohem's thoughts on the loyalty of his people. Rema was right, people sucked. This was undoubtedly the officer that Ohem wanted to watch, the troublemaker.

There were looks of agreement and Ohem squeezed my shoulders before taking a step back from me.

Oh, so he wanted the dramatic reveal, huh? *I have been preparing for this day my whole life.*

I gave the red alien a nasty smile and shifted. There was no pain, the transition was smooth like it should be, thank god. I made a mental note to go back and thank Healer again.

The alien clothing stretched with my change to a point and then became tight, so I used my claws to tear it away from my body. I stood before the shocked officers in my full Rijitera glory. I gave them my loudest, most vicious War Howl. The sound that panics the enemy, making them run away from the battlefield in terror so we could hunt them down for the slaughter. All Rijiterans are born with it, we are taught how to hone it, and now I was thinking it's probably an unknown relic from our evil universe conquering days. It sounded absolutely nothing like a wolf howl and completely like something that crawled straight out of hell and was here to eat you alive.

Even Ohem had taken a step back from me, his Izi flashing. The Howl faded, and I bared my teeth in a silent snarl at the aliens. There were screams, and a few stumbled over chairs behind them. When I was satisfied that they believed Ohem, I turned and calmly walked to his side.

Fifteen

Okay, so I was a drama queen. Sue me.

When I didn't snap and slaughter them, the panic subsided into a tense silence. Ohem stared at the red alien, with all his Izi dark and the feel from him ominous. The red alien shifted nervously in his seat, not able to hold Ohem's gaze. When Ohem finally looked away to focus back at the room as a whole, the red guy slumped in his seat in relief.

He still mustered enough courage to glare at my mate in what I'm sure he thought was a discrete way. I caught it, though. I'd been hunting for it.

I didn't growl or call attention to him, I wanted to let it ride for a while, see what he did. I'd follow him around, see who he talked to, find out who his friends were. Then eat them for the offense paid to my mate. Make sure there were witnesses so others wouldn't make the same mistakes this asshole was. Ohem's voice rumbling out over the auditorium drew my eyes back to him.

"My wife is from a planet in the outer systems, far from the Unity's reach. Some of her ancestors escaped the purge to flourish there. They did not conquer or rebuild their empire. She has put her friends and her mate ahead of her own wellbeing time and again. She risked herself for strangers during her escape from her cage on an alien ship to save them. She released an alien that was strange, something she feared. She could have left me imprisoned. She is honorable and not looking to repeat the actions of her ancestors."

He paused and ran his hand over my furred head to cup under my jaw. I tilted my head to give him better access, leaning into his hand. He was staring at me with all his love highlighted over his body as his Izi burned star bright. "I love her. I trust her with my life and with yours. With my brother's treachery in the open, he will come for me. He wants power and a war will give him that. I have long suspected that Vero was preparing to launch attacks on independent planets outside the Unity's reach. I believe this is my brother's goal and Vero is simply following orders."

He looked away from me and addressed the officers, his hand still cupped under my muzzle. "I will stand against him. I will allow those who wish to leave the opportunity to do so."

There were a lot of offended faces in the crowd. It was like he said, most of his people would stand with him and it appeared to irritate them that he had offered them a way out. So maybe Rema and I were a little too cynical. We'd still been partially right so far. There were shady people, the red alien the first to show it.

"I will fight with you," I growled out at them. I left the part about murdering anyone who threatened Ohem unsaid, but a few of the smarter ones caught it. A few stared at the monster speaking with shock, but most smiled with a morbid glee. I was their great enemy, and while they had all the confidence in their General, having something you thought of as indestructible on your side probably helped when you were about to be going against an army ten times your size... maybe even a hundred times your size. I always loved a good brawl, and this one promised to be bloody. I was downright giddy about it.

Ohem nodded at me. "Together we will stop Rakis's path of destruction. We can not let them use whatever weapon they have found. Those who wish to leave, notify Rema within the next two days. We will make a transitional jump to an unknown sector to plan our next move. You will need to board the transport ships before then if you want to go home."

He paused and sighed deeply. "Do you have questions?"

Almost every single hand went up except Red's. He stood and bowed to Ohem before turning on his heel and walking out without being dismissed. Ohem just stared after him for a moment before flicking his gaze to someone in the front row and nodding at her.

The questions were endless, ranging from the crash, to Rijiteran numbers on Earth. I shook my head at Ohem to let him know to keep that a secret for now. He nodded to me and expertly evaded answering. There were concerns from a large alien in the front about my loyalty and my nature that Ohem crushed into dust and then some. I told them I'd kill the whole of the Unity and everyone on board this ship if Ohem's life was in danger. My answer satisfied the one who'd first asked the question, a big green giant that had a mean, blocky face. He seemed to respect my violent, protective nature, the burning look of approval almost giving me a sunburn. I bared my big teeth in a smile, and he threw his head back, booming out a rocky laugh.

With his approval, the rest that had been hesitant relaxed. I'd won over the hard case and his followers. Who would have thought my loose moral compass would win me allies on this ship? Certainly not me. I figured they'd all be out to kill me and burn my body to ash to make sure I didn't resurrect like a vampire.

It took nearly two more hours of questions before Ohem dismissed the room and we made our way back to the portal. I shifted back inside the tube and crossed my arms. "Do you think we'll find any ruins on the planet they were looking on?"

I was curious about my ancestors, but I mostly wanted to get ahead of Rakis.

Ohem hummed softly and tilted his head down. "I think so. All the reports say that the Axsia soldiers were there for weeks, and it seemed like they abruptly left, and that is a sure sign that they found what they were looking for."

What weapon did my ancestors leave behind? It would be easier if it was a big gun or some sort of AI that we could fight against and not some super nuke that would vaporize us before we could even put boots on the ground.

"How long will it take to get there?" I asked.

We'd been moving, but there had been no gut destroying wormhole jump, so I had no idea where we were now. The desert planet we'd been stranded on was nowhere to be seen through the many windows of the Solus.

"We will allow two days for the crew who wish to leave before we make the jump into deep space. From there, it will take roughly a week to reach the planet. We have taken to calling it Detritus. We will take the time between now and then to prepare and select the ground team."

Detritus was an appropriate name for a planet that had probably been a bustling civilization a couple thousand years ago. Relic would have been my first choice. It was going to be busy as hell here for the next couple of days. Chaos, even. The perfect time for Red to start some shit while everyone was distracted. It's what I would do if I was a backstabbing, power hungry little bitch.

The tube opened into the hall for our living quarters and I walked out in front of Ohem, anticipation gathering in my gut when only silence greeted me in the hall. The girls were still gone. Ohem and I were going to be alone in our quarters. I was eager to go hunt Red down to follow him, but more importantly, I needed to show my mate some affection before we became too busy for sex.

I'd passed out last night after he'd taken such good care of me before I could take advantage of the privacy of our bedroom, and then he'd let me terrorize his officers in the auditorium. He was such a good mate, and some things couldn't be helped.

The door slid open at my approach and I strode into our common room. As soon as Ohem passed through the entryway and the door slid shut, I turned towards him and sprang. He caught me effortlessly, and I curled my legs around his waist, wrapping my arms around his thick neck, and pressed my open mouth against his. His tongue slid against mine, his growl rolling through my body, and I ground my pussy into his stomach to assuage the ache he built in my body with just the sound of his voice.

He was already naked, the skin of his stomach hot and slick against me. He must have retracted his armor as soon as he'd walked through the door. Great minds think alike. I needed him. His dick would give me better focus so I could shake that red alien's bones right out of his body. It was as good an excuse as any to play hooky from our responsibilities for a short while.

I pulled away from his mouth to lick a path down his neck to my mating bite. I bit down, not quite breaking the skin, and let out a possessive snarl. Ohem groaned and walked a few steps to the table, where he pulled my mouth away from his skin with a hand in my hair and turned me to slam me, belly down, onto the cool stone tabletop. He barked a command, and the table rose until I was at the perfect height for him to move behind me.

His claws scraped my scalp as he fisted my hair and pulled my head back. "It is time I gave you that reminder I promised," he snarled into my ear and then he was thrusting into me so savagely that I jerked almost across the table, his hand in my hair and the other pressing into my back the only thing that kept me firmly in place. His tails wound around my legs and pulled them tightly together so I couldn't push against him or try to pull away from the pressure of his thrusts.

I screamed at the punishment, the pleasure/pain line blurring until I was a writhing, panting mess. My release coiled in my core like a great snake, spiraling tighter with every thrust Ohem pounded into me. He moved his fist from my hair to hold me down by the back of my neck, his other hand bracing against the table. Burning hot tentacles wrapped around both wrists and then my arms were being wrenched back and bound behind me.

Another snaked up the back of my thigh, leaving a trail of heat in its wake. It skimmed over the cheek of my ass, and I tried to struggle. Ohem snarled and tightened his many grips on my body. The tip of it dipped between my legs for a moment, touching where I was dripping wetness down my inner thigh and then the stiff peak of his wandering tentacle opened and one thick finger appendage was pressing into the tight ring of my ass with slick relentlessness.

I shuddered at the feeling. I'd been stuffed full before, but I was near bursting with him now. He started thrusting it into my ass in time with his cock. The heat invading my body was near unbearable now; I was whimpering and begging him mindlessly to make me come, but he kept his steady pace.

It wasn't until he wrenched my head to one side and his sharp, narrow teeth tore into my shoulder that I was blinded by the most intense orgasm of my life. The fire raged inside me, spreading from my core to the rest of my body, engulfing me completely in the inferno of his making. I was wailing and howling like a wild thing; the pleasure forcing me to try to arch back against him to prolong it as long as I could, but he held me immobile. He pulled his teeth from my shoulder, roaring as he surged forward one final time, so deeply that I slid forward, even with his tails and tentacles holding me still. He ground himself against me until I came again, my voice a croaked moan. Ohem had reminded me all right. If I wasn't a near instant healer, I'd be needing a cane to walk around for the foreseeable future. And one of those donut things people got for broken tailbones.

My neck was tingly and my pussy was pulsing around his still hard cock. The parts of his tentacle in my ass were still lazily thrusting inside me and I lifted my hips up for more. Someone was going to have to sanitize this table. It was beyond tainted now.

I chuckled, and Ohem's cock twitched inside me. "Laughing, Jack? Perhaps I haven't exhausted you enough yet." He moved his hand from the back of my neck to run his claws down my back, the sharp tips pressing threateningly into my skin. The tentacle in my ass pressing deeper inside me in warning.

I turned my head to grin at him. "Are you up for it, General?"

It was the last thing I said that wasn't cries for mercy or screams of pleasure for the next hour and a half.

• • • • • • • • •

Ohem hadn't let me shower. I'd hobbled my way on jelly legs into the bathing chamber to clean off, but he'd fisted my hair again and growled into my ear, "Leave it."

Lord have mercy.

So I'd dressed in another set of red clothes and some flats and scurried out of our rooms before he decided he wasn't done with me yet. It was a good thing I was hard to kill because Ohem had done his best to fuck me to death. I grinned to myself, remembering my fear of him in that tube prison. I'd been so worried he'd eat me. I mean, he had, but only in the best way.

Now I was energized and focused enough to hunt me down a rat. I slipped into the portal and touched the link around my neck. "Call Rema." I didn't know if I had to actually say 'Call Rema' or if just Rema's name would work, but better safe than sorry.

There was a chirp and then Rema's deep voice answered from my link. "Yes, Nin At'ens?"

I grinned at the fancy title and rubbed my hands together. "There was a red alien at the officers' meeting, he was medium height, creepy black eyes. Disrespectful and resent—"

"His name is Serail. He's the first flight officer in the forward attack wing," Rema said, cutting me off and letting me know Red was indeed their problem child.

I nodded even if he couldn't see me. "Thank you, Rema. I'm going to hunt him. I think he might try something before we transition."

"I'd tell you to be careful, but then one such as you has no need of it," he said. His voice deepened when he thought he was being funny.

"I sure don't, but I'll call if I end up needing help," I said.

"You do that, Rijitera. Try not to get blood everywhere," he said.

The link clicked, signifying he'd cut the connection. I laughed and touched my wrist link to pull up the map of the ship. "Show me First Flight Officer Serail."

The yellow line flowed across the map until it stopped at a mess hall all the way across the ship, Mess Hall 68. I repeated the mess hall name out loud so the link would connect to the portal and take me there.

The portal closed silently, opening again a few seconds later, and I moved into the corridor. The smell hit me before the noise of the hallway. Strange smells that mixed in the same way a perfume shop did, making it near overwhelming to me. I sneezed a couple times to clear my nose, but no dice.

There were aliens everywhere, walking along the hall and in and out of rooms. Some carried tablets and others were just going about their business. It was weird to be around so many beings when we'd been stranded on a planet and then sequestered to Ohem's quarters for most of the last two days. Or was it three days? God, I couldn't keep track of time in space. It was messing me up.

I walked like I knew what I was doing and acted like I belonged on the ship. Which I did. It was my territory now, since it was my mate's pride and joy. No one glanced at me or ran away screaming, so I moved along until the hall ended at a tall archway into a large dining facility. There were so many types of aliens and I made an effort to avoid staring at the freakier ones, but it was a losing battle.

There was an octopus just sitting at a table holding a mug in one of its tentacles, drinking coffee. This is my life now. I was on an acid trip from hell and the way out was blocked by a big, black, shiny sex god that kept me chained to him with his magic cock.

I scanned the area for one red, totally fucked, alien scumbag and spotted him in the middle of the room surrounded by a gaggle of equally fucked friends. Walking further in, I sat three tables from him, tilting my head to listen in on his conversation. I willed the background noise of so many aliens talking and eating at once to silence in my mind and narrowed in on his voice.

"He brought a Rijitera aboard this ship! Rakis will never allow it to stand. Now he says some nonsense about standing against the Unity? I'm telling you, he isn't fit for command. The whore female has clouded his mind. He's weak enough to be captured by Vrax, and now he has married a beast."

A whore. How original. It was almost as disappointing as that green button on the shark ship. I was going to rip his spine out of his body and use it to pick my teeth. I'd had plans to do this discreetly and save the 'warning the rest of the crew' to Ohem, but there was a large group of people around Red. They were listening and not doing anything. It was making me twitchy. It was disrespectful to my mate.

Maybe everyone counted on my General being an honorable male. They probably figured they'd get a prison sentence or just kicked off his ship. Like with any military, there was probably a loss of rank or pay cuts, too. Getting kicked out with a dishonorable back home was almost like having a felony on your record, so I'm sure with how serious they took their service, the aliens were treated the same.

Ohem would follow protocol and the rules like a good General. It just wasn't much of a deterrent when you had what was essentially the president telling you he'd have your back if you wanted to mutiny. Ohem instilled respect in his people, but you know what worked better than respect to keep people in line? *Fear.*

Rakis could whisper in their ears all he wanted, but if they had something they feared more than him? Well. Things just wouldn't go his way now, would they?

"I've contacted Rakis about the General's plans, we just have to sit and wait. The Unity fleet will be here to take care of the matter and capture the Rijiteran. They offered us a bonus for the alert," he said, smug as all hell.

That rat motherfucker.

A few aliens around me stood and drifted off to the exits. I'd noticed the dining room slowly clearing out. Were some leaving to go report to Ohem or Rema? Or was this just getting back to work movements? Either way, I'd made up my mind. It was still plenty full enough to make my point. Now some, like Callie, would tell me that this wouldn't help my cause. That they were already wary of me and I should toe the line and be a good little soldier and an upstanding citizen to earn their trust. Screw that. I was a Rijitera—we didn't need your trust or goodwill.

This was a war. You either were with us or you were against us, and those that were against us were going to die. It was my mate and my pack. If you weren't pack, then you were *food.* I only hoped Ohem wouldn't be fiery mad at me later. I wasn't planning on harming any of the lazy, no good, non-reporting bystanders. Just scarring them for life a little.

I stood and sauntered over to Red's table, elbowing past a couple of his buddies. The rest parted like the red sea. Dead Red stared me down without a care in the world, his black eyes cold and stupid. The type of stupid who thought he couldn't be touched because of his rank and the friends surrounding him, and the reassurance that his boss was coming to back him up. He was probably giddy that I'd foolishly walked right into his hands.

He just needed the corny villain hand rubbing and it could be a scene from a terrible movie. Bet they'd get an extra nice bonus if they subdued me before Rakis could get here. Idiots. Guess they hadn't been good students in history.

I pressed my palms against the top of the table and leaned forward. "You're going to die here today, that can't be avoided. I have a reputation to maintain, after all. But I'll make it quick if you tell me how many are in your little gang and when Rakis will be here. Who else does he have in his little circle jerk? You know, that kind of thing," I said to him, surgery sweet and smiling.

His friends laughed, and he scoffed at me and stood, leaning forward to get into my face. "You're alone, Rijitera. You're going to cooperate and come along quietly like a good female or we'll beat you bloody and drag you to the shuttle unconscious. The choice is yours," he said, his arms crossing over his chest.

Rookie mistake. Always leave your hands loose and ready. He'd also put his face right in front of mine, which was the bigger mistake. Did he think Rema wouldn't fight him? Or any of the other officers or crew? He was overconfident, and it was enough to make me wonder just what else was going down on this ship or was he really that stupid? How many did he have on his and Rakis's side? I'd have to find out the hard way then. It was my favorite.

I shifted and sank my fangs into his face. He screamed and his friends squealed like little pigs while trying to pull me off him. I shook them off, readjusted my bite, and pulled. His face tore off his skull. I let him drop onto the table and slide to the floor. He was clutching his face, screaming, and rolling around on the floor. He wouldn't be going anywhere anytime soon.

One of Red's buddies shot me with something and I turned fast, slashing my claws at the one nearest to me, spilling bowels onto the floor. Screams echoed off the walls, and I howled out a hunting song, moving through the crowd of his buddies, claws flashing. There were screams and crying from the bystanders bearing witness mixing with the dying sounds of Red's comrades. Some bystanders ran for the exit, but most cowered under tables and against walls, too frozen in fear to run. More of Red's friends joined the fight, firing weird pistols at me that burned my skin for a few moments before healing. I danced around, tearing an arm off here and a leg off there. Blood sprayed the black floors of the dining hall and all over the gray stone tables, splattering the terrified crew members hiding under them. I wrapped my hand around the leg of Red, who was trying to crawl out into the hall and dragged him through the pooling blood, shoving my claws into his back to sever his spine and leaving him there, paralyzed and screaming.

I tore the jaw off another alien with a hard slap of claws against his face; his buddy scuttled under an empty table to escape, so I picked the table up and crushed him with it. I bit through the throat of another and turned in a slow circle, looking for more, but there were none. Except for the still screaming, newly paraplegic Red still trying to crawl away.

"Not so fast," I growled out and laughed. The sound was a nightmare imitation of what a laugh was supposed to be, and the crawling Red started begging. I shifted back, turned him over and lifted him with my hand wrapped around what was left of his face, palm against his mouth.

"Shut up. You answer my questions and I won't start eating you until *after* you're dead."

I hauled him over to a table, laid him down on his back and sat down, my hands splayed across his belly. I looked around the room, catching the haunted eyes of the bystanders staring back at me, and grinned. No doubt I was covered in blood and viscera. It would make the legend that this would undoubtedly turn into extra special.

"These men disobeyed my mate. Your General has been good to you, he respects and admires your loyalty to him, and how do you repay him?" I asked, sinking a single claw into the stomach of my captive. He screamed and the cowering from the crowd got worse.

I chuckled darkly at them. "You do nothing! These idiots sat here in a crowded room and talked about their involvement in a plot against my mate, and you sat there and did nothing," I snarled and sank in another claw. "You didn't link the General or Rema. You just sat there eating your lunch and ignoring it. I would kill you all for the disrespect, but my mate values you. I'm going to give you this one warning. There will be no others.

I will kill any who stand in his way. You may leave if you don't agree with him, as he has offered, or you can stay and do your fucking job. Betray him, don't inform him of a traitor, or assist any traitors and I will kill you."

I sank another claw and got one more tortured scream out of my captive. I rose over him to look into his eyes. "Tell me what you know, little rat."

His strangled voice rasped from a mouth without lips, making his words half mumbled. "Rakis has spies on the ship. He had me planted at the beginning of the officer's selection. I watched and reported to him."

He screamed when I dug my claws around in his insides. "Please! I brought reports of flight coordinates to the team aboard the ship that works for Rakis. They are professional soldiers. I don't know their names, they never met me in person. That's it, I swear!"

I snarled at the room and tore into his stomach while the rest watched. His agonized screaming turned to wet gurgles and then silence as I pulled his organs out and laid them on the table. I sat back down and kept my promise.

I only started eating him after he was dead.

Sixteen

Rema ran into the room with Ohem close behind him just after I'd finished my meal of traitor tartare and was sitting back, rubbing my full belly. No one had said a word while I'd eaten their crew mate in front of them. Oh, there'd been some vomiting and sobbing, but everyone had been too terrified to move.

Rema came to a stop and looked at the massacre with assessing eyes. They came to land on me, sitting at a table with a hollowed out corpse on top and my food belly jutting from my gore covered body. He looked both sick to his stomach and impressed. I had that effect on people.

"I said not to get blood everywhere, Rijitera," he said, his voice mild and casual. Rema was going to be my bestie, he just didn't know it yet. Or maybe my bestie in-law since Patty was my best friend and Rema was doomed to holy matrimony with her.

Ohem's presence had a profound effect on the atmosphere in the room. There was an easing of tension and terror. I didn't blame them, Ohem could probably kill me if he truly wanted too. Oh, it would be a hell of a fight and he would never lay a hand on me in anger, but I understood why he was their savior. It probably made them feel like my leash had arrived. In a way, it had.

"I see you caught my brother's spy," Ohem said, he didn't sound angry and his Izi was a pale glow so I wasn't sure what was going on inside his head right now. I tried not to fidget in my chair like a naughty school kid caught passing notes.

"They weren't exactly being subtle about it," I drawled. My eyes never leaving Ohem's face.

He walked further into the room, his tails raised so they wouldn't drag through the blood, and circled the scene, his feet making sticky sounds in all the blood. He came to stand in front of my table and looked at the body of Red splayed out on top, and then started going through Red's clothes with his tentacle clasper fingers, his hands resting on his hips. He was angry, I could tell now in the calculated way he held himself. I just didn't know if he was angry at me for blowing my semi-peaceful persona of a friendly wife, or if he was mad that Red had been on this ship in the first place.

A heavy thudding from the archway had me glancing up in time to see the big green officer from the meeting walk into the room and survey my artwork. He was grinning like a madman. I had one in my corner at least.

He walked with heavy steps to where I still sat in front of my leftovers and looked down at me. "Have a pleasant lunch, Nin At'ens?"

I shrugged my shoulders and answered him honestly. "It was more for the shock value, but yes, you aliens are tasty little snacks." My smile was wintry when I met his eyes. "If they'd been loyal, this never would have happened. I respect loyalty. I even respect indifference, but I don't like traitors to my mate."

Big guy nodded and swept his arm out. "I agree with you. I have long said we needed to clean house. Rakis was always an oily little male. I never liked him."

My new fan was a lizard-like alien, a crocodile that stood on two legs like a man. He didn't have a tail, and his face was human looking, complete with a hook nose that looked like it had been broken a couple times and he'd never had it fixed properly. He had big round orange eyes that were laughing at me.

He was built like a brick shit house, too. Shorter than me by a few inches, but twice as wide, and I was a big girl with big shoulders. He had teeth that shone white like a crocodile too, conical and sharp, that he flashed at me when Ohem approached.

Ohem sighed and crouched down in front of me to take my bloody hands in his. "Did they tell you anything before you slaughtered them?"

He didn't sound angry at me or resigned, like I'd fucked up and he was going to have to clean up my mess. He just sounded tired.

I nodded. "Yes. Red—Serail—was a plant from the start. Your brother has been planning this for a long time." I squeezed his hands in sympathy. "I know they called Rakis and told him our plans for letting people leave and for our jump in two days. There are also more of his people on the ship. He said there was a team of soldiers here, but I'll sniff them out. It'll be harder since I lost my temper a little here, but I'll find them just the same."

Ohem nodded and stood to glance around at his people coming out from under their tables and from their huddled corners. "Any traitors will die. We can not afford leniency right now. Not with what is at stake. If you see or hear something, report it. Do not approach them on your own. What has happened here today was in my mate's nature to defend and protect me. I don't necessarily condone it," he said, but he touched my cheek in reassurance. "But I understand it. I would kill her enemies as well. She will not harm you if you pose no threat."

I looked at the scared and traumatized faces and nodded my agreement.

I wasn't a complete psychopath. Just a partial one. Like seventy-five percent. "I will not kill you for no reason. I'm not a total savage. I love your General and it offends me that someone would go against him. You don't have to agree with him, just don't actively work against him and you will never see my teeth in anger," I said to the timidly growing crowd. None of them would ever want to be my bosom buddy, but that was fine with me.

Ohem flared his Izi in approval at my words and helped me to my feet, he turned to the big green lizard guy and pointed at the bloody remains on the table. "Would you have this room sealed and sanitized, Aga-Ush?"

The green male winked at me. "You may call me Aga, Nin At'ens." He nodded at Ohem. "I will see this done for you, General," he said and bowed. Aga started barking orders into his link. He then sternly told the crowd to scram and to see counselors. They would need it. I'd made quite the impact statement with my early dinner.

Ohem held my hand in his all the way back to the portal with Rema staying behind to help with the cleanup and crowd control.

The portal closed us inside, and he looked down at me. "I understand you thought you had to take action against my enemies, my *ursang*, but perhaps the next time you do you can take it to a secure room without giving my crew nightmares for the rest of their lives." There was amusement in his voice that made the tension melt from my shoulders.

I shrugged. "I needed them to witness what I was capable of and tell the rest of the crew on the Solus what they'd seen. I won't have to do such a public execution again."

"Ah, I see. Yes. I imagine you won't. Our remaining enemies will try to stay hidden now. They will also understand just how lethal you are. I will have Rema investigate Serail's comings and goings. We will find who else he conspired with. I will also move the departure date for those leaving to tomorrow morning."

They should have already been tracking him, and maybe Rema already had. He appeared untrusting of anyone but Ohem, and he'd pointed out to his General that even a seemingly loyal crew could be snakes in the grass.

The portal opened in our hallway and Ohem gently nudged me out. "Go get cleaned up, I have to see to the departures. We will have to postpone our celebratory night for a later date. I am sorry, Jack, that my ship hasn't been the haven I had wanted for you and our friends."

He was so solemn and genuinely upset that I'd had to kill some people. Silly male.

I smiled up at him and reached up to pull his face down to mine so I could kiss his jaw, leaving behind bloody smudges on his face. "I live for this shit, Ohem. My life back home was boring as hell. This is awesome. Patty and the girls are fine. I'll kill anyone who threatens them, and I think Callie enjoys the challenge. Sam wants to help, and Patty is a wildcard that lives for chaos. Don't apologize. I'm here to help you. This is me helping. I'll worry about the spies. You get your people situated and get us to where we need to go. I love you," I said and started walking towards the metal door of our rooms.

"And I love you. Be careful," he said, and the portal door closed around him.

I called Patty and the others to check in after I'd washed all the blood off of me. Patty was with Sam in the labs where Rema had dropped her off when he'd gotten the call about my incident in the cafeteria, and Callie was grilling the pilots in one hangar. They were all safe and being watchful. I told Callie to be extra careful being alone, but apparently she'd found the big boss of the pilots and was sticking close to him. Her voice had an added huskiness to it when I called. It might have to do with more than just the fancy alien spacecrafts she was interested in. Sexy alien men would do that to a girl.

Once I was dressed, I figured it was time to do a little exploring myself. I french braided my hair to keep it out of my face and tied it off with some weird rubbery hair ties that Ohem had left for me.

I entered the portal and touched my wrist link to bring up the map. There were a million cargo bays, docking bays and ship hangars. So many crew quarters it was overwhelming to look at the numbers running on the side of the map. Kitchens, dining halls, common rooms, gyms. Entertainment rooms? Might have to check those out. Gardens, pools, theaters, training grounds. This ship was gigantic, and I'd never see all of it. I'd start with the entertainment room farthest from me and work my way back. We were towards the front of the ship, closest to the bridge. The entertainment room I selected was almost completely at the ass end of the Solus, towards the bottom. There were so many levels on this thing.

"Entertainment room 473, deck level 234," I said to the portal, and the door opened a few seconds later. I stepped out into the corridor and followed my map to the left. There were hundreds of aliens crowding the wide hall, moving back and forth, that it was almost like walking around in the Mall of America. I kept my ears open for snippets of conversation as I walked, and I took notice of how they parted around me, avoiding my eyes. Word traveled fast on the ship. Good.

The glowing line on the map turned right down a side hallway. I followed it to a swirling neon lit door. It slid up at my approach and the map pinged to let me know this was the place. I touched the link to close the map and walked into the room. If you've ever been to Dave and Busters, then imagine that, times a thousand. It was dark with neon lit games and virtual reality sections.

There was music here. Bass pumped from invisible speakers and aliens grinded along to the beat on a pulsing dance floor in the center of the room. The dance floor was a sunken section that had steps wrapped around it. It was probably the size of a football field. Everything on the Solus was larger than life. How awesome. I weaved my way through the crowd to a long bar on the far side of the room. It was like a dance club in here, dark and confusing, so no one would recognize me. Cue evil hand rubbing.

The bar was red neon with glowing mushroom like bar stools all along the front. I snagged one as an alien vacated and surveyed the wall behind the bar. It was red with floating white shelves that highlighted all the various sized bottles covering the wall. The bartenders were six-armed slender creatures that wore illuminated paint on their bodies like rave dancers. I met one of their many, many eyes and locked my muscles so I didn't bug out like a coward. They had faces full of eyes! The bartender smiled at me and I shuddered.

It approached and placed a wavy glass in front of me. "Nin At'ens! What an honor to serve you! What can I get you?"

I couldn't tell if it was male or female. Its voice was deep, and it was slightly larger than the others, so we'd go with male. He was staring at me, practically vibrating with anticipation, and I felt a little bad at being so put off by his appearance. I looked at the bottles again until I snagged on a glowing pink liquid that looked interesting,

I pointed at it. "Whatever that is. Can you make me something with that?"

He didn't even turn his head, just some of his eyes glanced back and it was a herculean effort not to gag.

He twittered and waved his many hands enthusiastically. "Yes! I will make you the very best drink. I am so honored," he said and turned to grab bottles off the shelves.

I turned and bobbed my head to the beat, and studied the crowd. If I didn't know I was in space on an alien ship this would look like something Earth would think up. Combination nightclub-arcade with bar. The alien crew weren't dressed in the typical crew red either. There were all kinds of attire out there. Short club dresses transcended Earth, it would seem. Some dancers had no clothes, just painted bodies that glowed under the lights. This was my favorite room, hands down. I was going to bring the girls here later, and we were going to get drunk and dance. I was going to drag Ohem's big body onto that dance floor to grind all over him. I needed to have some club dresses made asap and paint my exposed skin to really drive him wild.

The trill of the bartender had me turning to see him place a wavy glass in front of me filled with swirling pink liquid. The rim was crusted with gold flakes and there were glowing balls floating in the drink that were dissolving into foam that threatened to overflow the glass. He stood there and watched me take a cautious sip, my eyes widening at the fresh, sweet flavor and the kick of alcohol. It was delicious, and I took a longer taste.

I flicked my eyes to his many, many eyeballs, and finally settled on two large ones in the center, and smiled over my glass. "This is amazing. Thank you. I'll be sure to only come to your bar for my new favorite drink," I said.

He wiggled and his thousand eyes blinked rapidly at different intervals that threatened to bring my drink back up. I swallowed it down and held my smile in place. It wouldn't do to throw up his drink right after I promised to make him my personal bartender.

"I call it the Nin Rijitera! In honor of you," he said, his voice overly emotional at my compliment.

I dipped my head at him and drained my glass. "How do I pay you?"

He tittered and raised his hands in front of him. "The General has instructed that all expenses be passed to him."

Ohem, my alien sugar daddy.

I nodded. "Add a bonus for my appreciation for you," I said, not knowing whether they'd know what a tip was or if it was even something you did in space, but judging by the way he vibrated, it was the right offer.

I asked for another drink and he quickly had another prepared and I took it to walk around the room. I was on my second rotation when I heard Ohem's name. I casually stopped and backtracked to where the voice had sounded over the music and games. There were five females seated at a table off to the side of the dance floor, backed against the wall. I bobbed my way over and notched myself between two different groups of chatting aliens and focused on their conversation.

"I think she's a perfect match for the General. She's strong enough to challenge him and help him destroy his enemies, but beautiful in her warrior way," a blue-skinned bird lady said. She was ethereal, and I stared at her in shocked wonder. If I hadn't been happily mated, she'd be the first alien I'd approach, hands down. Her small beak was a darker blue than her skin and feathers, and was more malleable than an actual bird's beak, as she could smile with it. She had gorgeous blue wings rising over her shoulders, starting as light blue then blending into the dark blue of her long flight feathers. A crest of feathers on her head rose and fell as she talked, much like a cockatoo.

She had her pert breasts exposed and painted with neon orange paint in swirling patterns, her dark blue nipples were pierced and her slim thighs flashed underneath her ribbon skirt, bird feet and talons painted the same bright orange as her body. She was sexy as hell and I was momentarily transfixed until one of her companions spoke.

A raptor-like female tilted her head. "She slaughtered thirty crew members in minutes and then ate one in front of the others left alive," she flashed a toothy predator smile, "I like her. We will have to set up a meeting, she could use allies and guides." The others voiced their agreement.

Oh, I liked these ladies. Girls supporting girls!

I listened for a few more seconds to their chatter. They weren't spies. I moved on to complete another long circuit of the room. I caught talk of the murder spree in the mess, and others wondering about my human friends, but no talk of Rakis. The hairs on the back of my neck had raised during my circle around the room, and the burning feeling between my shoulder blades told me someone was watching me. I finished my glass and sat it down on a table, waved at the bartender and left the room.

I checked two more similar entertainment rooms, and it was much the same. Horrified comments about my savagery and others that admire me for it. The feeling of being watched followed me to each new place. I moved on to some cargo holds and found them empty except for massive metal crates. Still being followed, I turned my head slightly and didn't see anyone behind me. I couldn't smell them either. Whoever they were, they were good.

I'd been gone for hours and checked in again with Ohem and the others. They were all back in the common room and I was told dinner was going to be served in an hour. I told Ohem about my shadow in a hushed voice so my watcher wouldn't overhear. Ohem chuffed and told me to continue as I was, that he was watching. It gave me the warm fuzzies. I checked more rooms in the halls and pretended to be oblivious.

They tried nothing, just followed and watched. My wrist link chimed and I tapped it. A small message holo screen popped up from Ohem. It said to lose my shadow. He'd turned off my tracking link to everyone but him and Rema. I grinned, turned a corner, and sprinted to the portal. It opened again in a different area, and I walked down the corridor. I entered another portal and then another until I came to a completely empty hallway. I exited the portal and wandered around for over an hour, checking the rooms until I was sure the feeling of being watched was gone. I was in one of the maintenance levels, all the rooms were full of tools and desks with various objects in different states of repairs.

Time to wrap this up for the day. My link pinged again with another message that said to check a room that they'd followed my watchers to. A small offset room on the map was highlighted. It wasn't labeled and looked like a storage closet to me, but I'd check anyway before I left this section of the ship. The map pinged outside a plain metal door, and I pressed my ear to it and listened. No sound, but I could smell aliens inside and the tang of ozone that I remembered from the plasma gun battle on planet Hellhole. Bingo! Did they not think my mate would have me monitored? That he'd not track them down easily while they followed me around? Between Red and these new assholes, I had little respect for Rakis's lackeys.

I narrowed my eyes at the closed door. It hadn't opened at my approach. I pushed it, but it didn't open so I typed a quick message on my link to get Ohem or Rema to open it. It clicked softly and slid open less than twenty seconds later. It was a dark hallway. There was another dark door at the end and I walked on silent feet to stand outside it. There were murmurs of conversation inside. I leaned close to the door and focused.

"Bring her to Bay 3. We'll take care of the rest," a male said in a deep, raspy voice. I would bet my life I was who they were talking about. "We have brought enough soldiers to capture her. Rakis wants her alive. Kill the General."

My lips pulled back from my already shifted fangs involuntarily, a low growl clawing its way up my throat. I clenched my teeth to keep quiet, and backed away from the door. Pivoting quietly, I left the hallway before I rushed in and killed everyone. I didn't want to repeat the cafeteria slaughter. I was going to be responsible. I'd get the others first and then let their plan play out. I'd find out what it was when they either "captured" me or after I was lured to the bay. Just to be safe, I'd warn Patty and others about it and have them stay in our rooms. I made it to a portal and waited until it closed before I touched my link. "Call Ohem."

"Yes, my *ursang*?" Ohem's Mount Doom voice even rumbled over the link.

I gave him a quick rundown of my day and what I'd heard at the door to the unmarked room.

He hummed. "Patty and the others are here with Rema and I. They will try to take or lure you tonight. The shuttles are leaving first thing in the morning with those who wish to leave, and then we are jumping to a restricted sector. They don't have time to delay. They won't know where you are right now. We turned off your tracking locator so you could lose your shadow and I could track them when they went to report you'd evaded them. I left ours on so they will see we are in our quarters, but I will turn yours on now. Let them come to you. Go back to the entertainment room and feign drunkenness. We will monitor you and I will meet you when they lead you away."

It was a simple plan, and it would work. It always did. I don't care if you were a super advanced alien race, if your target was isolated and inebriated, you acted. I walked back out of the portal and returned to my bartender.

The club was even more crowded than before and the music was louder. I ordered a bunch of my drinks and slammed them quickly until there were several empty glasses in front of me. I waved the bartender away when he reached to take them. Alcohol burned through my system, leaving me buzzed for a few seconds before my metabolism swept it away. I sat sipping my last drink and swayed in my chair, my eyes shuttered and talked loudly to the bartender. He was more than happy to stand and chat with me.

I learned his name was Ket'ak, and he was a Morlens. His wife was the pretty blue bird lady I'd overheard earlier. He'd called her Izari and was very fond of her. I smashed my judgy, human from Earth nonsense into powder, and kept the surprise off of my face when he'd told me Izari was his mate. Maybe he was the pinnacle of beauty to her species and I was an asshole for thinking otherwise. We set up a double date, and he looked like he could die happy at any moment. He and his mate were adorable. I told myself I could get used to his eyes.

I'd been here only ten minutes when a wide eyed pixie looking thing buzzed over to me on dragonfly wings. It was about three feet tall and I wanted to squish it like a bug. It had that shifty look of someone that was doing something bad and liked it. It took a seat next to me and met my eyes. I gave it a sloppy smile and swayed harder in my seat.

"Hi! I'm Jack!" I slurred and stuck out my hand.

The bug looked at my hand, and then ignored it to meet my eyes again. "Nin At'ens." It looked around and then leaned forward. "I know where there are other traitors."

Its eyes narrowed slightly, and I didn't miss its cocky little smile on its bug mouth. I widened my eyes and leaned back, almost falling over before I grabbed the bar to steady my poor, drunken self and popped up from my seat to wobble forward, looking over my shoulder at the bug who was hovering behind me.

"Show me."

The bug's eyes lit with triumph and he flew ahead of me. I weaved slowly through the crowd, almost falling a time or two, trying to really sell it. It came back to buzz at me impatiently a few times; I swatted at it and purposely missed, growling at its smug little face. We made it out of the club and into the portal, where I leaned against the wall and closed my eyes. I even snored a little. I should win an Oscar for this performance.

The bug muttered under its breath and tapped my cheek to wake me when I didn't move for the opening portal door. I blinked blearily at it and followed its lead out into a cavernous cargo bay. I stumbled to a halt, but the bug didn't stop, just flew up and disappeared into the maze of towering crates.

"Hello? Is anyone there?" I said, like I couldn't hear them rustling around. I added a little nervousness to my voice and walked into the narrow gap between the wall of crates stacked in front of me. They should really, *really* brush up on the Rijitera in their histories. I'm sure even in the washed out public versions it mentions heightened senses. I could smell, hear, and taste them in the air.

Idiots.

Movement in the shadows above me had my eyes flicking towards the ceiling. It was hundreds of feet above, but I saw Ohem clinging to it. He came to give me some backup. He was a darker shadow against the black cavern of the ceiling. I moved my eyes back to the front and continued walking. It warmed my heart that we were hunting together.

Past the first mountains of crates was an opening with, what I was assuming, were the cranes to lift the cargo. They had faint lights glowing on them. It gave the large square clearing the perfect feel for an ambush. I heard them moving to box me in and hid a smile. A single male stepped out of the dark and into the glow of the machines, his plasma rifle pointed at me. He was grim and had that practiced movement of a trained soldier. This was their ringleader, no doubt about it. He was here to take care of the hassle of killing me himself. I laughed at him when his people melted out of the shadows behind him. There were only twelve of them. Elite soldiers, but they'd only brought twelve.

My voice echoed inside the hold and I quoted my favorite movie husband, the opportunity too good to pass up. "You made three mistakes. First, you took the job. Second, you came light. A twelve man crew for me? Fucking insulting. But the worst mistake you made," I looked up and watched Ohem drop behind them and rise, his Izi lighting up slowly from his feet to his helmeted head. Other shapes took position along the top of the crates, Ohem's soldiers were here. I turned back to the ringleader and smiled. "Was thinking I came alone."

Seventeen

The enemy soldiers didn't hesitate, their weapons spitting out plasma fire that lit the area in a chaotic display of light and deafening sound. The smell of ozone filled my nose, making my eyes water. It took precious seconds to shake the disorientation. The soldiers had split into teams to keep Ohem and I under a constant barrage of burning hot ionized gas. Ohem's men rained down hell from above, burning up the enemy soldiers. The plasma shots slicked off Ohem's armor and the faceless helmet that covered his entire head.

I wasn't so lucky in my plasma proofness this time around. Only my berserker was immune to the blue fire and the shots that hit me burned chunks of skin and fur off my shifted form. Gaping holes blown in my body healed rapidly enough, but the pain was intense, and I hissed between clenched teeth every time I was touched by the shots. I ducked and weaved, slashing with claws to sever arms from bodies, but the soldiers from our side were damn good and killed most of the enemy before I even got to them. I think I only killed two and maimed one more before all of them were dead except for Ringleader. The whole fight lasted only a minute or two. It was all very anticlimactic. Anger sparked in my gut at having my kills stolen from me, but I shoved it down deep and didn't snarl at the good guys when they jumped down to surround me, weapons at low ready. They faced away from me, watching the dark for any more targets.

Being protected had my hackles raised.

The weight of Ohem's gaze watching me from behind his faceless helmet pulled my eyes to him, and I knew he was laughing. He had the ringleader kneeling on the floor in front of him, bleeding in various places all over his body and one arm was a smoking stump, the plasma having cauterized the wound so he wouldn't die before we could question him.

As irritated as I was at the unwelcome fire support, I still admired my deadly male as he stood over his enemy. Ohem's armor was bulkier than before and it was the darker red black of old blood. He'd put on his war pants for me. How romantic.

I was going to let him soothe my pique later. He was going to have to sex my irritation right out of my body. I was going to work up a real good MAD, so he'd have to work twice as hard to make it right. Calling in backup in an ambush? The nerve. I wanted compensation.

I grinned at Ohem, and his arms crossed over his chest. His shoulders shook slightly with silent laughter. I sighed and barely avoided melting into a puddle of lovesick goo at his feet.

Ohem's helmet melted away from his head and he met my eyes briefly, their glow full of heated promise, before they went dark and cold as he turned his attention towards Ringleader.

"Take him to Aga," Ohem said to one of the Solus good guys standing off to the side of him.

The good guy's helmet dissolved and his nasty smile told me that my new friend Aga wasn't someone you wanted to interrogate you. Given his admiration for my more violent tendencies, I wasn't all that surprised that Aga was a persuasive interrogator.

A soldier walked up and handed me a set of folded red clothes with a pair of flats placed on top and turned his back for me to shift. Ohem was watching intently, his upper plate pulling away from his teeth at his people who stood around me until they averted their eyes. It was cute that he would snarl at them while I stood naked for the whole two seconds it took to pull my clothes on.

The clothes stuck to the blood spattered all over my body, and I grimaced at the feeling. Once dressed I told them it was safe to use their eyes again and two of Ohem's men dragged the ringleader through the cargo crates and out of sight with the others falling in behind them, leaving my mate and I alone.

He wrapped a hand around my upper arm and pulled me into him. "Are you angry that I brought support?"

I shook my head, "My instincts want to rage about the stolen kills, but my brain says it was smart. You can still make it up to me, though."

Ohem's hand squeezed my arm harder as he laughed, turning to pull me along after him towards the exit. "I will do just that, *ursang*. I can't have my wife angry with me, it's bad for morale."

I was still laughing when we entered the portal that took us to the security headquarters where Aga had already started the interrogation in another room. Ohem led me to a table in a staff break room and I sat to wait until Aga had some information for us.

Ohem went to the sink built into the wall and waved his hand in front of a panel that slid out to reveal purple cloth stacked neatly inside. He picked one up, wet it at the sink, and then came to kneel beside my chair and started washing the blood from my face. I closed my eyes so he could scrub the stubborn blood that had already dried into my eyebrows.

When he was satisfied with his work, he placed the soiled cloth in a retractable bin and gathered me into his arms before sitting in his own seat. I rested my head against his armored chest and sighed. We sat in silence for a few moments until I couldn't take it anymore and asked the first thing that popped into my head to beat back the boredom.

"Is kissing something your kind do, or is that something you picked up from the girls on the Vrax ship?" I asked. I was curious, of course, but waiting patiently had never been a strong suit of mine. I could never sit in silence for long before starting a conversation just for the sake of talking.

Ohem's chest vibrated against my cheek when he chuckled. "Did you think only humans had found a use for every orifice on the body when it came to sex or intimacy?" He laughed some more, which was a little uncalled for.

I pushed off his chest and sat up in his lap to give him my best glare. "A simple 'yes, we kiss' would have sufficed."

If his horns wouldn't have punched through the wall behind us, I think he'd have thrown his head back and laughed until he cried. I slapped my palm against his chest, which only made my hand sting. I shook it out and tried to hide my smile so he wouldn't be encouraged.

"Well, what about the way you were all touchy feely right before we crashed and then down on the planet? I hadn't told you we were mated yet."

He glowed cheerfully and shook his head then tapped my nose with a claw. "I have very good hearing, Jack. And neither you nor Patty were trying to be quiet as you discussed your jealous rage in the Vrax dining facility or your desire for me to fuck you."

I scrunched up my face in mild embarrassment. "You heard me?"

I slapped his chest a second time when he started laughing again. My cheeks grew hot and I covered them with my hands before glaring at Ohem. He grabbed my shoulders and gave me a little shake while he got himself under control enough to speak.

"I had been fascinated by you the moment I saw you outside my cell, as I've already told you before. I wanted you. You were bold, even in your fear." He glowed a little softer and tightened his grip. "You rubbed your nose in my chest and moaned. I was lost to you in that moment, or at least to the lust you ignited," he said and winked two of his four eyes at me.

"I didn't moan."

Ohem nodded his head. "You moaned. You stuck that little nose against my skin, inhaled my scent, and moaned. I remember it clearly, *ursang*."

I could practically taste the smugness in the air. I leaned further back so I could take him all in. He sat with his back straight as a board, shoulders squared, head held tall. He was the picture of male arrogance. I grinned wider and shook my head. He was adorable.

I leaned forward and wrapped my hand around one of his black horns and pulled his face to mine so I could kiss him. He cupped the back of my head and rubbed his hard lips across mine before slipping his tongue inside. Things were getting heated when Rema burst into the room, chest heaving like he'd sprinted the entire way here, with a tablet in hand.

I had been so absorbed by my mate that I hadn't been paying attention to the sounds outside the break room. Really stupid, since we were under attack from spies. Ohem, however, didn't look surprised to see Rema, so he'd heard him coming. Man, my mate was way better at multitasking than I was.

Ohem hugged me tighter to him and shifted his body to face Rema. "What's wrong?" he asked.

Rema looked both angry and devastated, and my heart stuttered before it started racing.

He took a deep breath and then waved a hand over the tablet to cast a screen onto the wall and a video started playing. It was of Rakis. Ohem stiffened against me and I leaned harder into him, grabbing his hand to clasp it in mine. Rakis was addressing a large crowd in front of a massive black glass palace. He looked so like my mate, only slightly smaller in stature and covered in fine burgundy robes. His Izi was shining dimly and strobing in distress as he spoke to the crowd.

"It is with deep sadness that I address the Unity today with news of my brother, General Ohem At'ens, who has conspired with the criminal Councilor Vero to incite a war with our independent trade partners. I have no other choice but to issue an order of arrest for the General in all Unity sectors. He has been stripped of his military rank and status as a Unity citizen. He is cast out from his House."

White hot *wrath* spread through my body like a slow river, lazily licking at my nerve endings. I looked back at Ohem and his Izi was strobing slowly with an odd mixture of amusement and irritation. He was taking this much better than I was. I turned back to the viewscreen. I could be stoic for his sake. I would not rage kill the furniture in this room.

"Be aware that he is still in possession of our warship Solus Geshgid and should be approached with extreme caution. Please report any sightings to your local security forces who will immediately relay the messages to me." Rakis looked directly at the camera and his face was a perfect mask of solemn sadness.

What a joke.

"To Ohem's loyal crew, I say this to you; I honor your loyalty to my brother, but know that you serve a traitor. You will be given full amnesty from any crimes you were ordered to commit under his command. The Unity will welcome you back with open arms, free of judgment. We only ask that you report your false General's whereabouts. You will be rewarded as a hero and loyal citizen of the Unity." Rakis's face grew hard and his Izi dark. "Any who aids my brother will be branded a traitor to the Unity. You will face the full consequences of our laws for your continued association with Ohem."

The video ended and Rema stared at Ohem, his face stiff with rage. "I had been monitoring the feeds since our communications were shut off for security and saw the broadcast. It was sent out to the broad net. It's everywhere now."

Ohem sighed and stood, allowing me to slide down his body until I landed on my feet in front of him before his arms fell away from me. "I had wondered when he'd make his announcement."

Rema blinked at him. "You knew he'd do this? He's branded you a traitor to the Unity," Rema shouted as he paced the room.

Ohem approached the agitated male and placed his hand on Rema's shoulder to stop him. "Yes. It was the next logical course for him to take.

He will want the whole of the Unity's military might behind him. The other Councilors will be on board with him if they have a common enemy. With my apparent alliance with Vero, the council will now have all the incentive they need to launch a full assault." Ohem sighed and released Rema's shoulder. "Even if my escape from capture went against his original plan, I'm afraid it gave him an even better course of action. My brother was always a shrewd tactician."

Rema closed his eyes, his wings pulling in close to his body like he was trying to shield himself from the news. He opened his eyes again, and gave us a hard look. "What do we do about this?"

Ohem flashed his Izi, shaking his head. "What we have been doing. Shuttling any who wish to leave off this ship and investigating the Rijitera ruins on Detritus. What we find there will determine our next move."

Rema nodded at us, saluting before he turned on his heel and exited the room.

I looked at Ohem, and his shoulders dropped. He ran a hand over one of his horns and down his face before he met my gaze. "It would seem you were dragged into a war when you were taken from your planet. I can still take you back to Earth. You and our girls."

I snorted and wrapped my arms around his waist. "I'm not going anywhere. You're stuck with me forever, mate. Though it was nice of you to offer." I leaned back and bared my teeth at him. "Do it again and suffer." I smiled sweetly at him, and he chuckled and gave me a squeeze.

"You can offer the other ladies an out, but you'd have to pry this life of space adventure out of Patty's cold, dead hands." Ohem chuffed and shook his head. "Callie might take you up on the offer, though. She's got a loving family and a career back home. Though I'm not sure how that career will hold up with her weeks' long absence." I shrugged. "And Sam is enamored with your super fancy science and medicine, so she's staying forever and I think she has a crush on your science doctor."

Ohem sighed and hugged me tightly, and then stepped back with his hands on my shoulders. He bent down until he could look into my eyes at face level. His eyes glowed softly, and when his hands moved up my shoulders to cup my face I knew he was about to make me cry by saying something sweet.

I girdled my loins and waited for his emotional bomb to drop.

He closed his eyes and tipped his forehead against mine. "I love you, my *ursang*. My brother betrayed me. There is a war brewing that will no doubt rip the fabric of my nation apart. I will lose friends and soldiers under my command. All of this turmoil and I feel *strong*. I feel secure knowing that we will prevail. You make me feel strong." He lifted his head away from mine to look into my eyes again, his palms hot against my face. "I have found a miracle in all this chaos. Not a Rijitera, just you. I found *you*. You have given me a new family. I love you more than any of my words could say. I am so very, very glad that my brother was a treasonous bastard, and I ended up on that Vrax ship."

Tears spilled over my cheeks to wet his hands and I breathed out a shaky laugh. "Damn, Ohem. You sure know how to make a woman feel all warm and mushy inside." I lifted my hand up to grip his forearm and smiled at him. "I love you too, my creepy alien mate. Tentacles, tails and all. Wouldn't change a thing. Don't you worry about that brother of yours. He's on my shit list."

Ohem laughed softly and rubbed his face against mine, careful not to knock me out with his horns. We were a sappy mess when Aga walked into the room, casually wiping blood off his hands with a cloth. Ohem stood tall and looked at his officer. Aga gave a nasty smile and shrugged his wide shoulders. "He held stronger than most, but I got some *very* interesting things out of him before he died."

I grinned at the green giant, and his eyes twinkled at me. We understood each other.

Eighteen

Turns out there were way more people on the ship that aligned with the Unity and Rakis than Ohem had expected. I don't know if they were just scared to go up against the bulk of a larger army, or if they were truly loyal to their nation. Either way, it hurt my mate. He didn't show it outwardly, his Izi glowing a steady neutral, but I could tell in the stiff way he held himself, tentacles and tails still behind him. We stood in the largest hangar in the ship watching the progression of thousands boarding shuttles that would make the jump out of the system. I slid my hand into Ohem's and gave it a hard squeeze.

Once the last shuttle was lifted by the claw and placed in the launch tube Ohem looked at me and nodded, before doing the same to the officer's that had gathered to oversee the exodus.

Aga was one of them, his eyes hard and his mouth twisted with disgust at the people fleeing back to the Unity. He met my eyes, showing me his sharp teeth in a silent snarl. I shrugged my shoulders and mouthed, "Pussies."

Aga's face relaxed, and he smiled. I liked Ohem's torturer. Aga was the equivalent of the director of the CIA, only a lot meaner and greener.

I'd been informed of all this during our conversation after Aga's interrogation of the ringleader spy. It meant King's Guard or something like that. Basically, Aga was a badass and my new coach on all things violent and bloody. We were two peas in a pod and it was making poor Ohem nervous.

We'd been grinning at each other like gleeful idiots since he'd told us what he'd learned during his interrogation. Rakis's ships were in the star system to take back the Solus with orders to arrest Ohem, and failing that, to kill him. It was only a matter of time before all out war started, because Ohem had many more allies on the independent planets that would welcome our help against Rakis's campaign to conquer a large part of the universe. We'd also gathered more intel on Rakis's involvement with Vero.

We knew where Vero was going next, how many soldiers he had, and where he planned to strike first. The unlucky planet Korsal was going to be the first battleground, and it had made Aga a very, very happy crocodile. He'd told me the aliens on Korsal were a fierce warrior race and it was a horrible mistake for Vero to choose them first.

It was an underestimation of the planet's more primitive species. Aga had rounded up the remaining enemy spies on board with an extra pep in his step, probably killing them with a little more joy than normal after the news. I hadn't had time to ask for details, as we'd spent our night in meetings with Ohem's officers. I'd made a valiant effort not to fall asleep and failed after the sixth hour of endless military talks. I'd been woken by Ohem a few hours later in our bed. He must have carried me there after the briefs and was rudely waking me up for the shuttle departure I'd asked to be a part of.

I'd wanted to be there for moral support and it was a good thing I hadn't missed it.

Ohem's heavy hand landed on my shoulder and squeezed. "We must make our way to the bridge. We have a jump to make."

I nodded and waved to the officers, who saluted Ohem as we passed by them on our way to the portal door with Aga bringing up our rear.

"Don't let this weigh on your mind, Ohem. More stayed than left. Only three of your officers are among the *fleeing*," Aga said with a sneer.

I snorted, bumping my shoulder into the big green alien's arm and he smiled at me.

Ohem chuffed and shook his head. "I know. It is for the best that those who don't have the will for what is coming to leave. We must now focus on finding out what my brother and Vero have discovered on Detritus."

It sounded like he was talking more to himself than to us. Aga nodded his head in agreement and led the way out of the portal when the doors opened.

I followed and then stopped for a moment to stare in shock. I'd been expecting a command deck with desks and special chairs for the commander, like in the shark's ship or in a Star Trek movie, but what greeted me was so far off from what I expected. There were no desks or chairs to be found on the bridge, only an immense window that took up the forward part of the room and rows of pods. I'd been told that the windows weren't actually windows, but display monitors that had a constant feed from external cameras to give the illusion of a view into space. It still didn't make me feel any better about them.

This one was the largest window I'd seen so far on the ship and it cast an eerie glow onto the creepy pods that formed semi-circles three rows deep across the room. The pods were the same shiny black glass that made up the walls and floors of the ship. It was utterly silent on the bridge, adding to the creepy feel. Ohem strode into the center of the room and the window lit up with a display of numbers off to the side of a map of the stars, with the Solus being a glowing yellow mini ship on the map.

Ohem stared at the map for a few seconds and then turned to the pod that was nearest to him. "Sound the alarm for transition," he said to it and a soft warbling alarm sounded in the room.

I approached one of the large pods and cupped my hands against the surface to look inside. I couldn't see anything and I took a step back to frown at it in confusion when suddenly it cracked. I yelped and leaped back to practically climb up Ohem's side when I bumped into him walking up behind me. The pod folded into itself and inside was a smiling alien I recognized. Izari, the pretty blue bird lady I'd seen in the club the other night.

"Nin At'ens, a pleasure to meet you at last. My husband has only nice things to say. You have a friend for life in Ket'ak." She rose gracefully from her lava chair inside the pod and I almost swooned at her feet. She was even more beautiful up close. She smiled at me and her large blue eyes literally twinkled. I was about to embarrass myself in front of her by saying something cringe worthy about her level of hotness, but the whirring vibrations coming from the floor pulled my attention to my feet. The entire ship felt like it took a deep breath before Izari's pleasant voice sounded from in front of me and from my wrist link.

"All crew prepare for a transitional jump."

Three slow pings sounded out over the ship and Ohem's powerful arms wrapped around me to turn me to look out the window to watch. The ship let out its breath and a purple light shot out in front of the Solus like a sword, piercing the blackness of space.

"You can't really see the light. It is being displayed on the screen for you," Ohem whispered.

A black hole erupted into existence in front of the ship.

"Prepare yourself," Ohem whispered again.

He held me tightly, and the ship shot forward so fast that time seemed to be bending around us. My stomach roiled in protest as we passed into the void. It was a hellscape where nothing made sense, and my body was both upside down and spread out everywhere at once. There was no sound, just a pressure like I was being crushed by a planet. If it wasn't for the steady, firm presence of Ohem at my back, I'd have started screaming. It only lasted a few seconds before we passed through to the other side, but it was more seconds than I ever wanted to experience again. I'd finally found something about this ship that I hated more than the windows.

I shuddered, wrapping my arms around myself. "That sucked."

Ohem chuffed above me. "Yes. New crew members always find the transition to be unsettling. You will get used to it with time."

The hell I would. I was going to make the good doctor Ghix knock me out next time, and then I remembered my poor friends. Shit.

"What about Patty and the others? They must have freaked out," I said, and pulled away from Ohem to look for them, but he held me still.

"They are fine, Jack. Rema and Dr. Ghix were with them. They are being brought to us now."

I let out a slow breath and relaxed back against him. The endless star filled expanse of space glared at me through the fake window and I glared back.

I loved my mate, but damn, why couldn't he have been a non-space traveling barbarian species that would stuff me in a cave and keep me naked and pregnant for the rest of my life? This space travel bullshit was for the birds, but I bet Sam had the time of her life during the jump. A good natured sneer spread across my face as I shook my head. At least one of us was having a good time during all the space travel.

I was going to have to get used to it, eventually. Maybe someday the sight of the vacuum wouldn't make me want to run away and hide under my bed. My ancestors were probably rolling around in their graves at the shame of one of their own not liking space travel.

Patty and the others entered the bridge, and I turned to see if Patty hated the transition as much as me, and her still pale face confirmed it.

She came to stand next to me and Ohem, blowing out a breath. "That sucked ass."

Ohem chuffed in amusement. I elbowed him in the stomach, earning a sore elbow for my efforts. I cursed and rubbed it, frowning at Patty. "Next time we ask for the good drugs and sleep through it."

She snapped her fingers and groaned. "Damn. I was right next to Dr. Ghix and didn't think to ask that! Next time for sure."

Sam giggled, raising her hand sheepishly. "I thought it was fun. Kinda like a roller coaster ride."

"Yeah, from hell," Callie said and slid down the wall to sit with her head braced on her knees.

She'd looked sick when she'd come in so we had one more vote for transition suckery, and Sam was overruled. Sam went to sit on the other side of Callie while Dr. Ghix tried to coax Callie into drinking something green and glowing.

I made a face in sympathy before turning back to watch the screen again. I didn't need to witness Callie throwing up. It would just start a chain reaction and I didn't want to ruin the creepy feel of the bridge with my vomit. I forced my focus on space, hoping to calm my stomach, but it didn't help.

This space didn't look any different from the space we had just left. Just endless blackness filled with stars. We were going to be traveling a whole week before we got to Detritus. Hopefully, enough time to maybe get over the jump before we had to do another one. I wanted to make sure I got my hands on some sleepy bye pills before then.

Before I worried about drugs and the peacefulness of nothingness, I wanted to get some more tests done by Dr. Ghix and run through some basic self defense with the girls. Get them familiar with the alien weapons so I wouldn't have to worry about something happening to them while I was down on the planet. It didn't seem like enough time to prepare them for whatever was going to happen, but I wanted to get them started on being ready for anything as soon as possible.

They were going to be alone on the ship without Rema, Aga, Ohem, or me. Just the crew of the Solus... a crew I wasn't entirely sure we could trust with all the treachery that had happened so far.

I hadn't told them they were not coming with me to the surface. It would be a fight. Patty was going to be pissed, and I was already preparing to lock her into a closet to keep her ass on this ship. It was too much for me to worry about trying to keep an eye on them while also watching Ohem, who didn't need my help or protection—but tell that to my new trauma induced paranoia.

I couldn't be effective in a fight with my attention split in so many ways. I just needed to somehow explain that without making them feel like I thought they couldn't handle themselves, or that I was trying to mother them. They were adults and could very well make their own decisions, but I would not budge on this. I'd knock them all out if I had to.

"I want you and the girls to train while we're traveling. Self-defense and with whatever weapons they've got on this ship. We've only got a week to prepare and I want you ready," I said without looking away from the screen.

Patty moved closer to me and I raised my arm so she could tuck herself into my side. I wrapped my arm around her shoulders and hugged her to me. "It's not too late to go home. This isn't your fight, Patty," I whispered. It was my fight against the threat to my mate. Ohem loved his people. He wanted to save them and I would help him do that. I was a good wife like that. I would destroy worlds for him if he asked me too and, though the girls liked my mate and considered him a friend, it wasn't the same.

Being abducted and then thrust into an intergalactic war in the space of a few weeks was a lot to ask of the human women.

Patty looked up at me, smiled sweetly, and then bit the side of my boob hard with her evil little human teeth. I jerked back with a squeal and glared at her while I rubbed the spot she'd tried to take a chunk out of. "Ow, bitch. What the fuck?"

Patty was giving me a smile worthy of any Rijitera, all shining teeth with mean intentions. "Since violence seems to be the only thing you understand well enough not to question, I figured I'd give that a go."

She took a step towards me and I backed up into Ohem. Small though she was, the woman scared me sometimes.

"I'm not going anywhere. This *is* my fight, Jack. Someone wants to kill you and Ohem. That makes it as much my fight as it is yours. You think you're the only one that has protective instincts? The only one that wants a little revenge? Fuck that and *fuck you*. I may not be an all mighty werewolf monster, but I can pull my weight," she said with a soft tone, but the underlying menace was daring me to say something.

I did not take that dare.

"I'm sorry. Of course, you're not going anywhere. It was a stupid thing to say. Won't happen again," I said, my hands held up to ward off an attack.

Patty sniffed and nodded before she tucked herself back into my side and I slowly put my arm back around her shoulders. It was like hugging a honey badger that liked you well enough, but just one wrong move and it was game over, man.

Ohem leaned down so he could put his mouth next to my ear and whispered, "She is frightening."

I turned to him with wide eyes and whispered back, "I know, right?"

Patty snickered beside me. Both Ohem and I shuddered, and her snicker turned into laughter. I smiled down at her, hugging her tighter to me. I loved her to death. I was very much going to wait a while before dropping the 'you're fucking staying on the ship or I'll hog tie you and put you in the closet' bomb. Let her cool down first so her anger didn't build into something truly dangerous. Better to ambush her with it later and then run like hell while Ghix tranqed her.

As much as she wanted to be a part of whatever battle was going to take place, she couldn't. Not until she had all the training. Every type of training there was. Maybe a full exoskeleton battle suit, complete with laser cannon. If I could bite her and turn her into a Rijitera, I freaking would. Anything to keep her safe. God, she would be terrifying as one of my kind. She'd give my mom a run for her money. If only it was that simple.

"I will have Rema set up a training schedule for our girls," Ohem murmured to me.

I leaned my head into his arm and nodded. It was all we could do for now. It would do a lot to keep us occupied while we waited for our arrival on Detritus. I looked over my shoulder at Sam and Callie, still seated against the back wall of the bridge.

Callie was still hiding her face behind her knees trying to keep her stomach contents where they belonged, and Sam was rubbing her back and making comforting noises at her.

I looked back at Ohem and blew out my breath. "Maybe we wait until Callie doesn't feel like she's dying."

Ohem chuffed, "The glowing liquid that Ghix is trying to give her will cure her of the jump sickness."

Patty sighed and pulled away from me to march over to Ghix and snatched the medicine from his hand, making the spider doctor squawk in surprise. She smacked the back of Callie's head with her palm. Callie jerked her head up in outrage and Patty struck. Callie's mouth had been partially open with whatever she was about to yell at Patty for hitting her, making it easy for Patty to grip her jaw and dump the glowing green gunk down her throat. Patty dropped the glass and slapped her hand hard against Callie's mouth until she stopped coughing and gagging.

Once she was sure that Callie had swallowed it all and wasn't at risk of throwing it back up, she released her and stood, brushing her hands together in a job well done motion and then casually walked back to us. Callie was busy trying to light her on fire with her eyes as she walked away, but judging by the smile on her face, Patty didn't give a shit.

See? *Scary.*

Callie stood to follow but then paused, her face brightening for a moment before settling into a begrudged scowl. She continued her forward motion until she stood in front of us, her arms crossed. "While I don't appreciate the method, I suppose I'm thankful for the results," she said, fixing Patty with narrowed eyes.

I had my lips pressed tightly together, but despite my best efforts, snorts of laughter still escaped. Callie slowly turned her head towards me and bared her teeth. I pulled my mirth deep inside and smothered it until it died. Best not antagonize her further. She was liable to bite me too, and I had been bitten by enough human women tonight, thank you very much.

Callie gave me one last glare before she returned her attention to Patty, who shrugged with a grin. "You were being a baby and needed to take your medicine."

Callie sighed, dropping her arms to her side. "You're a real bitch," she said with no real venom, the twitching at the corner of her mouth belying her stern expression.

I slapped my hands together and smiled at them. "Since you feel better, it's time to hit the gym, ladies," I said, and laughed at their confused expressions.

Nineteen

Callie's fist connected with my ribs with a dull slap, and I grunted at the impact. I wrapped an arm under her armpit and tossed her across the mat. She landed with a whoosh of escaping breath and stayed down. We'd been at this for four hours. Callie was well trained and the nanos had given her an edge, but fighting with me was a losing battle and she had gotten angry and sloppy the longer I smacked her around.

"How many times do I have to tell you not to move in close? Stay outside of my reach. Quick darts and then retreat. Tire me out! Why the hell would you let me get your hands on you?" I ground out through clenched teeth. My irritation was leaking out into my voice and I took a breath before walking to where she lay prone and crouching down next to her. "If that had been an actual fight, Callie, I would have ripped you in half. Stay away from me until you are confident you have a good shot. Throat, knees, or eyes. Those are my only vulnerabilities in my human form," I said quietly, slumping back onto my butt and resting my arms on my raised knees.

Hopefully, the weapons training went better. With armor and extensive training with the various weapons on board the ship, they might stand a chance in the coming war. Callie wanted to fly the nimble ships Ohem called Ùll, which literally translated to harass.

Callie had started calling them Magpies. I didn't think it was quite a deadly enough name for the mean-looking ships, but what did I know? I wasn't a pilot. She'd been in one simulated training session so far and the very stern bossman pilot had been impressed. She'd floated into the gym on cloud nine and then I'd tossed her right off it in our sparring session. Guilt pricked at me when I looked at her defeated face.

"I thought if I got close enough it would make it harder for you to hit me," Callie mumbled.

She had her arm thrown over her eyes and was turned partially away from me. I reached over and tapped her shoulder. She turned to look at me from under the protective covering of her forearm.

I gave her a small smile and shrugged. "It puts you right in biting range. Never get close to the teeth." I sighed and rubbed the back of my neck. "We have to get you girls to use your smaller size to your advantage. Quick and nimble. We just don't have enough time before the drop onto Detritus," I said slowly, watching her out of the corner of my eye.

She sat up and blew out a breath. "We can't go down onto the planet with you, can we?" she asked with resignation.

"No. I'm sorry, Callie. I don't know what's going to be down there. It would be risky to bring you three with us," I said.

She nodded and got to her feet with a grunt, turning to look down at me with a shrug. "It's okay, I understand. We'll continue training on the ship. I may never take you on hand to hand, but I'll be the best pilot these aliens have ever seen. See how much your strength matters when I'm shooting missiles up your ass," she said with a grin and extended a hand to me. I laughed and slapped my hand into hers, letting her pull me to my feet.

"They're rail guns, actually."

I turned and spotted a very wrung out looking Sam walking towards us from her mat. I cocked my eyebrow at her in question and she smiled. "The weapons on the Magpies are rail guns. High velocity projectiles that use electromagnetic force to fire a metal rod. It uses its own mass and kinetic energy to inflict a massive amount of damage. It's much more effective than a missile," she explained and then bent over to brace her hands on her thighs. "I am so not cut out for fighting."

I patted her back in sympathy. We'd pushed them hard today. They were all going to be bruised and sore tomorrow, just to go through it all again. Patty was still dodging Aga's swipes and getting more and more frustrated by the fact he was barely trying and still getting in front of her repeatedly. I gave Sam one more pat before approaching Patty's mat, stopping right at the edge and crossing my arms to watch.

Patty feigned right and rolled out of Aga's swing, right into his kick. It sent her flying across the mat. I stepped to the side to catch her. She impacted into me with a grunt and I helped steady her on her feet once she got her breath back.

She brushed me off and pointed a finger at Aga with a snarl. "Let's go again."

Aga shook his head, his arms braced on his hips in a disapproving manner. "That's enough for today, little bug. You will have plenty of time tomorrow for more squashing."

Ouch.

Patty's shoulders stiffened, and she raised her chin in defiance. It didn't bode well for Aga. As strong as he may be, Patty was a survivor, and a devious one at that. While I didn't want her coming down to the planet with us this time, it didn't mean that with proper training and some armor, I wouldn't want her on my team in the future. He'd better sleep with one eye open for the foreseeable future.

I suppressed a flinch when she whirled around and pinned me in place with a hard stare. She held my gaze for a long moment before she sighed and her shoulders dropped in defeat. "I can't go with you, can I?"

I shook my head and Patty closed her eyes, swallowing hard before opening them again. She sniffed and lurched forward, wrapping her arms around my waist.

She squeezed me as hard as she could and I wrapped my arms around her, hunching my body over hers. "What if you die down there, Jack? What am I going to do without you?"

I tightened my hold on her. "I will not die, Patty. Ohem would never allow it and I'm hard to kill. I'll be fine."

Sam placed her hand on my bicep. "And if she gets hurt, I'll be here to help put her back together."

Callie came and slung her arm around Sam's shoulders and grinned at Patty within the circle of my arms. "I'll be here to lecture the Amazon on being a dumbass, and back you up for the ass whooping she would deserve for being careless enough to get hurt."

Patty sniffled, stepping away from me. I let her go and straightened, grateful for the girls' support. I'd been dreading this conversation, expecting a blow up fight from Patty. I should have had a little more faith in her. She wasn't stupid.

"See? Nothing to worry about. I'll be fine. Aga is going down with us and he's like our own personal walking tank. I have no worries. Ohem will be there to watch my back too," I said and shrugged. "We don't even know if there is going to be anyone there. Reports say they left. We could get there and find absolutely nothing."

Patty gave me a skeptical look before she nodded to herself and turned to face Aga. "I'll see you tomorrow then."

Aga showed his teeth in a nasty smile and left the training room.

Rema approached from where he'd been standing off to the side while we'd had our moment, flaring his wings a little. "I will have Izari monitoring our links while we are on the planet's surface. You are welcome to watch the feed on the bridge if it would give you peace of mind."

If women could melt into puddles of emotional goo, they'd be scooping us up with a bucket.

Patty stared at him for a long moment before she sprang at him, slamming her body into Rema's, her arms wrapping around him in a tight hug. The male's wings flared wide in surprise and he took a step back before a small smile tipped the corner of his mouth and he hesitantly wrapped his four arms around her, blushing the whole time.

He looked up and caught my eye; I grinned at him, wagging my eyebrows. His smile turned into a grin and he hugged Patty tighter to him, earning a sigh from the small woman. Callie came and slipped her arm around my waist. I rested mine across her shoulders and Sam hugged my other arm. We watched Rema look down at the top of Patty's head in wonder.

"Have you finished teaching your lesson in futility, then?" Ohem's voice sounded from behind us and everyone jumped and shouted in alarm, even Rema. The male had clutched Patty to him, putting his body between her and the perceived threat. Ohem could sneak up on anyone, it would seem. Even men who'd served with him for years.

Bells. He needed bells.

I untangled myself from Callie and Sam to turn my glare on my mate. He was leaning against the door jamb, looking pleased with himself.

"Shit, Ohem. Make noise when you walk," Patty scolded. Ohem's deep chuckle was his only answer. He came to stand before me and I crossed my arms, tilting my head back to stare at him expectantly.

He cocked his head at me and gestured to the large mat in the middle of the room. "Would you care to spar with me, *ursang*?"

Excitement slicked down my spine and I grinned at him, bouncing on my toes a few times.

Hell yeah, I wanted to spar with him. I turned my head and looked over my shoulder at the girls and Rema. "Y'all wanna take bets?"

Patty cackled and rubbed her hands together. "I am so recording this and starting the alien version of TikTok. Make me famous, Jack."

I turned back to Ohem and wagged my eyebrows. "What do I get if I win?"

Ohem shook his head and reached out to cup my chin in his palm, his claws pricking my cheeks. He leaned in close to my face until we were almost touching.

"Win, Rijitera?" he purred.

I growled at him, shoving his chest with both hands. Ohem laughed as he sauntered over to the mat, turning to cock his head at me in a silent challenge.

A sly smile stretched across my face as I pulled my shirt over my head, followed by my bra. Ohem's low growl made me snicker as I chucked my shoes and pulled my pants off. I added an extra swing to my hips while I walked to my mate, taking my place in front of him on the mat.

I let the change roll over me. Once my Rijitera form was complete, I crouched down into a fighting stance, flexing my claws. Ohem chuckled and *moved*. He was fast enough to blur from my sight, but the air stirred to my left and I dodged out of the way just as he popped back into existence where I'd been standing.

"Come, Rijitera, you must be faster," he mocked, blurring again.

I cocked my head and kept my muscles loose and ready. *There.* The air shifted behind me and I jumped straight up, twisting my body in mid-air like a cat to land behind Ohem. I swiped my claws across his back, scoring him shallowly. Thin lines bled yellow, dripping slowly down his skin. I'd drawn first blood, score one for me.

Ohem pivoted quickly, leaving me no time to react or move out of the way of his backhand. The blow landed solidly across my muzzle, snapping my head to the side. Shaking my head to clear it, I bared my teeth at him. Blood trickled down my lip and I licked at it, my body heating as I watched him. Score one for Ohem. I ducked his next blow, dancing around him, slashing at his exposed side and missing by centimeters. Ohem's tails lashed out, wrapping around my calf, nearly pulling me off my feet. I snarled, slashing at it with my claws. Ohem hissed, and a tentacle snapped out, catching my forearm in a bruising grip.

I lunged into him rather than trying to get away and our bodies collided with enough force to knock Ohem off his feet. He rolled with me, trying to pin me beneath him and end the fight. I gave a short bark, jerking away from him during the roll, breaking his hold on me and coming to my feet with a wolf smile.

I wasted no time and pounced on him. I hit only an empty mat, rolling out of the way in time to miss being stomped on. I popped to my feet, but Ohem was rushing me and I had to quickly dance out of the way, my claws scoring his side as he passed. More yellow blood. Two points.

"Come, General, you must be faster."

Ohem kick hit me square in the chest. My breath rushed out of me with a hoarse whoosh as I was flung backwards, barely keeping my feet. The eerie chittering sound that emerged from him made my hair stand on end as he rushed me again. I kept dodging out of his way, trying to catch my breath. His tentacles snapped in the surrounding air, and his tails tried to trip me up or wind around my legs, but I bobbed and weaved, jumping when I needed to, just managing to evade capture.

Growling, I leapt to the side, landing a punch into his wounded side, slashed with my other claw, drawing blood along the outside of his thigh. Three points. Ohem chuckled, disappearing from in front of me to reappear behind me, and the fiery burn of claws across my back signaled another point for him. We got increasingly faster until our bodies blended together across the mat, each landing blows until I lost count on who was winning and who was losing. Teeth and claws flashed, yellow and red blood spattered the mat beneath our dancing feet.

It was *glorious*.

Blood pounded through my veins in rich rivers of battle fueled lust. Ohem pulled back and crouched low, tentacles raised behind him, opening and closing threateningly. His tails thrashed around on the mat, all the lines on his body lit up. He tilted his head at a downward angle and let loose a deep, low roar. His teeth pressed forward out of his mouth, his eyes bright against the black of his face plates. It was a terrifying threat display. He was done playing with me. My hair stood up along my spine and I snarled back at him in defiance.

Ohem disappeared from in front of me. I whirled around and had to step back to avoid him, and step back again, and again. He just kept coming, too fast for me to escape, all I could do was block his blows. He wasn't clawing at me, just pushing me, herding me. My back hit the wall, and his big body pressed against mine, pinning me.

I struggled for a moment, trying to gain enough leverage, but the battle was lost. Ohem snarled into my face, all four tentacles slamming into the wall behind me. I wasn't going anywhere anytime soon, so there was only one option left to me and I was all aflutter about it. It was beyond arousing to turn my neck to him and submit. He purred, pressing his mouth firmly against the scales on my throat, biting down lightly. Every single strand of fur stood on end, and a full body shiver cascaded over me.

He released my neck after a moment, running his face up until our cheeks were pressed together, my fur against his hard plates. "I win, my *ursang*." His hand ran up my armored stomach. "You are magnificent," he murmured into my ear.

The heat between us threatened to light the gym on fire. I had enjoyed that fight entirely too much. It wasn't every day a female Rijitera found more than her match.

Just when I made steps to jump into his arms, fur and all, the clapping started. I peaked around Ohem and caught Patty collecting money from Rema while the other girls cheered.

That traitorous bitch.

I narrowed my eyes at her when she turned my way. She just grinned, shrugging her shoulders as she pocketed the silver coins the aliens used for physical currency. That she made Rema bet with real money and not the more commonly used digital stuff meant she'd wanted me to see it exchange hands. She was a psychopath.

I loved her crazy ass *so much*.

Rema was sweet for thinking I'd win. I'd file that away for a later favor owed. Still, I'd have bet against myself too. Ohem was a beast. It was almost a shame neither of us could actually hurt the other. I was very curious about which one of us would come out on top of a life or death fight. The little cat scratches we'd given each other were nothing but foreplay.

I tilted my head up to catch Ohem's eyes, and he winked two of his four eyes at me in a gesture he'd picked up from us Earth girls.

He'd win.

I was pulled from my ogling by Sam trotting up to us, a big shit-eating grin on her cute face.

"That was amazing! I got a little nervous for a second, thinking you two were fighting for real."

She was so adorable, I just couldn't handle it.

I shifted back, crossed my arms over my naked chest, and leaned into Ohem's side. "Just a little friendly competition. I couldn't actually hurt the big guy, but a few love taps? That's totally on the table," I said, nudging Ohem with my elbow.

He chuckled, laying a hand on my shoulder. "She couldn't hurt me, even if she tried her hardest."

The smug sonofabitch. I elbowed him harder, and he caught me in a bear hug, laughing. I wriggled out of his arms to glare at him. It only made him laugh harder. My lips were twitching, so I tightened them into a thin line. My mate needed no further encouragement.

Patty came and handed me my clothes, still smirking. "Yeah, he totally whooped your ass. He was going easy on you and *still* whooped your ass."

First the betting and now the trash talking? This bitch.

We really were best friends.

I pulled my clothes on before draping an arm around both Patty and Callie's shoulders, steering them out of the sparring room. Sam trailed behind us discussing the fight with an overly enthused Rema while Ohem stalked behind us, his eyes burning holes into my ass. I added some extra sass to my steps.

"Have y'all been to the nightclub yet?"

Twenty

The blue-gray planet took up the entire vid screen on the bridge. It was probably twice the size of Earth, with more land masses, and what looked like a nasty storm system brewing right over where we were supposed to land.

Detritus looked like a hellhole of mass proportions, and reports from the drones the Solus sent out told a story of high humidity, violent thunderstorms, and enough jungle to make this trip extra shitty.

The last week had flown by, so much so that looking at the planet now, I didn't know if I was quite ready to leave the girls behind. I swallowed hard and my hands shook where I had them tucked into the crook of my elbows. What if something happened on the ship while I was down there? We'd run the girls ragged with hand to hand training, and learning how to handle all the various weapons Ohem thought they could handle, like the plasma rifle they'd tested out when I'd first visited Dr. Ghix.

Callie was a crack shot and would be armed while we were investigating the surface, giving me some more peace of mind. Patty had improved a lot fighting with Rema instead of Aga. Rema was more patient, though no less hard on her. They'd been adorable to watch. Sam was still hopeless, the poor thing. She worked hard, though, I'd give her that. The woman didn't quit. She'd earned a lot of respect from the instructors we'd had working with them just by taking her licks and getting back up every time.

We'd run through security checks a dozen times, with Aga questioning anyone who threw up flags. We'd set up monitoring systems that ran an algorithm that would raise alarms if certain trigger words were said by anyone, and Aga had an entire crew of thoroughly vetted members monitoring the feeds at all times. He was sure the ship would be fine, but security was up, guards were on alert, just in case. The Solus was on top of its people.

So why couldn't I shake the feeling of dread? Maybe I was nervous of finding the ruins of my people down there, or nervous we'd find nothing and all this was a waste of time. I didn't know for sure. Something had my hackles raised. Ohem had sensed my restlessness over the last few days and done his best to fuck it out of me, to no avail. We'd gone to the nightclub, I'd danced all over him and had been pulled into a dark corner with his hand clamped tightly over my mouth while he made all my dreams come true, and I still had a stone of anxiety sitting heavy in my stomach.

The girls and I had explored all over the ship, finding some wild stuff. One being a jungle in a room that gave the illusion of having no end. They had the tropical version of Central Park on a damn spaceship. It had walking paths, animals, and different kinds of flowers. It really felt like we were in the jungle and not in space. Ohem had said it was necessary for some aliens on board, so they could relax in something close to their natural environment. The Solus had literally everything.

Callie had taken us on several simulated flights, where I discovered I got violently air sick when multiple barrel rolls were performed.

That was a fun revelation.

Callie was one hell of a pilot and had all the flight officers fighting over her. I was happy for her, I just never wanted to fly with her again as long as I lived.

She'd gotten a kick out of finally having something over me. I was still tempted to smack her around a little. She'd been way too maliciously gleeful during those sims. Patty had cackled her head off the whole damn time and screamed for more. She and Callie had bonded while I vomited into a bucket provided by a grinning Sam.

I'd had my double date with Ket'ak and Izari. That would have been a lot more fun if Ket'ak's eyes didn't split in so many directions when more than one person was talking. Ohem had been overly amused at my valiant efforts to keep my dinner down. Izari had winked at me and hadn't seemed bothered by my reaction to her husband's eyes. They were obviously deeply in love with each other, and it was nice to have a couple to hang out with until Patty sealed the deal with Rema.

The highlight of the past week, however, was the weight lifting competition Patty had egged Ohem and Aga into. They'd had to bring in crates from storage when the metal weights weren't heavy enough for the two males. The training room had been filled with aliens shouting and taking bets. Patty and I had made out like bandits. Why anyone bet again Ohem was beyond me. Aga was a tank, to be sure, but Ohem was a *monster*. He'd trounced Aga in the end. Aga had laughed and been good natured about the whole thing. He hadn't been put out at all about losing. We'd also become very good friends during this week since I was always with him, helping with security.

I'd also gone to a few therapy sessions with one of the Healers to deal with the nightmares and separation anxiety I got anytime Ohem wasn't in the room with me, as a result of his brush with death. It was helping, but I still had nightmares and—if I was lucky—nothing on Detritus was going to make that worse. Looking at the planet, I didn't think I was going to get that wish. The dread ball in my stomach was warning me of something bad.

I squeezed my eyes shut and took a deep breath to calm my anxiety. I was a big bad Rijitera. I could handle my shit, dammit. I would protect Ohem and my girls. Nothing bad was going to happen to them. I repeated that mantra in my head over and over until Ohem's hand on my shoulder had me opening my eyes to look up at him.

"It's time to go, Jack. The shuttle is ready."

I nodded once, my heart pounding in my chest and I turned to give Patty and the others a bone-crushing hug goodbye.

"You stay safe down there, Jack. Don't make me come and get you," Patty whispered to me.

I kissed the top of her head. "I'll be fine. Stay on the bridge with the others. Love you guys," I said and left the bridge before I changed my mind and turned this ship around.

"They will be fine. The bridge is on lockdown while we are gone," Ohem said.

I just nodded. The sooner we got to the planet's surface and got this done, the sooner we could get back on the ship.

Please God, don't let any of these alien motherfuckers on this ship try anything.

We took the portal to the hanger the humans had dubbed Hanger Force One or HFO for short.

Rema was waiting for us with Dr. Ghix in front of a mean-looking transport shuttle. Two large rail guns were mounted underneath it and it was heavily armored. Ohem was taking no chances. There were thirty of the same transport shuttles all being filled to bursting with red armored aliens carrying big guns. We were taking a small army down with us. What was really badass was Aga. The big green crocodile was in the deadliest looking armor I'd ever seen. It was dark forest green with nasty spikes over the shoulders. He had a sword over his back.

What medieval fuckery was this?

I moved closer so I could get a better look at the sword. He was standing behind Rema and Dr. Ghix, directing crew members into the right shuttle, so I stepped between the two males and tilted my head. It *was* a sword in a scabbard and everything.

Aliens had swords? That was some mind bending shit. Did all of us evolve from the same person or something? Green buttons, kissing, club dressing, and now swords.

Aga glanced over his shoulder and caught me inspecting his weapon and turned to face me. He reached over his shoulder, pulled the blade out of its sheath in a smooth, practiced motion, and held it up for my viewing pleasure. The blade was blue metal and looked wicked sharp, like a razor blade. It was thinner than I expected.

"Why a sword? Why not something that shoots plasma?" I asked him.

His smile was predatory. "I enjoy the close up kill. Can you really claim to be a warrior if you don't watch the life drain from your enemy's eyes?"

I looked at Ohem with wide eyes. "I can see why you're nervous about our friendship now. Never send me and Aga out alone together."

Aga laughed, pointing a claw tipped finger at me. "There would be no one left, Rijitera. We would kill them all." He was still laughing after he put his sword into its sheath and went back to directing.

Ohem pinched my chin with his thumb and forefinger, tilting my head up. "No fighting alongside Aga."

I grinned at him. I would promise nothing. Ohem growled at me and pulled me over to stand in front of Dr. Ghix. The good doctor smiled at me and handed over a box. I scowled at it in confusion, but took it. He'd poked and prodded me a couple of times over the last week, and I was a little twitchy around him now. I opened the box with a dramatic amount of caution, hearing Dr. Ghix sigh in exasperation had me snickering. Inside the box was a black cloth. I frowned at the doctor while I pulled it out and held it up. It was a black bodysuit.

I gave it a shake and raised my eyebrow. "What's this?"

Dr. Ghix smiled. "Just put it on, Jack."

He gestured behind me and I turned to see a raised cloth changing room set up between crates waiting to be loaded. Shrugging, I went to put on the catsuit, snapped the curtains closed behind me, and quickly shucked off my clothes and shoes. I stared hard at the suit, trying to figure out how to put the damn thing on. There was no zipper and the neck hole wasn't big enough to step into.

I pulled on it to see if it stretched and the back split open so fast I thought I tore it apart. Oh, right. Everything they used on this ship was magnetic. They didn't even know what a zipper was. I stepped into the legs, pulling it over my body. It was a very soft material. As soon as I had it on properly, the back sealed up on its own. Smart clothes were so cool.

I slipped on my red flats and walked out to see Dr. Ghix holding up a pair of socks. I sighed and bent to put them on, too.

"Leave the shoes off. The cloth you are wearing will harden into a type of armor more akin to a shell. It shouldn't rip when you change and isn't made from any technology. Just a special type of fabric made from the secretions of an insect found on my planet. It should be hard enough to protect you from most plasma blasts. I know you heal quickly, but Sam wanted to negate the need to." He smiled at me. "She worked very hard to find something your nanos wouldn't reject."

My throat got tight. I cleared it, smiling at the doctor. The smile crumpled with the urge to cry. I took a couple of breaths and cleared my throat again.

"You tell her thank you for me. Tell her I love it, and I love her," I said.

I was proud my voice didn't wobble. Damn human woman, making me an emotional mess. I could have told her on my neck link, but I didn't feel like blubbering right before we left. It would ruin my reputation with the crew.

Ohem placed his hand on the small of my back. "Monitor our friends, Urli," Ohem said to Ghix.

I turned my head towards the doctor, mouthing, "Urli?", as Ohem ushered me into the ship. I caught the doctor's grimace before the door shut us inside. It was a terrible name for a huge spider man. Ohem used his hands on my shoulder to gently push me into a seat and pulled a hard harness made from the same porous fibers as the joints of his armor down over me. It snicked into place in the seat back at my hips and he jerked on it a few times to make sure it was secure before taking a seat next to me, pulling his own harness down.

Rema and Aga took their seats across from me, and a few other soldiers settled in around them, filling the empty seats quickly, but no one sat on the other side of me and I couldn't help but snicker at Ohem. He gave me a long look, but didn't rise to the bait. I reached across to give his thigh a squeeze and waited for the liftoff.

I didn't have to wait long. The clank of the claw connecting to the hull of the shuttle set my teeth on edge. We were lifted smoothly; the engines hummed to life and then we were accelerating down the tube and out into space. The door became transparent, giving me an unfettered view into space.

The shuttle shuddered for a moment as the engines fired us faster across the void. In under five minutes, we were entering the atmosphere. The shuttle dropped twice and my stomach dropped with it. Spaceships should be immune to turbulence. It wasn't right that we were on a super advanced alien craft and the air currents still battered us around. I closed my eyes to think happy thoughts, anything to keep my gorge from rising.

The ship dropped sharply, shuddered, and rose again. The pilot spoke over our links. "Storm is pretty bad. Brace yourselves."

Understatement of the fucking century.

The ship jerked like it was being tossed back and forth between a giant's hands. I had a death grip on Ohem's thigh and his warm hand over mine did absolutely nothing to calm me down. I hated flying.

Hated. It.

Callie was a goddamned crazy person for wanting to do this.

I cracked an eye open to see if anyone else was having a hard time. Aga was smiling, *the psychopath*. Rema was *sleeping*. The elf was passed out cold, like none of this was happening. His head jerked from side to side when the ship dipped up and down. The rest of the soldiers looked bored. I peeked at Ohem to see him leaning back, body relaxed, just going with the flow.

All aliens were crazy.

I shut my eyes again and waited for it to be over. I never used to be this way on Earth. I'd flown all over the world and didn't get sick. Wonder if it had anything to do with falling out of space in a glorified U-Haul?

I was going to need so much therapy after this war was over. Funny how ripping someone's spine out didn't send me into a tailspin of anxiety, but add some turbulence and I was a mess. The Healer on the Solus had said it was all about control and losing it. Killing someone was me in control, falling out of the sky was me *not* in control. Made sense to me.

A thud rattled us around like rocks in a can and my eyes flew open. Rema opened his eyes and yawned, stretching his arms over his head, and shook his head as if to clear the sleep from his mind. He caught me staring at him and smiled.

I glared at him. "You disgust me."

Rema frowned in confusion and looked at Ohem, who just shrugged his shoulders and lifted his harness. Panicking that he was trying to kill himself, I made a move to slam his harness back down and he grabbed my wrist, chuckling. "We've landed, Jack."

Twenty-One

I looked out the window. The entire planet was a jungle of gray, with wind whipping gray trees and bushes around. We'd landed in a valley that ran the length of the treeline for miles. It almost looked like it had been clear cut at one point in time, and short gray grass had taken over the space. It was weird that the jungle hadn't reclaimed the cleared out spaces after thousands of years of no maintenance from my people. It didn't look natural.

Rain pounded the glass of the door, and when Ohem stood, the door slid away, letting the howling sound from the storm inside. I shielded my eyes from the sting of the rain with my forearm. Someone tapped me on my shoulder, and I turned to see Rema holding out a black ski mask with a face of solid plastic instead of the mouth and eye holes. I pulled it on and almost yelped when it hardened into a helmet, letting out a hiss of air when it pressurized.

Rema's grin disappeared behind the red helmet that melted over his face, but I hoped he could still feel the heat of my glare. I sighed, at least we were on the ground and the rain wasn't in my eyes anymore.

This helmet was uncomfortable as all hell, though. I ran my fingers along the seam at my neck and couldn't find it. It had melted into my suit. I clawed it, but my nails only scraped along the hard surface.

I was panicking again. Ohem's hand closed over mine. "It's voice activated, Jack. Retract," he said, and my helmet lost its firm feeling and went back to cloth. I pulled it off, sighing in relief, and was immediately bombarded by the rain and had to pull it back on. It hardened again automatically, but this time I didn't panic now that I knew I could take it off.

"Thanks," I said.

Ohem leaned down. "You need to keep it on until the storm dissipates. Do not take it off, Jack. I'm watching you."

I stuck my tongue out at him and, like Rema, his amused look was swallowed up by his helmet covering his face.

I hoped they both got water under their armor and it caused a rash.

I followed Ohem out of the ship and into the storm. The wind almost knocking me over when I stepped out of the shuttle and I had to grab onto Ohem's arm to get my balance. Why couldn't I ever land on a planet that was temperate? Was it too much to ask? Keeping a firm hand on Ohem, I looked around. Gray trees, gray grass, horrible gray sky.

This planet sucked. Everything was just varying shades of gray, from black to almost white. It was depressing. What had my ancestors seen on the planet to settle here? Maybe it was like a way station or something. Those always seemed to be in the most remote, shitty spots.

We gathered with the rest of the soldiers and crew that Aga had insisted come with us, the big crocodile was in the middle of it all issuing orders and scowling at people. He wasn't wearing a helmet and didn't seem bothered by the stinging rain pelting his eyeballs. He caught sight of us and waved Rema over, the two joining forces to get everything organized. Cargo vehicles were being unloaded from some shuttles and crew members were piling into them, forming a convoy line of sleek black hovering machines that vaguely resembled the armored transport vehicles back on Earth. Only without the wheels or obvious guns.

Ohem ushered me into one vehicle. There were no seats inside, just hand holds hanging from the ceiling. I reached up to grab one and immediately regretted it. It was squishy, like I'd grabbed a fist full of jellyfish for stability.

Ohem's head was turned, no doubt watching to see how I'd react. I swallowed my shriek of surprise and disgust to give him a smile. He and Rema had enjoyed enough entertainment from me today, thank you very much. Looking over I saw that Rema and Aga were leaning into the vehicle waiting for my screams, Rema's shoulders shaking with silent laughter. Pricks.

I gave them all the bird and held on tighter to the jellyfish handle. Why make it squishy? Did it help mold to your hand or something? *Aliens were fucking weird.*

Once everyone was loaded into the vehicles, the line started forward. Mine and Ohem's craft was in the middle, the command vehicle protected from front and back. Aga and Rema had taken the lead vehicle. It was an odd feeling to be riding in a truck-like thing but not have wheels on the ground.

Hovering only a few feet over the ground made for faster travel. I'd asked why we didn't just fly there and they'd told me that Vero had very good ground to air weaponry, making an approach from the air dangerous. We were going to ride in from the ground into where we thought their left flank was. Intel still had found no sign of Vero's soldiers. The drones were unable to get good images in the storm, so we were treating this like there were enemy soldiers waiting for us.

I'd been slightly disappointed that this super advanced alien civilization didn't have robots or drones that wouldn't be knocked out by the weather. Ohem had explained that AI was unreliable and dangerous at the best of times so no sentient race trusted them, and that drones were small flying crafts, so of course, weather affected them. Science fiction was so off the mark on a lot of things. I was going to have a sit down meeting with some Hollywood directors back on Earth one of these days and make a damn fortune with a new, more realistic movie.

The vehicle shuddered as the wind battered us around and I kept my feet by sheer force of will. The soldiers and Ohem were completely at ease with the tossing, their stance widened for stability. A booming crack of thunder made me jump, it was followed by another and another. The winds picked up and tossed us around some more before our transport came to a gradual stop. Ohem's head tilted to the side, and I tapped him on the back. He turned, his helmet retracted, revealing his grim face.

"What's going on?" I asked him, looking around at the confused soldiers around me.

Ohem dropped his hand from the jellyfish holds. "We've stopped. Much too soon to have made it to the ruins." He went still in a way that let me know he was talking through his link, probably to Rema.

I watched his face as emotion rolled over it. For having stiff plates instead of skin on the upper part of his face, he was very expressive now that I knew what to look for. The widening and then narrowing of his eyes, the tensing of his lower jaw, the smooth black skin pulling tight over the muscles there, Izi lighting softly, then going dark. Surprise and then disbelief followed by despair.

Something big was going on. Something bad. I stepped closer to him to press my palm against his chest. He had his war armor on; it was rougher than his regular wear, like a shark's skin.

Ohem placed his hand over mine. "Rema said they have found a settlement. We need to get out."

He turned to the door that opened on the side of the transport and stepped out, the wind and rain rushing in behind him. I checked to make sure my helmet was on securely before following him out.

The storm had reached new heights, lighting lancing across the sky, blinding me every few seconds, but the clear face of my helmet darkened after the third flash of lightning, saving my eyes from the blinding effect. Thunder boomed near constantly now and the wind was trying its best to pick the convoy up and toss it away like a bunch of errant toys. Whoever was driving each vehicle deserved a raise for keeping them where they needed to be.

"We have to reach Rema. He is with Aga at the front. Stay close." Ohem's voice came from inside my helmet, not from my neck link like I'd been expecting. I followed behind him up the line of hovercrafts, leaning into the wind to keep my feet.

I ran into Ohem when he stopped abruptly, smacking my forehead against his back where his ridges rose through his armor. I stepped around him, scowling and rubbing my helmeted forehead like it would help. My hand dropped to my side in shock when I turned to see what had stopped him. Through the dust and rain, was a settlement. A dozen domed tents were scattered over an area of open valley no bigger than a football field. That wasn't what was causing the sinking feeling in my stomach though. There were bodies laid out all over the settlement... some of them were too small to be adults.

There were children laid out on the wet ground, out in the rain. I made to rush to the kid closest to me, but Aga's hand on my shoulder jerked me to a halt. I turned to glare at him, but his face was hard.

The grim line of his mouth quelled whatever rebuke I was about to say. "They are dead," he said, his voice flat.

I looked back at the little form in the rain, my heart beating painfully in my chest. A knot formed in my throat as I watched the mud and water flow around the small shape.

Why'd they leave a kid to die out in the storm? I looked at the other bodies spread across the settlement, dread making goosebumps spread across my skin.

"What about the rest of them?" I asked Aga.

He shook his head before dropping his hand from my shoulder. "They are all dead. The whole settlement. Fifty adults and fourteen children."

Kids. I couldn't handle dead kids. They were almost sacred to my people. We fucking loved children.

Rema walked out from between the domes, his body stiff. He stopped in front of Ohem, shaking. His helmet melted away from his face, his already pearly skin was bleached of color, eyes haunted by whatever horror he'd just seen. He took a few steps away from us and retched. When he was done, he stood wiping his mouth with the back of his hand and came to stand in front of Ohem again, who placed both of his hands on Rema's shoulders.

"What have you discovered, my friend?" Ohem asked, softly, his hands trembled where he'd placed them on Rema.

"It's a disease of some type. It—it melted their skin. There is another settlement just past this one. It is the same there. They couldn't have been here long, these are quick shelters, and there are crates still needing unpacking." Rema's voice was tight with emotion.

I went to him and placed my hand on his arm. His eyes met mine as tears gathered in them. "There were babies, Jack. Little babies," Rema said around clenched jaws, whatever tears he was shedding were being swept away with the rain and wind.

I closed my eyes, trying to block out the image of dead babies from entering my mind, and swallowed. "Was there anyone alive?" I asked, voice hoarse.

Rema's face was terrible, he shook his head slowly. "No."

"This is a dead planet, they should have never come here," Aga murmured, more to himself than to anyone around him.

Ohem stepped around Rema, closing the distance between us and the first corpse in a single leap. I watched as he crouched next to the body to examine it. I let my hand slip from Rema's arm as I passed him to join my mate. I walked until I was close enough to see the body in the rain. I wished I'd stayed away.

It was a female; she had her arm outstretched towards the little body slumped on the ground near to hers. Her green tinted skin was covered in oozing lesions. It appeared as if the skin had melted in spots, the muscle and bone showing on her arms and legs. Her teeth were visible through the wound on her cheek, bright white against the carnage of her wounds. Her face was a ruined mess of flesh and blood. The sickly sweet stench of rot lingered under the smell of the rain, only reaching my nose when the wind shifted.

I didn't want to, but I had to make sure. The child was slumped forward over its legs, like it had taken a seat and then collapsed forward out of exhaustion. I reached out a shaky hand to touch the little one's shoulder and pulled it back. Its head flopped sideways, exposing a neck that was hanging on by tendons alone, the skin and muscle melted away. Its face was gone, much like the mother. I couldn't even tell what sex the child was.

I gently laid the poor thing on its side and then wrenched away to crawl a short distance, croaking "retract" so I could pull my helmet off and vomit. I threw everything I ate that day up and then dry heaved for several minutes. Ohem's hand touched my upper back between my shoulder blades. I wiped at my mouth and looked up at him from my knees.

"What is this, Ohem?" I was crying, and the storm was stinging my eyes, but I didn't care. We came to fight soldiers and found dead kids instead. I couldn't fight a disease. My claws couldn't seek justice for that baby lying in the mud, just out of reach from its mother.

Ohem pulled me to my feet, encircling me in his arms. "It's a sickness. We will task some of the crew to bury the bodies and send samples to Dr. Ghix." His voice was filled with a raw grief that made me cry harder into his chest. Rema had said there were babies. *Oh, god*. What was this?

When my sobs subsided, Ohem helped me pull on my helmet again. I looked back at the child on its side where I'd left it. Diseases were supposed to be an Earth thing.

"I thought the nano's cured everything. How could they die from a disease?"

"They don't have nanos," Aga said. I looked up to find him in front of me, still without a helmet in the rain. His fists were clenched at his side. "They don't have nanos," he repeated.

I didn't understand. I spun to look at Ohem, a question on my face.

Ohem shook his head. "That's not possible."

Aga snarled and pointed at the domes. "They don't have nanos. They've died from sickness." He looked at me. "They are separatists. Those that leave the Unity to set up colonies on unclaimed planets. This one is dead. Meaning it is off limits. No one should have been here." Aga was well and truly angry now. I'd only ever seen him good natured, even when threatened. I still didn't understand what was going on. Ohem was flashing threateningly, and Aga was still growling at him.

I stepped between the two males and held up my hands to both of them. "What's going on? What does that mean?"

Ohem bared his teeth at Aga before answering me, "Separatists are a rumor. There are none. These people are from outside the Unity."

Aga laughed, his voice filled with bitterness, and pointed a claw at my mate. "You are still blind, my friend. Even after the betrayal of your brother, you choose to believe his lies. The Unity's lies. These are separatists. They flee the Unity for a better life. Open your eyes and *see*." Aga gave Ohem a final sneer before turning on his heel and stalking off to the group of crew members gathered by the convoy.

I watched Ohem's face, watched his internal struggle play out across his body with whatever all that had meant. His Izi had flared brightly with his anger and then died as Aga had talked.

"What is he talking about, Ohem?" I asked, keeping my voice soft.

Ohem's eyes flicked to my face and his hands flexed at his side. "There are rumors of Unity corruption. That all is not what it seems to those of us living a life of privilege. Rumors of starving people, of forced labor. Sex trafficking, slavery, death sentences. Rumors of people fleeing to out planets like this one. To start a new life free of the Unity. I did not believe them. I still did not believe them even after Rakis tried to kill me, thinking it was only my brother and Vero and not the entire system of government." Ohem raised a trembling hand and ran it down his face. "Am I a fool, Jack?" he asked me in an anguished voice. His body was hunched forward, like he wanted to curl in on himself.

I went to him, wrapping my arms around his waist. "Not a fool. Just a male that believed in his people."

Having your illusions shattered was a jarring and traumatizing thing. Ohem looked like this was the very worst day of his life. These people had run from their planet, just to die from some stupid ass disease. Why didn't they have nanos?

"A fool all the same. I would see things, hear things, and ignore them. Aga has been vocal about the Unity and I would dismiss him. It is a terrible thing to understand at long last." Ohem shuddered, pulling me tighter against him. His heart was thudding in his chest. He took several deep, trembling breaths, and then sighed.

"I will try to make this right. That is all I can do," he croaked.

We walked back to the shuttle together, my arm wrapped tightly around Ohem, offering my support while he went through his existential crisis. Ohem left me with Rema while he went to Aga to get the dead buried and the samples gathered for Ghix.

"Why didn't they have nanos?" I asked.

Rema started, looking down at me like he was surprised to see me. He blinked a few times and flicked his wings. "They take them out when they flee. They believe in starting over in truth, from what I understand, and that means rejecting anything the Unity has handed out. Like nanos. Their children would be born pure. Foolishness. It has led them to their deaths." Rema's wings closed in around him, protecting him from the worst of the rain. He still hadn't put his helmet back on, his hair was plastered all over his face, torn free from his braid by the violent winds. He said nothing more, and I didn't want to push him. The male looked haunted.

I watched as the crew and soldiers worked together to dig in the storm, setting up a system that kept the water out of the graves so they could place the wrapped bundles into them and cover them up. They'd brought all kinds of equipment for excavating any ruins we'd found. Now that equipment was being used to dig graves. Ohem and Aga were off to the side having a deep discussion by the looks of it. Aga nodded and embraced Ohem. The two males hugged for a long moment before breaking apart.

"He has been gone for many years. He barely goes home to Stellios, and then he only goes home to see his mother and family," Rema said. I gave him a confused look, and he smiled sadly. "He has been on the Solus for years. He doesn't understand what has been going on with the Unity. He goes where he is needed. There have been many, many wars that have kept him away from Stellios. He barely knows the people he fights for."

I nodded, understanding.

"It would seem that almost every time we were due to come home for a time, a war would break out with some out planet and we would be called away again." I looked sharply at Rema and he nodded. "Considering Rakis's actions, I think we were kept away intentionally."

My eyes widened. This was some deep government conspiracy shit. Rakis hadn't wanted Ohem to look too closely at things back home, what better way to keep the born warrior away than to send him off to war.

"Why didn't you say anything to him when you suspected that was the case?" I asked. I dreaded his answer, but Rema only smiled that sad smile again.

"I didn't know until Rakis attempted to kill Ohem. Why would I? We had always been told from young children that the Unity was a harmonious government that took care of its people equally. I am not from a family as well known or as exalted as the At'ens, but my own House is connected well enough. I noticed nothing amiss in my travels on Stellios and Axsia. All appeared well. I joined the fleet when I came of age and have rarely been on Stellios since then. Only Aga has made comments about the corruption. He is from an out planet annexed during the last war on Xemia. He would understand better than most the true nature of the Unity."

Holy shit, my poor mate was having his reality stripped from him. He'd been freaking Red Pilled. And poor Aga. He was the Morpheus in this equation, and no one had believed him. Rema's face got that far off look when someone was talking via their links and I waited for the news. It came from Ghix's frantic voice from my link. "Enemy incoming!"

Twenty-Two

I HAD TAKEN A single step towards Ohem when the first blast incinerated a soldier a few yards in front of me; the percussion throwing me backwards with enough force to dent the side of the transport shuttle when I impacted into the side of it. Something crunched in my back, ripping a scream from me.

The pain flared white hot for a single moment, stealing my breath, then I was up and running towards Ohem. I passed a down Rema on my mad dash across the space between myself and my mate. I couldn't stop to make sure he was okay. Icy fingers of fear were wrapped around my heart, trying to crush it. I couldn't see Ohem.

Another blast exploded ahead of me and I rolled aside to avoid being thrown again. The valley erupted into chaos, with soldiers and crew screaming in pain or yelling orders, links forgotten in the fight. The storm still raged around us like a hurricane, the rain and wind making it almost impossible to determine where the hell we were being shot at from.

I heard the roar from my right, like wrath incarnate. I tore the helmet from my head with a clawed hand and shifted my form to leap over a transport shuttle rolled onto its side and found Ohem engaged in a vicious fight with a huge alien creature. A cross between a rhino and a dog, the thing had three large horns on its face that it was using to try to gore my mate. It roared again when Ohem opened a gash along its flank.

I felt the shot coming this time and jumped out of the way in time to watch one of the transport shuttles engulfed in a fireball. The movement drew the creature's attention to me and it charged me while I picked myself up from the ground where I'd landed to avoid being blown to ash. Ohem snarled, grabbed the thing by its leg, and dragged it backwards away from me. The rhino dog whirled around to snap its great teeth at Ohem.

Ohem bitch slapped it with all six claws, tearing away one horn from its face. I looked to the sky to spot whatever craft was fucking shooting at me, but I couldn't see shit through the storm clouds and had to dodge out of the way when it shot at me again.

This blast caught the rhino dog's hip, shredding its back legs. The unholy sound that came from the beast's mouth had me covering my ears with both hands. Ohem jumped up to straddle its neck and wrenched its head violently to one side, breaking its neck in a satisfying crunch of bone. The shrieking stopped, and I lowered my hands to look at my mate. He stepped away from the dead creature, his helmet retracting away from his head as he came to stand in front of me and met my gaze, his eyes alight with rage.

The air whined. I snarled and pushed Ohem back as hard as I could. The shot hit right between us. White sweltering heat blinded me. The skin burned away from the front of my body, my right eye searing in its socket. I screamed, my tongue melting in my mouth from the heat, choking me. I was thrown back, landing on my side with a crunch of bone. My body swelled for a second, and then the pain was gone. I was healing damn near instantly. Whatever we'd done to my nanos, they were now working double time.

I lurched forward on all fours to where Ohem lay. He was already getting to his feet, his armor smoking where deep rends showed his bloody skin on his stomach and chest. Fresh liquid armor was filling the torn spaces and solidifying again, self patching.

"Are you okay?" I panted.

Ohem cracked his neck before nodding. "Yes, *ursang*. Only a few scratches. Where are they shooting from?"

I shook my head. I didn't know. I had seen no ships. It was only the whine of sound and then the heat from the shot. I searched the sky, but could only see the lightning in the clouds. I looked towards Ohem's crew, Aga was pulling the wounded to the treeline. I was relieved to see Rema limping after him, shouting orders at the soldiers still able to walk on their own. Thunder boomed, but it sounded further away. The rain was also lessening in intensity, though the wind was still trying its hardest to sweep us off the planet.

I returned my gaze to Ohem's. "I didn't see it. Only heard it."

Ohem bared his teeth at the sky. "We must make it to the trees. They will have a harder time targeting us under the canopy."

We sprinted towards the tree, but no one shot at us again. A feeling of foreboding settled over me like an ominous cloud. They'd been hell bent on killing us, they had the element of surprise, and we were running. Why stop?

I skidded to a halt just inside the treeline, Ohem stopped with me. Soldiers were still fleeing deeper into the forest, with others holding a line to cover their backs. Aga was with those staying to cover our retreat, holding a rifle in hand and looking mean.

I trotted to him, stopping just beside him. "Where are they coming from?"

Aga cringed while giving me a side eye. "You sound horrible in this form, Rijitera."

I snarled at him. I wasn't in the mood for jokes. Someone had ambushed us and sent a damn mutant dog after my mate.

The corner of Aga's mouth quirked. "It is an Aš. A small, fast craft we fondly call the Insect. They have it cloaked, but I saw the shimmer as it passed by. Don't worry, Jack. We brought something just for this occasion. Had we not been stopped by the separatist village, they wouldn't have ambushed us." Aga raised his weapon's muzzle to the sky. "That was only a scout. There will be more coming our way soon. We caught him by surprise. I don't think they expected to find us here. It's the only reason we are still alive." Aga jerked his chin in the fleeing soldier's direction. "They are regrouping further in. Go with them. I will cover your back."

I nodded and went back to where Ohem was waiting for me. He hadn't moved to approach Aga with me and had instead watched the sky beyond the trees. I didn't know if it was just him wanting to make sure we weren't being followed or that he didn't want to speak to Aga. Either way, I was over this planet already. The rain slicked down his armor in rivets. When he turned to look at me, his face was cold.

"Aga says to stay with the rest of the crew. He'll follow us further into the jungle."

Ohem glanced at Aga before turning his yellow eyes to me. "Very well. Lead the way, *ursang*."

I hesitated for a few seconds before turning to jog after the rest of our crew. I wanted to ask him if he was okay, wanted to hug him, but shit kept happening. Up ahead, Rema's voice was an indistinct murmur giving quiet orders. The sound of weapons slapping against hands and the grunts of the wounded being moved broke the eerie quiet of the jungle.

We got to them quickly. Most of the soldiers were on their feet, looking ready for some payback. They had their rifles in hand, forming a solid line on four sides, with Rema and the wounded in the middle. They parted to let us through, left fist over chest salutes as we passed each row of soldiers. I repeated it back to them, my lips pulled back over my teeth.

Rema's wings flared out when I got close to him, his eyes meeting mine in a brief shared look of relief that the other was alive. "I am glad to see you both well." He eyed the shiny parts of Ohem's armor where it had patched itself after the rhino dog almost eviscerated him. "If a little worse for wear."

I shrugged. "There was a mutant dog."

Rema's eyebrows pinched in confusion. "What is a dog?"

I waved his question away with one clawed hand and then pointed at Ohem's stomach. "What was it?"

Ohem gripped my finger in his hand and pulled me to him with it. "It was a Khuuks. They are used for tracking. It was set loose to find something, the Aš was following it." I ran my claws down the sealed tears in his armor, they slashed down his chest to groin. If he'd been wearing his usual gear, it would have spilled his guts all over the grass.

They'd sent their hound to sniff out something, with its handler close behind, and had stumbled onto us by accident. Had they been checking on the settlement? Everyone there was dead.

Or would they have stumbled onto the same horror we had? Too many unanswered questions. We still needed to find the ruins of my people. Obviously, Vero's people hadn't left like we thought, and now they knew we were here.

"What now?" I asked, dropping my hand from Ohem's chest and shifting back to human.

"We take care of the Aš and then continue on our path."

A muscle twitch in my face. "How do we take care of something we can't see?" I asked with the infinite patience that I totally had.

Ohem's Izi flared briefly in what to him was a broad smile. "We use bait."

• • • ● • ● • ● • • •

When he'd said bait, I thought he'd meant a person, but no. A team of three slunk to the edge of the trees and threw into the clearing a small black ball, about the size of a grapefruit, and then hightailed it back to our position like their asses were on fire. We were maybe two hundred yards from the treeline. Close enough to see our abandoned transport shuttles, two of them still smoldering, and the black, scarred dirt where the rail gun rounds had killed a few of our people. Rema had explained what the weapon was, and it made sense.

Plasma didn't have a percussion wave as it didn't use projectiles, but the rail gun fired metal rods at faster than light speed. It had been a light and fire show I wouldn't soon forget. Nothing on Earth could compare to that kind of raw power. If it had hit me dead on, I would have died. No super healing was going to fix that.

I kept my eye on the ball, waiting for something to happen and when it didn't become apparent what the hell the thing did, I gave Ohem a questioning glance.

"Just wait," he murmured to me. I scowled at him, but did what he said. Ten minutes passed with nothing, and I worried that whatever plan Ohem had cooked up was a bust, when I heard the telltale hum of the hidden engines from our attacker. I leaned forward on all fours with my ears straining forward, trying to track its approach. It was coming in from the direction it had left, likely having done a large loop. Whatever the ball was that they'd thrown out there, it was drawing it back to us.

"Get ready," Aga said to all of us.

I heard weapons whine as they powered up. The soldiers were behind us in lined formations, ready to follow us out. I'd pointed out that usually the commanders came in behind the soldiers back home. Aga had sneered and called the leadership of human military history lowly cowards. Apparently, leaders in the alien armies always led from the front. If you weren't good enough not to die, then you didn't become a leader. Sounded pretty risky to me, but then I was a brawler and not a leader. I left that stuff to those that didn't have the urge to rip the heads off of people who annoyed them.

The humming grew louder. If the wind wasn't blowing, I was sure we'd see the dirt and grass stir under the craft as it hovered over the ball. The shimmery distortion in the air, like a mirage, was more obvious now that Aga had told me what to look for. Aga stepped forward, hefting a gigantic cannon over his shoulder, a feral light in his eyes.

I cocked my head and took a step back when Aga winked at me. The cannon fired. The blue fire of the plasma exploded out with a deafening crack, burning the air in its wake, closing the distance between it and the enemy craft in an instant. The shimmer erupted in blue flames, revealing the black of the hull under the cloaking, then the fire turned red, and the enemy's ship broke apart into pieces. No one cheered.

The jungle remained silent while we watched the craft burn.

"Let's go," Ohem said. We marched out of the jungle and into the remaining shuttles to continue on our hunt.

Twenty-Three

We made it past the separatist settlement without incident. The storm had died, leaving a muddy mess with fallen branches and jungle debris all over the valley floor. Even the grass was churned up in many places. No one shot at us, nor did we see any signs of enemy movement. Still, we proceeded with extreme caution. The rail guns we hadn't had the chance to fire last time were primed and ready, rotating slowly in every direction, just daring someone to try us.

No one did.

We remained incident free until the clear cut valley ended. A wall of trees tall enough to put the empire state building to shame loomed in front of us.

The dark gray trunks of the trees were wider than houses. I pressed close to the transparent door as we passed under the behemoths. It was so dark in this part of the jungle that I found it hard to see even with my exceptional night vision. There were thick vines crisscrossing between trees, scattered with black flowers, and ferns covering the ground all in differing shades of gray. It was a really odd color scheme for a jungle.

Not a single vibrant color to be found, nor had I seen any sign of animal life. No bird calls or even insects. It was unsettling as hell. I almost preferred the howling of the storm. Now it was only silence broken up by the sound of our own convoy humming along at a steady clip.

"We will be at the ruins soon," Ohem said from a spot behind me. I twisted to look at him, eyes wide.

"You just jinxed us," I said, flicking his chest with my fingers.

I'd changed back when we'd entered the transport, thankful for the handy armor that Sam had helped make me. It kept Ohem's growling at the crew to a minimum. It hadn't hindered my shift at all, except for the helmet, which was long gone. I hadn't bothered to locate it before we left the settlement.

Ohem chuffed. "I do not believe in curses."

I stepped into him and his arm that wasn't holding onto the jellyfish hanging strap wrapped around me.

"Well, I do. So keep the jinxing to a minimum," I said, rubbing my cheek on his armored chest. Ohem's hand stroked down my spine in a soothing manner.

"Yes, *ursang*. In that case, we will encounter all the bad things."

I smacked his chest with my palm. "Smart ass."

Ohem chuckled and covered my hand with his own, pressing it hard against him. "Such violence towards your mate."

I opened my mouth to give a retort when one soldier started coughing. It was violent enough to prompt him to retract his helmet and bend over at the waist. One of his buddies next to him slapped his back a few times, and the coughing subsided. When he straightened, his alien features were the picture of embarrassment.

"Sorry," he mumbled, and his helmet flowed back over his face.

I frowned at him, my hair standing up on end. I know it was probably paranoia but coughing after finding an entire settlement of dead, diseased bodies was making red flags raise in my mind. Everyone had been elbow deep in corpses while they dug graves and buried them. Including Ohem.

I took a step back away from him and stared. They were all so confident that no disease could touch them with their nanos working to kill anything that might enter their bodies. Maybe they were right. Something was just so off about this whole thing.

One scout and his mutant dog? No backup soldiers or storming cavalry? With their links, the scout could have relayed our position immediately. We should be in the middle of a major fight right now and yet we were driving through a silent jungle, unhindered.

Another soldier coughed. I whipped my head around, trying to pinpoint which one it was. An alien at the back was having a coughing fit. Icy fear settled deep in the pit of my stomach.

Holy shit.

They were fucking sick. They shouldn't be coughing at all. The nanos kept them healthy. The first I could brush off as someone sucking spit down the wrong pipe, but two? It was a hacking, wet cough that lasted a minute before tapering off and the soldier recovered its composure.

Then another coughing fit by a different soldier. I brought my wide, fear-filled eyes to my mate's. Ohem cocked his head to the side in question and started coughing.

Oh god. I clutched his arm, my heart pounding in my throat while he hacked. He was joined by a few others on the shuttle. I hadn't even realized we'd come to a stop until the door slid open and Aga stuck his upper body inside our craft.

He met his gaze with my own and there was worry in his eyes. "We have arrived. I think you both need to see this. The crew will stay in the shuttles."

Ohem's coughing ended, his Izi flaring in slow pulsing patterns. "I think we are sick, Aga."

"I know," Aga answered, his voice grim. Aga reached in, wrapping a hand around Ohem's forearm, and pulled him out of the shuttle gently.

Ohem turned to the soldiers in our shuttle. "Stay here. We will get answers soon. If it gets worse, link me immediately."

The crew saluted him. I followed behind Aga and Ohem quickly, looking back over my shoulder at the soldiers and crew gathered just inside the shuttle door. Most had their helmets retracted, and worried eyes followed us as we walked away. Aga had his hand hovered over Ohem's back, guiding the larger male towards a scattering of large stones. They towered over the shuttles that floated a few feet away from them, shining bone white in the gloom cast by the gray skies with pocket marks of wear and tear all over them.

When Ohem and Aga came to a stop in the middle of the stones and faced out beyond them, I stopped beside them and looked to where they were staring. I sucked in a breath at the sight of what appeared to be a military encampment down a shallow slope just past two tall stone columns. There were dead bodies everywhere. Laid out like they'd fled and collapsed in the rush. Bodies were hanging halfway out of the shuttle doors, piled on top of each other like they'd tried to fly away.

Tried and failed.

"What the fuck?" I whispered, taking a step to investigate, but Aga placed an arm in my path.

"Wait. We don't know what's going on. Better to wait for Dr. Ghix to get back to us with the results of the samples we sent," he said, his face a mask of grim determination. He flicked his eyes to Ohem, who, despite being black as pitch, looked pale. His Izi was phasing in and out in a pattern I'd never seen before. Very slow and halting. He was swaying a little on his feet. Fear, like I'd never known, surged up to wrap its claws around my heart and squeezed. We didn't have time to wait. These people had died quickly.

"It's too late for that, Aga. We need to look around their camp. See if they left anything out that can explain what's going on here. Maybe their links can tell us something," I said, my voice shaky.

"Jack is right. We look. Get Rema, he is adept at cracking open links. Have the others set up camp around our shuttles. We will set the dead into sealant and send them back to the ship," Ohem said, his voice stronger than before and a small splash of relief pressed back against the might of my fear. His color was a touch better. Perhaps his nanos were pushing back at whatever illness this was?

Aga grunted. "Very well. I'll go set the crew to their tasks, but go cautiously. We don't know if any still live. Even dying, they may still try to kill you."

Aga gave Ohem a rough pat on the back and went to get Rema. I watched some of the crew and soldiers stumble out of the shuttles, coughing. Others were looking dazed. Rema stopped talking to a female that was crouched low to the ground to speak to Aga. He looked at us and nodded to Aga before grabbing a passing crew member and ordering them to look after the soldier.

Rema's pretty face was bleached of color, his pearly skin dull. He was panting just from the short walk to where we stood. Sick. Like the others. Only Aga and I were the last remaining members of our party not affected. Yet.

Rema grimaced. "I think we should hurry. This is fast acting, some of the crew have already started developing rashes that will no doubt turn to the melting lesions we saw on the dead separatist. I had to sedate one of my pilots."

"Did you hear from Dr. Ghix?" Ohem asked.

Rema shook his head no.

Ohem sighed. "I have tried linking him several times and still nothing. We will continue on as planned. We are looking to take links and see if we can find anything about the illness or Vero. Flag any mention of the Rijitera and send the data to me."

"Understood. I'll start on the west side. Aga will join me in a few moments. He's sending instructions to the Solus for quarantine," Rema said. Ohem's body tightened at the mention of quarantine. It was likely unprecedented for aliens so reliant on their nanos for their health and longevity.

"Let's get this done," Ohem said.

Rema waved to us and jogged slowly to the camp to search his portion. I didn't think any of us should be alone. I planned to look quickly and then round the males up. I pressed my lips into a hard line and started walking.

I passed through the towering column, noting them in a distant part of my mind not focused on saving everybody from flesh-eating disease, that they looked like they'd been part of a towering door. Thirty feet, at least. Just beyond them, the ground sloped gradually like maybe it used to be stairs, and then we were inside Vero's camp.

The smell was overwhelming now that we were standing right on top of it. It was cloying. I breathed only through my mouth, but then all I tasted was dead things. I crouched down next to a body and turned it over with a careful hand, trying to keep my touch only on the clothed areas. It was much the same as the others. The skin and muscle had been eaten away, all the soft tissue dissolving into a soupy mess on the ground around the body. My gorge rose and I had to swallow hard to keep it down.

I straightened and continued on, checking each body, hoping for some identification marking one of them as Vero. Ohem trailed to my right, checking links and bodies for information. I occasionally caught him watching me, checking on me. I did the same to him and drifted between the tents to catch sight of Rema. He was fine, but slow. They both were moving like they'd aged a hundred years.

My mind was spinning. Ohem was sick, Rema and the others were too, but why weren't Aga and I the same? Did we not touch as many dead people as they did? I didn't understand and it was driving me insane.

I ripped the door off a white plastic dome tent, peeking inside to find metal containers labeled food. I checked the three next to it and found more containers and some lab equipment. I was pilfering through the lab finding absolutely nothing when Ohem's voice spoke over the link, making me jump like a scared cat.

"Jack. I found Vero. Center of camp. Come quickly."

I tore out of the lab and down the center of a few dozen of the white domed tents. The males of my group had managed to drift away from me and it set my teeth on edge. I had to weave around the bodies spread throughout, trying to keep a tally of the dead. I stopped counting at one hundred. In the center of camp, was a massive dome dominating the center of Vero's encampment. It was placed in a sunken pit about two-hundred feet wide. The very top of the dome was still twenty feet tall, even with most of it buried.

Doubled doors were open, and I passed through them to find hundreds of white tables in rows with artifacts laid on them. There were scientists-looking aliens lying dead in the aisles between tables. In the center was a massive round table without a center, like a ring. Ohem, Aga, and Rema all stood in the center over a single body.

Ohem waved me over. "This is Councilor Vero."

He gestured to the male on the floor. Vero had been a large male in life, bulky with muscle and a severe face. It had a pig-like quality to it, complete with a short mushed snout that was half melted off. He had tough, dry looking tan skin that was covered in short quills, at least what was left of it.

He wasn't as bad as the others. Likely because he hadn't come to the surface until after his men had secured the area. Vero was lying next to an opening in the ground. Massive stone doors were laid open on their sides like a cellar, with stairs that led down into the dark.

"They found the ruins," Rema stated, staring down into the dark of the staircase.

I turned my head to take in the entire room. It was large, like a ballroom. It was filled to the brim with relics from my people's past. Sudden territorial rage filled me over it all. No one should touch these things, least of all my enemies. Vero was a piece of shit for digging up the ruined evidence of my ancestors. I curled my lip at Vero's rotting corpse.

"I'm sorry, Jack. We will take the utmost care of the artifacts in this room. They will stay with you on the Solus. Perhaps we can dedicate a room as a museum," Ohem said to me softly. My heart fluttered in my chest, and I wanted to tell him to bury it all again. It belonged here.

"Thank you, Ohem. I'm gonna have to think about that, love. Let's just worry about finding out whatever we can to get you healthy again."

I went up to my tiptoes, pulling his face down to plant a kiss on his mouth. Ohem sighed and leaned into me. God, I missed him. He was standing right in front of me and I missed him. We'd been so busy the last few days that all we'd had time for was some pre-sleep cuddling.

"I love you," he whispered against my lips. Another knot formed in my throat and I had to wait a few breaths before I could reply.

"I love you, too." Tears burned in my eyes. I blinked several times to clear them, taking a step back from my mate. I blew out a breath and turned to find Aga and Rema watching us. Rema had a soft smile on his face, but Aga looked like he'd like to hang himself. I sneered at him and he answered me in kind. It made me feel better.

"Let's get this shit done. I've got a war to plan," Aga said.

Ohem snorted at him, but Aga had already turned on his heel and was taking the stairs down into the ruins. Rema smiled at me again before following Aga. I took Ohem's hand when he offered and together we made our way into the echoes of my ancestor's lives.

Twenty-Four

It was a long descent down a stone staircase before we reached the bottom. A long, wide tunnel stretched out into the dark ahead of us and Aga pulled a metal globe out of his belt and twisted it. The globe floated into the air and lit up like a spotlight. I squinted my eyes against the glare. He'd just ruined my night vision. I growled at him and opened my mouth to say something when Ohem gave my hand a squeeze.

"Rema and Aga cannot see in the dark."

Weaklings. I caught Aga's eyes and he glared at me. I smiled at him, flashing fang. Aga snorted and turned to continue forward.

The ball drifted forward, illuminating open doors along the hallway walls. We followed it slowly, looking into the rooms as we passed. Artifacts were still in some but most were empty. Some type of storage facility based on the way things were stacked in the rooms with crates inside. I was a little baffled at the stonework and the lack of technology of what was supposed to be an advanced race. Most of the artifacts upstairs had been bowls and tools. Basic things.

We kept following the hallway that curved to the left as we walked when suddenly the stone floor and walls gave way to metal partway down the hall. The metal was still a shiny silver, with no dust covering it, like someone had polished it to a high shine. It had carvings all over it. I crouched down to run my fingers over some. It was writing. Millions of carved words were all over the floors, walls, and ceiling. The longer I looked at them, the more familiar they were to me. Like a memory I couldn't quite grasp. Ohem's hand on my shoulder pulled me from my inspection, I glanced up at him.

"Let's keep moving, Jack. We can come back when we know more," he said. I nodded and stood to follow Aga and Rema. They'd stopped further up in front of a door. It was smooth, shiny metal with no carvings on it. They nearly fell over themselves when a hard voice spoke in a language that resonated so deeply within me that I was momentarily frozen in place. It hit me like a bomb going off. Like I'd been missing something my whole life and had only just found it again. I forgot what was at stake. I even forgot that Ohem was standing next to me. Goosebumps rose on my skin, euphoria flooding my veins.

Access denied. Final Protocol initiated. Disengage or die.

I was shaking as I approached the door. Someone called to me in the background, but I couldn't stop. When I stood in front of the door, I raised my hand to it and pressed my palm against the smooth metal. It was warm, comforting, like coming home.

DNA match. Welcome Home, Rijitera. I've been waiting.

The door slid apart silently. I took a shaky breath and stepped inside.

Friends of the Rijitera are permitted. Take nothing and live. Disobey and die.

I frowned and looked behind me. When my gaze landed on Ohem, it snapped me out of my stupor, but didn't take away the wonder or the feeling that I was where I belonged, at long last.

"Jack?" Ohem reached out to me and I took his hand.

The large room was all clear glass walls in a circle with an oval metal table in the center. I approached the glass, but what was beyond was dark and I could only see my reflection. I looked shell-shocked. My hair had escaped the braids I'd put in and was tangled around my head in a windblown mess. My eyes glowed with the inner fire that all Rijitera had, but mine looked more vibrant than I remembered.

Ohem stood behind next to me, his head turned downward to stare at me while I gazed at myself in the glass. His Izi were lit up in concern, so I tilted my head to smile at him in reassurance. I was still me, but different. Something had clicked into place when I heard the language.

"What did the AI say?" Ohem asked me.

I frowned. "Did you not have a translation?"

Ohem stared at me for a long moment before he shook his head slowly. "No, Jack. It spoke Rijiteran. No one has heard it spoken in over five-thousand years."

I turned to him slowly, my eyes wide. "You didn't understand it?"

The AI spoke before he could answer me.

I have their languages integrated. Stand by.

Rema and Aga were staring at me. I shrugged my shoulders and waited. I counted in my head. At fifteen seconds, the AI spoke again. This time in common.

Take nothing from this room, Friends of the Rijitera. Do so and I will kill you. You may call me Anu.

The males all bristled at the same time. I was oddly protective over Anu, and a low growl escaped my mouth before I could stop it. The others blinked at me and Ohem's hand came down on my shoulder.

"We will not harm Anu," he reassured me. Guilt settled in my mind that I'd just warned off my mate and friends from a computer program. It wasn't rational.

"There is nothing in this room that we could take, Anu. The room is empty," Rema said. Skepticism settling deep into the lines of his pretty face. It wasn't a good look for him, and I wanted to smack him.

You look but do not see, Neldre. Not that it matters, you are not permitted to see.

I stepped away from Ohem and did a circuit around the room, looking into the glass at random intervals. I couldn't see anything. I frowned at my feet.

"Am I permitted?" I asked Anu

Yes, Rijitera. All access is granted. You may see whatever you wish. You need only ask.

I approached the table in the center of the room. It was the same material as the door. Smooth silver metal. The others gathered around it as well. Ohem's arm snaked around my side and I leaned into him, letting his heat soak into me, soothing the nerves that were flaring up.

"You said you were waiting? Why? What is this place?" I asked.

This is the Archive. All Rijiteran histories and technology are stored here. It was the last thing the few survivors of Ara'Ama did. They tasked me with safeguarding the Archive until a Rijitera returned to retrieve their lost heritage. I have been waiting for five-thousand two-hundred years and eighty-four days.

My heart kicked into high gear, drumming in my chest like it was going to burst out and run a marathon. I hadn't much cared that my people had lost so much when Ohem had first told me about it. But hearing that all our history had been saved, that the survivors of the war had taken time out of fleeing to make sure that everything we were was preserved, made me want to howl with joy. I was out of breath, shaky.

"All of it was saved?" I whispered to Anu.

Yes. All. There is a message left for you to see. Would you like for me to play it now?

A tear rolled down my cheek. "Yes."

A holo screen shimmered into existence above the table, and a golden Rijitera faced me. She was larger than any I had ever seen. She had gold armor on, parts of it covered in blood, with a gold circlet around her brow. Her black eyes bore into mine.

"We are dying." Her voice was deep and guttural, the form of her jaws perfect for the language of our people. There was a slight delay and then her words were translated into common for the others.

"I am Empress Yenes. The last of my line. The others have succumbed to the wasting disease set upon us by the Orixas. At'ens had come here in the guise of diplomacy and left us with death."

I sucked in a breath, looking at Ohem. That was not the version he'd been told. My mate was staring at the Empress with a stricken expression.

"At'ens has taken the coward's way. Instead of meeting us in war and dying like a true warrior, he has used a weapon that kills all without a chance to fight. A disease that attacks the very cells of the body, killing the victims quickly. Even with our superior genetics, the virus has taken its toll in only six months. Millions have died. Our scientists have been working on a vaccine to administer to the survivors, but we have only been partially successful. We won't die from it, but it must run its course. Only a few thousand of us remain. Mostly children. We must leave our sacred Mother for another planet."

Her face took on a feral light, and she snarled, her long fangs white against her gold fur. "*We are destroying all that we have built. No enemy will ever touch our great works. We have set termination for this evening. All histories, technology, buildings, art, everything that has made us the greatest civilization until this point will be destroyed. Only this Archive will remain, deep under the Palace. Our vast collection of DNA for genetic research will stay here as well. Anu will guard it. She is our most sophisticated AI yet. We take nothing with us but what we need to survive. We are weak now and cannot afford for At'ens to find us. Our ships will take us to the farthest reaches and we will wait and grow strong again. May the Golden Light of the Mother forever shine upon you, Rijitera. Learn all you can from our history. Use our technology. Be Reborn.*" She bowed her head and gold seeped from under her skin to cover her head in a helmet like some ancient Egyptian god, complete with navy blue wings just below and behind her ears.

The video ended.

Ohem was shaking. I drew in a shuddering breath and placed my hand on his arm. He flinched from me.

"Ohem?" I said, uncertain.

He bowed his head before looking at me, the glow of his eyes dim. "Has nothing my family ever said been truthful? The histories we have state At'ens led a great army to battle the Rijitera and won after years. The entire Unity is based on this story."

That is incorrect. There was no war. At'ens came to make demands veiled as diplomatic trade deals for Rijitera technology. We refused. He came again, leaving us a gift. A box, said to contain a single large jewel, to signify that there were no grudges held. When it was opened, there was a beautiful gemstone inside. Less than a week later, people started getting sick. Six months after that, they were dying. In a year, most of the Rijitera on Ara`Ama, the Mother, the planet you now stand on, were dead. The disease even killed the wildlife on the planet. You are all infected.

Ohem closed his eyes. "And the purge afterwards? At'ens' history tells of the hunt for survivors. Of us destroying all that mentioned or belonged to the Rijitera."

No. The Rijitera destroyed all that was left. The only survivors were those that escaped the plague on the last ships, bound for the outer reaches. At'ens conquered the planet without a single shot fired. What he was left with was a wasteland. There was nothing for them to use. No technology. No art. Nothing. We made sure our enemies were the victors of a dead planet. All of our colonies were destroyed. Planets were broken.

Aga and Rema stepped away from the table, coming to stand next to Ohem. Both males placed a hand on his back in support. My mate was furious. His Izi blazing brighter as Anu talked. He trembled with rage by the time she fell silent. I had both arms wrapped around him. My face pressed against his chest.

"You are not your family, Ohem. You are fighting to make things right," Aga said.

Ohem grunted. "Somehow, Aga, that does not make me feel any better, but I thank you for your words." Ohem took a breath and fixed his eyes on the table.

"Do you have the capabilities to tap into interplanetary feeds brought by the soldiers here?" he asked Anu.

I do.

Ohem's lips pulled back from his teeth, his arm coming around me to hold me to him in a crushing hug. "Can you see if only my brother, Rakis At'ens, is involved with the soldiers that came here? I want to know how deep the corruption goes."

Stand by.

I rubbed my cheek against him. "I'm sorry. I don't know what else to say to make it better, but I love you. Now and always." Ohem picked me up and sat me on the table. It was warm, which made me nervous, but I met his eyes all the same.

"Thank you, Jack. I will come to terms with this in due time. It is an unpleasant shock. A bitter revelation. I was ashamed that the purge had happened, even when I believed the Rijitera were planet conquering tyrants. Now to learn this?" He shook his head and placed his forehead against mine. "It is almost unbearable. My ancestor was a genocidal coward that didn't have the bravery to meet his enemy in battle. Using a biological weapon is the highest of dishonors."

You are mates.

Anu said it like a statement and not a question. Smart cookie.

"Yes. He's my mate. I was taken by some other aliens from my planet, drugged, stripped, and found myself on a ship with some human women. I found the big guy in a glass cage," I said.

You cannot be drugged. I have run an initial scan on your biology. No substance in the Unity could render you unconscious.

I narrowed my eyes and leaned back away from Ohem. "Well, I was. They were powerful enough to knock me out for a few hours. Disoriented me when I woke up."

Not possible. Only drugs manufactured by Rijiteran scientists could be potent enough to incapacitate you.

I opened my mouth to argue with her when the screen shimmered back to life again on the table and I hopped off to watch. I backed into Ohem, my back to his front, and sighed when his arms wrapped around me.

Scans indicate the corruption in the Unity government goes back generations. It is spread throughout. Your House is the tip of the spear.

Ohem's growl was rough with pain. It dissolved into coughing and he sank to his knees, taking me with him. Aga and Rema knelt behind him, on either side, and wrapped their arms around us. We sat that way for a long, long time. Ohem's quiet crying was the only sound in the room. I cried with him, our tears mixing. His brother and House had conspired to capture him, and now they were trying to kill him. For more territory. More money.

Their own flesh and blood. It was an even greater offense to me than the millions or billions that were going to die over this war. They had betrayed my mate so badly he was weeping in my arms. My strong mate had been brought low. I would kill them all. They were going to pay for this. For everything.

Forgive me for breaking your solace. There is a disturbance on the surface. An enemy craft is bombing your people. There is one of your own in the air fighting back. I know your people are dying from the wasting plague. You do not have long. I may be able to synthesize another vaccine but you will need to destroy the enemy ship so that I may collect samples of the two unknown aliens on board your war craft. I do not have their kind in the Archive. They carry your non-Rijitera form.

My heart lurched with dread at the mention of the enemy craft and then raced in excitement that she could make a cure. Now I was filled with horror. There was only one species that would be unknown to Anu and looked like me. One that had only recently been discovered on a Vrax ship.

Only two people were stupid enough to take a Magpie and come to our rescue.

Callie and Patty were here, on this planet. *Oh, god.*

Twenty-Five

All four of us were on our feet and running out of the room and down the hall in a desperate attempt to keep both women from getting off that damn ship. I'd witnessed Callie in the simulator. She could fuck up the bad guys, no problem, but then they'd land and want to check on us. They'd breathe the air. They'd get sick. The aliens were dropping like flies and they were hard to kill. It would be much faster for humans, nanos or not.

I burst out of the dome building over the Archive and into the gloom of the still cloudy gray skies. There were soldiers running all over the place. They were forming up into units, each surrounding a single cannon operator. The cannons were firing at the scout craft that was raining hell down on us. A few of them were lying still on the ground, not blown to red mist by the rail gun. I noticed their melting skin as I ran past. We were losing them to the wasting plague before the enemy could take them out. Why was it happening so fast?

A small arrow shaped Magpie hurtled past from above me, firing on the larger scout ship with its rail gun. The scout twisted, reversed course, trying to avoid Callie's ship. The Magpie was on the scout's ass, firing both guns in quick succession.

"Are they safe on the ship?" I yelled at Ohem, who ran slightly in front of me.

The cabin is sealed. As long as they do not open the door to the hangar, they will be safe from the virus in the air.

Anu's voice coming from my link made me miss a step. Ohem and the others met my gaze as we ran abreast of each other. We had identical wary expressions on our faces. While my ancestors trusted their AI with all their precious knowledge, I'd seen the Terminator. I was protective of her on some instinctive level, but she also creeped me out a little. Tapping into our links wasn't hard for Rema, much less a super AI from a super civilization, so it shouldn't have come as a surprise.

"Thank you, Anu," I said, just to be safe. Being polite was always a good choice when dealing with potentially killer computer programs.

I looked back to the sky in time to see the Magpie take the scout out. The enemy ship erupted in flames and fell out of the sky, crushing one of the domed tents and sending a blast of heat and debris towards us.

"Callie, don't land. Stay on the ship!" I yelled into my link.

No one answered me. I watched in horror as the Magpie wheeled around and landed next to the transport vehicles.

"Stay on the ship!" I was screaming. I heard the others making similar demands. Rema had taken to the air to try to get to them before us. The wind had picked back up and buffeted him around. It was too late. The belly ramp descended.

Patty stepped out. Her slight form appeared miles away. The distance between us stretched and expanded until I felt like I was running through molasses. Rema screamed. Patty looked around until she spotted us running towards her and smiled. The smile died quickly, taken over by confusion. She hesitated a step and then jogged to meet us. Rema hit her first, wrapping her in his arms, groaning in despair. I was the second to reach them. I pushed Rema's wing out of my way and reached past his arm to turn her to face me.

"Patty, no," I whispered in a ragged voice. "What have you done?"

"We lost comms after you found the first scout. They knocked out communication with some kind of jammer. We had to make sure you were all okay," she said slowly, still confused.

"Ghix wouldn't let us leave, so we stole a ship," Callie said from the ramp and I sucked in a breath, whirling to her. The world narrowed to a pinpoint. The breath in my lungs froze. I wanted to fall to my knees and wail. I pulled Callie into my arms, meeting Ohem's eyes over her head.

"We have to get them to the Archive."

Patty touched my arm, and I looked at her. "What's going on, Jack?" she asked.

I closed my eyes, hoping that when I opened them again that they wouldn't be here. They'd be back on the ship like I'd asked them. I'd said to stay put.

"Is Sam on board the Magpie?" Aga asked.

No. Please say no.

"No. She stayed on the Solus," Callie said, pushing away from me. I didn't want to let her go.

"What's going on?" Patty asked again.

"There's a virus. It's deadly. Everyone is sick. Some are already dead. We have to get you to the Archive." I didn't waste anymore time talking about it. I picked Callie up, ignoring her curses, and watched to make sure Rema had Patty before sprinting back to the Archive.

I didn't stop to help any of the crew members. Didn't stop to see if the others were following me. The sight of the sleek metal door opening in front of me barely registers as I barreled past it and into the room. The table was gone and in its place were two white pods.

Place the females in the medical apparatus.

I did as Anu asked, pining Callie with a glare to make sure she didn't give me anymore lip, but the woman was pale already, with beads of sweat rolling down her temple. She looked dazed.

"I don't feel good, Jack. I'm sorry. We were only trying to help," she said, her voice barely above a whisper.

"Hush. It's okay. You'll be okay." I watched while Rema placed a sick Patty in the other pod. He kissed her forehead and then stepped back. I jumped when Ohem's hand pulled me back by my shoulder. I looked around the room and noticed Aga hadn't come with us.

"He's staying with the men. He feels the most well out of all of us except you," Ohem said.

Jack is immune. Generations of the vaccine teaching the nanos have accomplished the job the scientists thousands of years ago set out to do. We will use those nanos to make a new vaccine. We have all we need here.

"Show me. I grant permission for my friends to see," I said, my voice hard.

Lights flashed beyond the surrounding glass, illuminating miles and miles of open area. Some sections had metal shelving as far as the eye could see. There were ships, machinery, crafts of unknown origins. Tall walls filled with blue cells took up most of the space. Mechanical arms moved all over them, rearranging things. Floating crafts followed the arms, waiting for the cells to be removed and placed on them. The crafts then took the cells off into the distance until I couldn't see them anymore.

The cells are DNA samples collected over hundreds of years at the height of the Rijiteran civilization. Taken from mates or from donors. I will use them in addition to your nanos to formulate a vaccine for each individual. These two females are more delicate. They will need special consideration.

A tube rose between the pods and opened. A single bowl, no bigger than my palm, sat in the middle.

Place your hand over the extractor.

I did as she asked and held my hand over the bowl; the sides digging into my palm. Air hit my hand, and there was a pulling sensation, but no pain.

Stand by.

Dozens more arms converged on the walls holding the cells. I was watching Patty and Callie intently and saw their skin flush red with rashes right before my eyes. Patty groaned once and then a mist sprayed over her from inside the pod and her eyes closed. Her breathing leveled out and grew calm. The same thing was done to Callie.

"They are just asleep, right?" I asked Anu, anxious that something had gone wrong.

Yes. The injections will be painful. They need to stay sedated for several days. The vaccine will use samples from various DNA to match the balance needed to combat the virus. Using only your Rijitera DNA would kill any who are injected with it, so we must dilute the sample with others. I must warn you, the vaccine has a forty-seven percent fail rate.

Ohem's Izi flared, strobing across his body, starting from his chest, and he stepped past me to stand close to the pods.

"Will this alter their DNA?" Ohem asked.

Yes. Their species is weaker than nearly all in the database. The virus is breaking down their cells at an accelerated rate.

I stared at my girls, and fear skittered through me. What if the vaccine didn't work?

Rema's jaw clenched and his wings tucked close into his side when I turned to look at him. He was staring at Patty with sad eyes. He looked up and caught me watching him. "Will there be side effects to this alteration?" His eyes flicked to the ceiling as he asked.

Yes. The effects will be unknown. I will monitor them for adverse reactions. I can adjust dosage as needed while they recover. It will be a continuous intravenous injection over the course of five days. They will need more for recovery.

I drew in a breath and let it out slowly. We needed the vaccine for the remaining crew, too. Ohem and the other males I cared so much about needed it as well.

"The vaccine for the rest of our people?" I asked.

As I said, the vaccine has a large failure rate. It will save some.

A small round table emerged from the floor next to me. On it was a box filled with thin cylindrical metal rods. I looked at Ohem and Rema in confusion. Ohem shook his head.

"I don't know how these work," Ohem said.

Hold to the skin for five seconds.

Ohem nodded and took the box from the table, turning to me. "I will take these to Aga. I will assist him for a while. Link me if you need me. I love you," he said, trailing the back of his fingers across my cheekbone. I leaned into his touch and grabbed his wrist to stop him.

"I love you, too, but hold on." I reached into the box and took two tubes out. I pressed one to Ohem's forearm and counted to five and did the same to Rema. "How will we know it's working? How long does it take?"

It will depend on how far the virus has progressed. Those in this room are in the beginning stages. They are a hardier species. Most of your personnel you brought with you to the Mother are not up to the genetic task of combating the virus. I fear most won't survive. If the vaccine takes, patients will feel an improvement in two hours. We will have to monitor for further signs of vaccine rejection.

"Be watchful. Bring the sick down here. We will open up the larger part of the Archive for recovery," I said to Ohem.

Ohem dipped his head at me and took the box with the vaccines out the door. I watched him go, my fear swelling the farther he got away from me. Nothing I could do now, but wait.

Before I could even pace the room, Aga arrived with the first of the sick crew members slung over his shoulder.

He looked around the room and then at me. "Where do you want me to put them?"

I frowned, glancing out the windows at the area below us. "Anu, how do we get down to the level below us? I need a space for the sick to be treated."

Stand by.

An echoing hum sounded from below. I approached the glass to look down. A round disk platform was rising from the ground towards us. The disk halted right at floor level and I jumped back when the window I'd been standing in front of suddenly wasn't there.

"Shit, Anu. Warn me next time," I barked into the air. The disk was directly in front of me and I took a cautious step onto it. It was solid, not rocking or bobbing like I'd expected it to. I glanced over the edge, feeling my stomach drop at the height we were at. The disk didn't have rails or anything.

"Anu, can you add some type of barrier to this? I don't want anyone falling off and dying before we can treat them for the virus." No sooner had the question left my mouth did a shimmer appear around the disk and solidified into more glass walls. I looked back to see if the wall leading into the room had come back, but it was still open. I touched the extra glass, a little weirded out by the tech.

The lift will take the sick to a designated area I have prepared.

"Right. Thank you, Anu," I said.

I nodded at Aga, who crossed the room to the platform. Once he was in the middle, it started descending. I watched until they made it to the bottom. A door opened in a wall directly across from Aga, a lighted pathway coming to life on the floor leading from the disk to the room like a neon walkway. Aga followed it, disappearing from my sight. I blew out a breath and turned to see Ohem with Rema, both carrying soldiers in their arms.

"There is a platform coming. Follow the lighted path and Anu said there are accommodations for them."

Both males nodded, boarding the disk when it appeared on our level with a now unburdened Aga.

"There are more medical pods down there. It's quite the facility, Jack," Aga informed me as he walked past to exit the room and head upstairs. I checked on Patty and Callie before following Aga to the surface to help gather our sick.

Do you require assistance?

I frowned at the air in the hallway. "Assistance for what?"

Assistance moving your sick to the medical area.

"Oh. Yeah, if you can."

I took a step away from the shiny metal floor when it seemed to liquify. Bubbles of it rising to hip level in front of me. They shivered and then flattened out into oval shapes, about the size of a twin mattress. They stayed perfectly still in the air until I took a hesitant step backwards and they followed me, moving in a steady line one after another. The way they moved looked unnatural, and it freaked me the hell out. I pivoted to continue up the stairs, coming out into the domed tent where Aga and about twenty of our crew waited. I looked around in confusion. "Are there more outside?"

Aga's mouth hardened in a tight line and he shook his head. "This is all that is left."

The air turned to ash in my lungs, burning my throat when I sucked in a breath. "What?" The question coming out as a croak.

Aga looked down at his feet and then back at me. "They are dead. Those that are left are fading fast. We have to get them into the pods quickly."

I gestured to the floating ovals. "Put them on these. Anu, can you take them to the room you set up for us?"

Yes.

Aga picked up one of the sick and placed her on the oval. Two liquid silver streams flowed over the crewmember, solidifying into bands that tightened, securing her to the platform. The red rash flushed up her neck from her chest as I watched. The soft green of her skin was wet with sweat. The female grimaced, her solid black owl-like eyes seeking mine through her pain. "Nin At'ens?" she whispered and tried to lift her arm that was held down under the metal strap. Her ridged brow scrunched in confusion and she started trying to fight against the restraints, her panic growing when they didn't budge.

I placed my hand on her shoulder and shushed her. "It's okay. You're okay. This is just going to take you to the medical center."

She stilled at my touch and relaxed, her eyes focusing on my face. "I'm scared," she whispered to me. My heart squeezed at her soft voice, so filled with fear.

"I know you are. What's your name?"

"Lerra. My name is Lerra," she said, her voice shaky with tears.

I slipped my hand into hers and squeezed. "Hi, Lerra. I'm going to be right here with you the whole way, okay? You just relax and we'll be there in no time." Her hand tightened, and she shook her head. I looked at Aga, and Ohem was standing in his place. My mate looked tired, his skin sallow again, but he had another crew member in his arms, ready to place onto the ovals.

"Go ahead, Jack. I'm right behind you," he said. I watched Aga and Rema load the last of our people onto the floating stretchers. The oval drifted next to me when I started for the stairs. I kept whispering encouraging words to Lerra on the walk to the Archive. I stepped onto the lift with Ohem following with his own stretcher disk, and the lift started its descent.

The space was cavernous. The closer we got to the bottom, the larger it was. It stretched all around us for miles and miles, disappearing into a dark void where the lights ended. Did it keep going into the dark? It was almost like my ancestors had hollowed the entire planet out for the Archive storage.

The lift came to a smooth stop, and I stepped out onto the glowing pathway, my hand still in Lerra's. We continued into the medical area, it had the same medical pods I had placed Callie and Patty into in strategic rows on either side of the room. The plain metal floors and walls added to the sterile feel. I stepped towards the first empty medical pod, waited a moment for the bands to retract automatically, and then lifted Lerra. I placed her in the pod, watching as the mist sprayed her in the face, causing her body to relax into sleep.

Blowing out a relieved breath, I stepped back and watched Ohem and the others help the rest of our crew into their own pods.

"Callie and Patty are down here, too," Rema said from my left. I turned towards him and followed his pointing finger to the corner of the room. Both of my girls were sleeping peacefully in their pods. The large medical apparatus all but swallowing them, sized for a full grown Rijitera. Their color wasn't any better, but it wasn't worse either, so I took that as a good sign.

"Thank you, Anu," I whispered.

A grunt behind me had me turning, my heart in my throat. Ohem had gone down to one knee on his way to me. I was by his side in an instant, terror making my hands shake as I reached for him. His eyes met mine before they closed and he collapsed into my arms.

"Ohem! Jesus. Aga! Help me get him into a pod," I screamed across the room, panic making my voice a shrill bark. I pulled Ohem's body against mine, when hands grabbed him from both sides and helped me lift him. Rema and Aga maneuvered Ohem into a pod that was across from Patty's. As soon as we placed him inside, a glass cover descended over it, closing around him.

A shiver fled down my spine at the realization that I couldn't touch him now. I was trembling, cold sweat breaking out over my skin, and I banged my fist against the glass of Ohem's pod. "Open this, Anu. Fucking open this right now."

It is for his own health, Rijitera. I am putting him into a frozen stasis. It will slow down the destruction of his cells to give the vaccine time enough to counteract the virus.

A shuddering gasp emerged from my lips and I pressed myself to the glass of my mate's pod, trying to get close to him. There was a rushing in my ears, drowning out the sound of Rema trying to comfort me. My heart was going to break apart at any second. When Rema touched me, as if to pull me away. I shifted and turned on him, snarling and snapping my teeth in his face.

"Do not!" I roared at him. Rema held up all four of his hands, stumbling backwards in fear.

Aga stepped in front of him, his arms held wide. "Peace, Jack. We are not trying to take you away." He spoke in low, soothing tones. They would not pacify me.

I crouched on all fours, lips skinned back from fangs, and growled at him. My heart raced, pumping the blood through my veins in a roaring river to my bellowing lungs, pushing my breath out of me in rapid pants. Sweat coated my sides, and I wanted to kill them. Rend their flesh from their bones. My mate. They trapped him. They were trying to take me from him. I stalked towards them, the green one held his ground, but I could smell his fear. The winged male behind him stank of it. I would kill them and take my mate from this place.

The green male bared his teeth at me, holding my gaze, before his face contorted in pain and he bent over at the waist, coughing.

The coughing cut through the fog of my panic. I whined, confused, and approached him. I stuck my muzzle into his face and whined again.

"Get your wet nose out of my face, Rijitera," Aga said, but his touch on my head was gentle and he didn't push me away. When he fell, I was ready. I caught him under his arm and stood, bringing him fully to his feet. Rema grabbed his other arm, slinging it over his shoulder, and together we got him to a pod.

"You will not eat Rema while I'm in here, will you?" he asked, his voice a rough rasp.

I shifted back and gave him a sad smile. "No. I'm sorry. I'm so sorry, Aga. I didn't mean it."

He grunted, laying back and closing his eyes. "Don't you worry about it, Rijitera. Don't panic. We'll be fine. Just need to rest." His voice tapered off as he fell unconscious.

I clenched my teeth, tilting my head back to draw in a steading breath before opening them to look at Rema's pale face. "Let's get you in a pod before you collapse too, my friend."

That Rema could walk on his own to his pod, and both Aga and Ohem had collapsed, spoke of a much hardier constitution than I had realized.

When he laid back into the white apparatus, I leaned over him, my throat raw. "I'm sorry, Rema. You're my friend and I'm sorry I snapped at you. Please get better." A tear hit his cheek, and I wiped at my face.

Rema gave me a sad smile, reaching up to brush a tear away. "It's okay, Jack. Remember that you're not alone. Ghix is just a link away. I would want no one else to watch over the lot of us but you. It's going to be okay. We are going to get better. Just hold on." He dropped his hand, and the mist sprayed over his face. I watched over him until I was sure he was asleep and then went to stand vigil over Ohem.

"Is he going to live, Anu?" I whispered.

He has a seventy-eight percent recovery rate.

The fist around my heart loosened a little. I'd take those odds.

"And the others?"

Most will recover. The one you call Aga has the highest chance of recovery at eighty-four percent. The Neldre is steady at sixty-two percent. The two females are unknown as yet. A DNA splice is changing them. Too many variables to say for sure until the process is further along.

I looked across the room at Patty and Callie's pods. "Forget variables. What do you think will happen?"

Anu hesitated, and the fist gave my heart another painful squeeze.

I think... that they will survive. I used Rijiteran DNA in their modifications. It will defeat the virus as it did before. With your antibodies, they will live.

My shoulders slumped in relief and I leaned my forehead against Ohem's glass covering.

I sat like this for over an hour, letting the adrenaline and fear work out of my system, leaving me exhausted. A bed had materialized out of the floor thirty minutes ago, the same silver metal as everything else in the Archive. It had a soft mattress added to it and a thin sheet. I wanted to sleep but couldn't bring myself to leave Ohem. I wished Anu had some sleepy time drugs to help with the anxiety. The thought of drugs tickled a reminder that I had wanted to ask Anu a question earlier, before the shit hit the fan.

"You said only something cooked up by our dead scientists could knock out a Rijitera?"

That is correct. Your own kind drugged you. Judging by the human women, their race isn't up to the technological standards of even the Unity. They are too far behind to have accomplished the task, and nothing the Unity has could do it. So, the logical answer is one of your people rendered you unconscious.

I'd been in a jail cell. Waiting for *my mom*. Then woke up on a Vrax ship.

Holy. Shit.

My mom drugged me. It was the only thing that made sense.

The 64,000 dollar question was, *why?*

Twenty-Six

About Author

ALISHA STARTED OUT WRITING short stories in high school about things she only wished had happened in her favorite books. She's evolved that skill into writing her own stories about sassy lady heroes who kick butt and win in the end.

When not writing, she can be found riding her horses or reading some other author's hard work.

Twenty-Seven

Afterword

Thank you so much for reading my very first book! It has been such a labor of love writing this thing. Jack is such a fun character to bring to life and I hope you enjoyed her as much as I did. Don't worry, Patty WILL get her own book. She would never let me skip her anyways. I'm hard at work editing book two, and in the early stages of writing book 3. I also have some bonus content on my newsletter if you're interested in seeing Ohem's POV and some scenes from Jack's past. You can find me at Alishasundy.com or on the reader's group Jack's Clan on facebook!

Welcome to the second edition... I hope you enjoy it because holy shit was this the worst thing ever to edit. Lesson learned the hard way y'all, good editors are worth their weight in gold. As with many new authors, I made some mistakes here and there, but now that I have some amazing people on my team, I'm hoping to be able to avoid those same mistakes in the future. So thank you to my new, amazing editor Lou, at Literary Maiden Editing, for taking this flawed first book and making it shine. Thank you to my awesome critique partner and friend, Trev, for encouraging me and hyping me up to write more, and to all the beta readers who helped me get to where I am now!

And thank you, the readers, who saw my unpolished potential and gave me a chance.

Book two, Zero Dark Bloodthirsty is out NOW on KU!

Printed in Great Britain
by Amazon